A MATTER OF MALICE

OTHER WORKS BY THOMAS KING

FICTION

Medicine River
Green Grass, Running Water
One Good Story, That One
Truth and Bright Water
A Short History of Indians in Canada
The Back of the Turtle

DREADFULWATER MYSTERIES

DreadfulWater
The Red Power Murders
Cold Skies
A Matter of Malice
The Obsidian Murders (to be published in 2020)

NON-FICTION

The Truth About Stories: A Native Narrative
The Inconvenient Indian: A Curious Account of
Native People in North America

CHILDREN'S ILLUSTRATED BOOKS

A Coyote Columbus Story, illustrated by William Kent Monkman
Coyote Sings to the Moon, illustrated by Johnny Wales
Coyote's New Suit, illustrated by Johnny Wales
A Coyote Solstice Tale, illustrated by Gary Clement
Coyote Tales, illustrated by Byron Eggenschwiler

A MATTER OF MALICE

A DreadfulWater Mystery

THOMAS KING

HarperCollins*Publishers*Ltd

Published by HarperCollins Publishers Ltd

First edition

HarperCollins books may be purchased for educational, business or sales promotional use through our Special Markets Department.

HarperCollins Publishers Ltd
Bay Adelaide Centre, East Tower
22 Adelaide Street West, 41st Floor
Toronto, Ontario, Canada
M5H 4E3

www.harpercollins.ca

Library and Archives Canada Cataloguing in Publication information is available upon request.

ISBN 978-1-4434-5707-1 (hardcover)
ISBN 978-1-4434-5517-6 (trade paperback)

Printed and bound in the United States

LSC 9 8 7 6 5 4 3 2 1

For my cousins John and Joanne,
who like good stories with cranky cats

ONE

Thumps DreadfulWater stood on his porch and considered the night and the high, bright sweep of stars overhead. He shouldn't be up. He had gone to bed in good order, had even fallen asleep. Yet here he was. Standing in the dark, awake, depressed, waiting for the dawn to find him.

Not a problem. He wasn't going anywhere.

For pragmatists, autumn marked the end of barbecues, swimming at the lake, and sunbathing in the backyard. For the more philosophically inclined, the cold skies and the fading light were a metaphor for old age and death.

Or something equally melodramatic.

Thumps liked the season. Cool nights. High mountain colour. The end of days for the bitey bugs. But this autumn hadn't started well, and he wasn't sure that it was going to improve any time soon.

* * *

First, there had been the trip to Seattle. Claire had not wanted him to come, had wanted to face the disease by herself. But he had insisted. In some ways, it had been a mistake. Yes, he had been there to support her through the interminable medical procedures, to take her to the hospital and back to the room they had rented at the residence motel, to be around in case she wanted to talk.

She hadn't.

The operation had gone well enough, but the chemotherapy had been difficult, and Thumps had been forced to watch the woman he cared about spend her waking moments in the bathroom or lying on the sofa, so close to death that there were times when he would reach out and touch her to make sure she was still alive.

But as bad as it had been watching Claire suffer, the time spent in the hospitals and the clinics had been worse. Thumps wasn't sure he would forget the faces of the people he saw in the waiting rooms or wandering the halls, or lying in beds or waiting on gurneys that were parked in the hallways like a funeral procession, people for whom life was over but not over just yet, people who understood that there was no hope but who were going to hope anyway because it was the only thing they had left.

He tried to pretend that Claire would not become one of

those walking ghosts, that she would rally and walk away from the slaughterhouse, whole and complete.

Over the course of two months, they had talked with a dose of doctors, each one hinting at the gains medical science was making in the fight against cancer. Towards the end, Thumps had raised the question of the nutritional and environmental causes of the disease, and the medical fraternity had just shrugged and offered up brochures on new drugs and innovative procedures that were showing encouraging results.

"If we were sharks," one of the younger doctors had joked, "cancer wouldn't be a problem."

Thumps and Claire had laughed at this, not because it was funny but because they needed to laugh at something.

SECOND, THUMPS HAD left his Volvo with Cooley Small Elk, and Cooley had gotten into an accident. A guy ran a red light and hit him. Roxanne Heavy Runner, the tribe's secretary, had called with all the details.

"Cooley busted up some ribs and got a bunch of cuts on his face."

Roxanne was not known for compassion or humour, but there had been the hint of empathy in her voice.

"He's fine, but your car is toast."

Okay, maybe not empathy.

"Not a big deal," Roxanne had told him. "It was an old car."

* * *

THIRD, FREEWAY HAD disappeared. Thumps had asked his neighbour to look after the cat. Virgil "Dixie" Kane had a large Komondor named Pops who looked like a pile of dirty laundry. The dog had a digestive problem that was toxic. Freeway didn't seem to mind and, so far as Thumps could tell, Pops was Freeway's only friend.

Two weeks after Thumps had left to go to Seattle with Claire, Freeway had vanished.

"I figured she'd come home as soon as she got hungry," Dixie had told him, "but she didn't."

The obvious answer was that Freeway had been killed, hit by a car, eaten by a coyote. "I wouldn't give up," his neighbour had said. "You never know with a cat."

THUMPS CHECKED THE horizon. Nothing. No silver glow to suggest that there was a dawn lurking out there somewhere. It was all a trick, of course. Dead dark one minute and then when you weren't looking, a soft blush, a smoulder, and then the light would magically appear in the sky.

Claire would still be asleep. He had tried to get her to stay with him, just until she felt better, but she had wanted to be in her house on the reservation.

Alone. She had made that part clear. Alone.

Thumps leaned against the railing and considered the day. There was the matter of his car. He'd have to find out where it had been towed, and he'd have to talk to Dolores Cardoza at Chinook Insurance about the accident. There was grocery shopping to do. The only things in the refrigerator at the moment were the shelves.

And his medical appointment with Beth Mooney. Was that today or tomorrow?

Tomorrow. It was tomorrow.

Thumps had made it his life's mission to avoid doctors, and Beth was no exception to this rule. Ever since she had determined that he was diabetic, she had insisted on doing regular blood tests. He had had blood work done just before he left for Seattle, and tomorrow's appointment was to go over those results. Thumps was sure that the numbers would be within the normal range, but Beth would probably want to do more tests. She'd certainly give him another lecture on his eating habits, and she'd try to convince him, once again, to watch the short film on the complications of the disease—blindness, organ failure, amputations—that the American Diabetes Association had produced.

That wasn't going to happen. If he wanted to be distressed and depressed, his imagination would do the job as well as any film.

And there was breakfast.

As a diabetic, Thumps had to eat regular meals. And since there was no food in the house, he was going to have to find someplace and someone willing to feed him. And that would be Alvera Couteau. He'd start his day at Al's and take it from there.

Thumps checked the canvas messenger bag to make sure he had his testing kit and the sugar pills, as well as his camera. He had bought the tan bag at a surplus store in Seattle, and it was proving to be more useful than he would have supposed. And it had the unexpected effect of making him feel tough and mysterious, as though he were a photojournalist on a dangerous overseas assignment.

He looked up and down the street in case the cat was lurking in the bushes or hiding under a parked car. Then he set his hat at a rakish angle, put the promise of dawn at his back, and started walking.

TWO

Al's was sandwiched between the Fjord Bakery and Sam's Laundromat, and it wasn't the easiest place to find. The café didn't have a sign, and the only clue was the turtle shell Preston Wagamese had glued next to the front door with the word "food" painted on it. Al's had originally been an alley until the new Chinook Convention Center was built and blocked off one end. The city figured that Otto Lunde, who owned the bakery, or Sam Maloft, who owned the laundromat, would buy the dead-end alley and expand their business.

But that isn't what happened.

THUMPS COULDN'T REMEMBER ever getting to Al's this early, and he expected to have the place to himself. But he didn't. Wutty Young Beaver, Russell Plunkett, and Jimmy Monroe were already there, perched on the three stools closest to the front door and the grill like a trio of crows on a wire. On the wall, at Russell's shoulder, was a large coloured poster that said, "Stop the Pipeline."

"Hey, Thumps!" Wutty sang out. "Long time, no see."

"But you're just in time," said Russell.

"That's right," said Jimmy, "just in time."

IT TURNED OUT that no one wanted a blocked-off alley, so it sat vacant, filling up with trash, beer bottles, and used condoms. Teenagers with nothing better to do, vagrants who needed a place to sleep, and the working women of Chinook all made use of what became known as the "Alley Motel."

The dead-end laneway quickly turned into a civic embarrassment and a Chamber of Commerce nightmare, and after two years of fielding complaints from the businesses along the block, the city put the alley up for public auction. There was one bid. Alvera Couteau offered one dollar with the promise to build a restaurant in the space. The city, happy to have anything that resembled a business on the site, agreed, and nine months later Al's opened for business.

Al's had great food, but it wasn't going to win any prizes for decor or atmosphere. The place was dark and cramped. Most of the space was taken up with a long, lime-green counter and a run of chrome and red Naugahyde stools, with a row of plywood booths staggered against the side wall. The only light came in through the plate-glass window, and the steam from the grill rose up in greasy clouds and floated in the air like a storm front.

Al's wasn't in any guidebook, and tourists in search of a tourist adventure who happened to stumble upon the café seldom stayed.

RUSSELL PLUNKETT WAGGED a knife at Thumps. "Wutty's trying to guess Al's age."

Jimmy Monroe, who was sitting next to Russell, started chuckling. "Man has a death wish."

"Al has been clear on the matter." Russell raised his voice, in case Wutty was hard of hearing. "Anyone tries to guess her age will be eating breakfast up at Shadow Ranch for the next year."

"Man has a death wish," repeated Jimmy.

"Yeah," said Wutty, "but she's not serious."

A few years back, Wutty had tried to push Al on her "no smoking in the café" rule. Wutty lit up a cigarette at the counter and dared Al to throw him out.

She hadn't.

Instead, she stopped serving him. No coffee, no food. Wutty protested, told her that she couldn't treat a working man like that, told her that the café was a public institution and that he was part of the public.

It took a month before Wutty apologized and another month before Al began serving him again. Even then she didn't give him a full helping of hash browns, and she didn't fill his cup all the way to the top.

Russell turned to Wutty. "I hear the French toast at Shadow Ranch is real pretty."

The French toast at the Ranch *was* pretty. A few months back, Thumps had gone to the resort to talk with Vernon Rockland about a photography show. They had discussed the exhibition over breakfast. Thumps had had the eggs and elk sausage, and Rockland had ordered the French toast. It had come on a long, rectangular plate with fruit purée squiggles and mint leaf garnishes, along with strawberry slices and blueberries arranged on thin orange slices like flowers. The bread was a thick multi-grain dusted with powdered sugar, each piece leaning against the other to form an abstract tipi. Thumps remembered thinking that the whole thing looked more like a goofy Plains Indian diorama than a meal.

Al turned away from the grill. "So," she said, looking each man in the eye, "which one of you boys wants to go first?"

"Hell, Al," said Wutty, "you know I'm only fooling."

Russell dropped a ten-dollar bill on the counter and grabbed his hat off the hook. "Got to get to work."

"Me, too," said Jimmy, as he attempted to beat Russell out the door.

Thumps had tried a piece of Rockland's breakfast. The French toast was drier than he would have expected, somewhat soft and chewy with a faint aftertaste that reminded him of fish. The syrup was good though. Real maple from Canada.

Wutty stayed put on his stool, but now he had his cellphone out and was looking intently at the screen. Thumps wandered down towards the pay phone and found his favourite stool.

Al walked the coffee pot down the counter. "So just how old do *you* think I am?"

Thumps settled his elbows on the counter. "Does it look like my head zips up the back?"

Al set a knife and fork wrapped up in a paper napkin in front of him. "You're never here this early."

"Thought I'd get a jump on the workday."

"You don't work," said Al. "You still on Seattle time?"

"Damn!" Wutty slid off the stool and held his phone up like a flag. "I got a callback." He dropped a five on the counter and banged out the front door.

Al watched him go and shook her head. "One of these days," she said, "I expect I'll have to shoot him."

"Sounds like he's got a job."

"Television show," said Al. "They don't care who they hire."

"Television show?"

"One of those reality thingies." Al turned a cup over and filled it. "Got a question for you. Could use a second opinion."

"Your coffee's good," said Thumps. "And I'm not guessing your age."

"Course the coffee's good," said Al. "And I sure as hell know how old I am."

Thumps took a sip of coffee. It was hot and black. "I'm good with that."

Al leaned her hip against the counter. "You think I'm unreasonably grumpy?"

"That's the question?"

"That's the question."

Thumps checked Al's face to see if it was a trap. "How about I try guessing your age."

"You know Roger Menard?"

"Head of the Chamber of Commerce? Smells like a car air freshener?"

"That's the one." Al pulled a brochure out of her apron. "So Roger comes in with this."

The cover art on the brochure featured a stylized cowboy standing in front of a stylized Indian. The cowboy was waving his hat over his head. The Indian was holding up a hand in a traditional Hollywood greeting.

"So, Roger tells me I should consider being more pleasant. Wants me to sign up for the Chamber's new 'Howdy' program."

Thumps could smell the hash browns cooking on the grill. His stomach was grumbling. He might have to have a second order of toast.

"Menard actually came in?"

"Got as far as the door," said Al. "Hey, I got some new salsa. Real bite. You want to try it with your eggs?"

"Sure."

"You want to know about the Howdy program?"

"Nope."

"That's just what I told Roger," said Al, and she walked back to the grill.

Thumps opened the brochure. Inside was a glowing description of the town and the surrounding area. "High Plains Paradise" was one of the accolades. "Western Wonderland" was another. Both came with the promise that "Chinook is open for business." There was a three-step program on how to greet the visitors and tourists, and a list of "westernisms" that merchants were encouraged to add to their vocabularies. "Pardner." "Reckon." "Mosey." "Purdy." "Grub." "Yonder." "Shucks."

Thumps was chuckling when Al returned with his breakfast. She set the plate in front of him and put her hands on her hips.

"Here's your grub, pardner."

Thumps tapped the brochure. "Don't see 'yahoo' in here."

"Must have been an oversight." Al cocked her head. "You actually read that?"

Thumps opened the brochure and held it up. "Step one is to say 'Howdy' to everyone who comes in."

"Howdy, huh?" Al took the brochure back and dropped it in the trash.

"Needs more enthusiasm." Thumps mixed the salsa into the eggs. "You could probably throw in a 'yippee,'" he said, trying to contain the smile, "but only if you feel like it."

The café was empty for the moment. In a while it would be full, and there would be a line waiting to be fed.

Al leaned against the cash register. "So tell me about Claire."

Thumps stopped smiling.

"Roxanne says they got it all, but that's what doctors always say."

"She's fine."

"Didn't expect to see you for a while," said Al. "Figured you'd be looking after her."

Thumps pulled his head into his shoulders and tried to let Al wash over his back.

"Everybody is worried about her." Al strolled back to the grill. "Worried about you, too."

He hadn't imagined that Claire would see him as a knight errant on a white charger, hero of damsels in distress everywhere, but he had expected that his efforts in Seattle would have strengthened their relationship, that he and Claire would have become closer, that the disease would have given them common cause. Instead, little by little, Claire had drifted away, had become withdrawn, had become silent.

Thumps had tried to draw her out, but the distance became more and more profound until he couldn't reach her at all. He had told himself that it was just depression, that the cancer and the drugs were to blame, that when they got home, things would be better.

But when they arrived back in Chinook, Claire dropped him off and drove away by herself.

"You been to that new place yet? Down the street from Budd's? Fancy bistro thingy with organic espresso and flavoured coffees?"

Thumps looked up. "What?"

"Mirrors," Al yelled over the sizzle of the grill. "Who the hell calls a coffee shop Mirrors?"

Thumps tried to look sympathetic.

"You talk to the sheriff yet?"

"Duke?"

"He was looking for you."

"Why?"

Al waved her spatula at Thumps. "Don't know, but when you see him, tell him 'Howdy' for me. And be sure to ask him about the hitching post."

THREE

The Chamber of Commerce was serious about its Howdy campaign. Red and yellow geraniums were hanging in baskets from light standards, horse-opera scenes were painted on the windows of storefronts, even the ones that were dark and empty, and the heads of the parking meters had "Howdy" stickers stuck to the front, so you couldn't tell how much time you had left.

The main street was festooned with banners that announced the "Chinook Summer Roundup."

Whatever that was.

"DreadfulWater!"

Thumps turned to find Sheriff Duke Hockney at the curb behind the wheel of his black and white Ford Bronco.

"About time you got back."

Duke had little concern with fashion. His wife, Macy,

16

bought most of his clothes, and she generally kept things simple. Long-sleeved shirts in the mid-tone range. Dark green whipcord slacks. A comfortable pair of workboots.

"You plan to stand there all day?"

"I'm relaxing."

"This is what happens when you don't have a real job," said Hockney.

Today the sheriff was dressed in a multicoloured, snap-button cowboy shirt, set off with a bolo tie, a leather vest, and an enormous gold belt buckle that said "Rodeo." Thumps imagined that if Hockney bent over, the buckle would cut him in half.

"I have a job."

"Photography isn't a job," said Duke. "It's a hobby. Like model airplanes and birdwatching."

The bolo tie, with its silver and turquoise slide, was somewhat ridiculous. Around Duke's thick neck, it looked as though someone had tried to strangle a bear with a piece of dental floss.

"Now police work is a real job," said Duke. "And you used to be a cop."

Thumps wondered if he should go out to the reservation and camp on Claire's doorstep. Maybe she'd forgotten that he cared and needed to be reminded.

"Get in," said Hockney. "I've got something for you."

"In that case," said Thumps, "I'm not getting in."

"Damn it, DreadfulWater, I'm trying to do you a favour."

The marshal star on Duke's vest looked like the very thing John Wayne might have worn in *Cahill U.S. Marshal*. Thumps wondered what else was lurking in the sheriff's new wardrobe. Chaps? Cowboy boots? Spurs?

"I'm enjoying the weather."

"There's fresh croissants and espresso."

Thumps tried to contain his disbelief. "How did that happen?"

Hockney rolled the Bronco forward. "Just get in the damn car."

THE OUTSIDE OF the sheriff's office looked pretty much the same as it had two months ago except someone had put up an enormous hand-painted sign that said "Sheriff" in a gilded font that reminded Thumps of cattle roundups and posters for turn-of-the-century Wild West shows.

"Is that a hitching post?"

Duke grunted something unpleasant, slammed the door of the Bronco, and stomped into his office.

Whoever had decorated the outside of the sheriff's office had been turned loose on the inside as well. Rusty animal traps, Navajo rugs, a brace of stuffed ducks on the fly, an oil painting of Plains Indians hunting buffalo. There was an enormous moose head hanging on the wall behind Duke's desk.

"Nice moose."

"Two months gone," said the sheriff, "and you're still annoying."

The head was angled as though the animal had heard

something in the trees and was trying to see what was coming up behind it.

"Where'd you get it?"

"Same place as the damn hitching post."

Beside Duke's desk was a brass spittoon. Thumps was sure that this was Hockney's office, but it looked more like a Western Americana thrift store.

"You watch much television?"

"Nope."

"Me neither," said Duke. "But Macy does. And what the woman loves most are those reality shows." The sheriff whacked himself on the side of his head as though he were trying to knock a bad memory out of his brain. "Other night, she forced me to watch something called *Exhibit A*. Had that Native actor you like so much . . . Graham . . . Graham somebody."

"Greene."

"Whatever," said Duke. "You know that joke about watching paint peel?"

"Sort of like men watching sports?"

"Nothing wrong with men watching sports." Duke stomped over to where his ancient percolator was sitting on a small table. "You want some coffee?"

Thumps had seen what came out of the old percolator. On a number of occasions, he had even made the mistake of trying Duke's coffee.

"I don't see any croissants."

The sheriff poured hot asphalt into a cup.

"Or any espresso."

"I didn't say I had croissants and espresso at *my* office."

There was a white paper bag on one of the filing cabinets with a logo Thumps didn't recognize. A dancing cartoon squirrel. "Skippy's" was stencilled above the rodent.

"Just opened," said Duke. "Good burgers. Thick and juicy."

"I don't need a burger," said Thumps. "You promised me a croissant and an espresso."

Hockney shook his head. "What you need is a job. Something to take your mind off your woes."

"My woes?"

The sheriff put the cup to his lips and worked his jaw back and forth as though he were trying to chew the coffee into manageable pieces.

"Have you seen your car yet?"

Thumps waited.

"You're going to be needing a new one." The sheriff cleared his throat. "You ever hear of a TV show called *Malice Aforethought*? They do cold case re-enactments. It's Macy's favourite show. And they're shooting an episode right here in Chinook."

"That should make Macy happy."

"Yes, it will," said the sheriff. "And they want someone to review their current case for them, someone with investigative experience, someone who knows police procedure."

"Not interested."

"You get to hang out with movie stars. They bring in fresh croissants every morning, and they have one of those fancy chrome espresso machines." Duke paused to catch his breath. "Maybe you can bring Claire on the set. Give her a tour of the behind-the-scenes stuff. Might cheer her up."

"Not interested."

"They pay really well."

"Why don't you do it?"

The sheriff made a face. "City frowns on moonlighting. Makes it look as though they don't pay me enough."

"They don't."

"And I have to run the Chamber's stupid Howdy program," said Duke. "Why do you think I'm dressed like this? Why do you think my office looks like a goddamn petting zoo?"

"What aren't you telling me?"

"Look, just meet with the producers and the team." Hockney was smiling now. Which was never a good sign. "Where's the harm in that?"

"So, what's the show going to be about?"

"About?"

"You said they do cold case re-enactments."

Duke banged his coffee cup against the edge of the table. The black sludge didn't move. The table did. "Trudy Samuels."

At first Thumps didn't recognize the name. And then he did. "Samuels? As in Big Sky Oil Samuels?"

"The same," said Duke. "Emmitt Tull was sheriff then. Her

body was found out at Belly Butte. Emmitt figured it for an accident. Nobody liked to talk about suicide in those days."

"But?"

"Trudy's stepmother, Adele Samuels, screamed murder, swore Trudy had been killed by her boyfriend."

"Always a good bet."

"Boyfriend was Tobias Rattler." Duke paused to see if Thumps was paying attention.

"The novelist?"

"Wasn't a novelist back then," said Hockney. "Just another kid off the reservation."

"Autopsy?"

"Inconclusive," said Duke. "But Tull looked at Rattler. In those days the Samuels family was royalty."

"And?"

"According to the police report, the night Trudy died, the two of them were supposed to meet up for a movie. But Rattler said she never showed."

"So, no alibi."

"No motive either," said Hockney. "And no physical evidence to tie him to Trudy's death."

"And this TV program is going to solve the case?"

"*Malice Aforethought* doesn't solve cases. Shows like that just kick up dirt and pick at scabs." Duke paused. "You sure you don't know the program?"

"I'm sure."

"Then why do you suppose they asked for you specifically?" said Duke.

"Me?"

"Specifically," said the sheriff. "Kinda curious, ain't it?"

Thumps considered the moose head on the wall. Probably the last thing the animal had heard was the crack of the bullet just before it passed through his body. But the sound could just as easily have been a friend asking for a favour.

"Production office is where Budd's used to be." Duke settled in his chair and put his feet on the desk. "Sydney Pearl and Nina Maslow," he said with a smile. "You can thank me later."

FOUR

I f Thumps had bothered making a to-do list, it would not have included working for a reality television program.

It would have included his Volvo. He hadn't seen the car yet, had no idea how badly it had been damaged, though to hear Roxanne and the sheriff tell the story, the car was a write-off. He tried to remember if he had collision coverage.

And the list would have included Cooley Small Elk. He hadn't talked to Cooley, hadn't gone to see him, didn't know how badly the big man had been hurt in the accident.

And it certainly would have included Claire. She would have been the first item on it, though he had no idea what he *should* do or what he *could* do. He hadn't seen her since they had returned from Seattle. All his phone calls had gone directly to her answering machine, and she hadn't called back.

* * *

Budd's Clothing—"Clothes for the Entire Family"—had been in business since 1943, a fact that Leo Budd was always happy to share with others.

And now it wasn't.

One evening, Leo and his wife, Fanny, had decided that enough was enough. They sold the merchandise and the fixtures to a jobber out of Missoula, put the building up for sale, and moved to Florida.

"Got a place in the Keys," Leo told everyone. "Right next door to Marathon. Not real big, but we got sunshine all the time."

Leo and Fanny had invited most of the town to come down and visit, though Thumps didn't know of anyone who had taken them up on the offer. Then, too, they hadn't stayed all that long. About six months after they had left, they were back in Chinook, a little plumper, a little tanner.

"Place was beautiful." Leo had photographs. "Ocean, no snow, friendly people. But all everyone did was sit around in their underwear and drink. Or they'd go out on a boat and fish, and then they'd sit around and drink. We tried the fishing thing once and got sick."

Someone had painted a cowboy and a bucking bronco on the big plate-glass window, along with a red and yellow "Howdy" banner flying over the man and his horse. To one side, taped to the glass, was a single sheet of green copy paper that said simply, "Veritas Productions."

Thumps had never been in a production office before, so he

had no idea what to expect. Still, the sprawl of mismatched desks, second-hand chairs, and the long folding table stacked with reams of different-coloured paper was, by and large, disappointing. There was a large copier in a corner where the shoe department had been, and someone had set a sheet of plywood on sawhorses and buried it in food.

Duke hadn't been lying. There were croissants. As well as fruit and cold drinks.

And espresso.

On a table, all by itself, was a sparkling block of chrome and gauges that looked as though it could power a small town.

Standing next to the machine was a slender woman with dark hair cut short. Her white shirt and jeans were two sizes too small. They weren't made out of rubber, but the effect was the same.

"I'm guessing you're Mr. DreadfulWater."

Thumps tried to keep his eyes on the machine.

"Nina Maslow," said the woman. "The sheriff has told me all about you."

Nina's teeth were a brilliant white, and the effect of her smile was much like a strobe going off in a dark room. Maslow held out a hand. Her skin was soft and glowing, all her nails trimmed and polished. Thumps's hand more closely resembled a chunk of wood that had been left out in the weather too long.

"I'd offer you a latte, but the machine isn't set up yet." Maslow made a face. "Someone misplaced the portafilter."

Thumps tried to look sympathetic.

"Course we could have gotten one of those new machines that are completely automated," said Nina. "No portafilter. No levers. Just a bunch of buttons. Have you seen that ad with George Clooney and Danny DeVito?"

"Nope."

"I thought better of those two," said Maslow. "The coffee comes pre-ground in little plastic cups, so it's stale before it even gets near the machine, but you can be a complete idiot and still make a mediocre espresso. So long as you don't mind all the waste that's created."

"Espresso for Dummies."

"Exactly," said Nina. "Doing it from scratch with fresh beans, a good grinder, and a professional machine is the only way to get a great cup of espresso."

Thumps was trying to decide between a croissant and cheese or fruit and cheese, and didn't see the guy as he rushed by.

"Have you seen this script?" The man was tall and slim, blond with soft blue eyes, perfect teeth, and a chin that could split wood. "Why am I off camera in the third scene?"

Nina tilted her head to one side so she could get a clean angle on the man's throat. "Mr. DreadfulWater, meet Mr. Calder Banks. Calder is the face of *Malice Aforethought*."

Thumps could see where Banks might be the face of something. The man was magazine handsome, glossy with a deep, resonant voice.

"I've seen the script," said Nina. "So has Sydney."

"And?"

There was something familiar about Banks, a vague memory of having seen the man before. A television show? A movie?

"Let's remember our roles," said Nina in a motherly tone. "You're not the writer. You're not the producer. You're the star."

"You might remind Sydney of that." Banks dropped the script on the table. "No Calder Banks, no show. She upstairs?"

"I wouldn't bother her right now," said Maslow. "She just got off the phone with head office."

"L.A. pricks."

"Yes," said Maslow. "The very L.A. pricks who pay our salaries."

"Okay." Banks took a deep breath. "Tell her to call me. We need to talk."

Thumps waited until Banks had cleared the area. "Wasn't he in . . ."

"The Troy Donahue of our generation," said Maslow. "Pretty, petulant, fights below his weight."

"But?"

"But they love him in Japan." Nina made a soft kissing sound with her mouth. "You want a career that is guaranteed to be short and miserable? Take up acting. Five years back, Calder had the lead in a surefire hit TV series and then, bang, it was all over."

Somewhere in the office, Bob Wills and the Texas Playboys started in on "Across the Alley from the Alamo." Nina grabbed her cellphone and walked to the front of the store. Thumps could see where he might have been mistaken. Maybe her shirt and pants were made out of rubber after all.

"He just got here . . . Okay . . . on our way . . ." Maslow slipped the phone into her back pocket, a trick Thumps would have thought to be impossible. "You ever wonder where L. Frank Baum got his inspiration for the Wicked Witch of the West?"

"*The Wizard of Oz?*"

"Your lucky day." Nina nodded. "'Cause you're about to meet her."

FIVE

Budd's had the only mezzanine in Chinook, a distinction that was probably lost even on locals who had shopped at the store on a regular basis. It was a balcony of sorts wedged between the ground floor and the first floor. Thumps wasn't sure who had come up with the concept, but he guessed it was a suspicious store owner who had wanted to watch his sales staff and keep track of the customers at the same time.

Mezzanines were largely a vestige of the past. While the openness made the ground floor feel spacious and airy, they gave up valuable space, and newer commercial construction had all but eliminated them.

Maslow bounced up the stairs. Thumps plodded along behind her.

"Sydney Pearl," said Nina, as though the name itself was enough.

"He someone famous?"

Nina stopped on the landing. "She. Sydney is a woman."

Thumps tried a smile. "Embarrassing."

"Sydney and I co-produce the show. She handles finances and head office. I pick the topics and do the research. Both of us beat up the talent."

"Sounds like fun."

"So, you'll have two bosses."

"If I take the job."

Nina frowned. "Why wouldn't you take the job?"

"Maybe I won't like her," said Thumps. "Maybe I won't like you."

"I'm a sweetheart." Maslow's laugh was almost as good as her smile. "But I can guarantee you won't like Sydney."

Thumps waited.

"No one *likes* Sydney," said Nina. "Woman can be a real bitch."

Thumps waited some more.

"And she's got a gun." Maslow smoothed her slacks. "But she's one of the best producers in the business."

From the landing, he could see the front door. The optics of an empty store made the distance seem farther than it actually was, and Thumps considered getting a head start on walking away.

"Doesn't sound like much of a recommendation."

"There's not much to recommend television," said Nina. "It's a miserable business. Film's even worse."

"So why do it?"

"It can be exciting." Nina shrugged. "Bright lights and travel. Booze, drugs, rock and roll."

"Sounds tiring."

"The main problem is the people. Either you're a self-centred, predatory sociopath or you're in it for the money and the sex." Maslow tried another smile, but this one had lost much of its wattage. "So, Mr. DreadfulWater, which one are you?"

The mezzanine was small and the ceiling was low. But the elevation allowed you to look down and pretend that you were in charge of something.

Leo Budd had had his office on the mezzanine. Thumps remembered couches and tables. And the walls. The walls had been covered with photographs of Budd and famous people who had come through Chinook and stopped in the store. Budd's favourite was a photo of himself and Willie Nelson, taken when Nelson passed through on his way to a concert in Missoula.

Budd's photographs were gone now, all the furnishings moved out or sold. There was nothing left of the life that had once been the clothing store. Maybe this is what people and buildings had in common. Now the half floor was empty except for a heavy library table, some chairs, and a long, lumpy sofa that looked as though someone was using it for a bed.

"Mr. DreadfulWater," said Maslow, "this is Sydney Pearl."

The woman behind the table was in her fifties. Maybe sixties.

She had thin, white hair that touched her shoulders and glistened as though she had been caught out in a freezing rain and a pair of thick-rimmed glasses that gave her the appearance of someone about to swim laps. Or weld something together.

"My car?"

"Tomorrow," said Maslow. "It wasn't serious."

"Next time," said Pearl, "a little more care."

"Rough country," said Maslow. On the edge of the table was a tall amber bottle. Whiskey.

Or Scotch. The seal still intact.

Sydney Pearl held out a hand and pointed it at the folding chair. "Sit."

Lagavulin. Now that Thumps was on the same level, he could read the label. Lagavulin 21.

"So," Pearl said, "this is your guy."

Pearl wasn't pretty or even handsome. Her face looked as though it had been drawn on her head with a black Sharpie. Her fingers were long and thin, the nails short and blunt, the skin on her hands the colour and texture of an old saddle.

"Nina tells me you're going to help make my life easier."

Sydney Pearl was wearing a pearl-handled pistol in a shoulder holster.

"So, tell me, Mr. DreadfulWater," said Pearl, "how much do you know about the Samuels case?"

"Model 85," said Thumps, gesturing to the gun. "Thirty-eight calibre? Galco classic holster?"

Pearl slipped the gun out of the holster and slid it across the table, next to the bottle. "Nina said you used to be a cop."

Thumps picked the gun up, barrel down, and turned it over in his hand. "Didn't know television was so hazardous."

"One of my first jobs was on *Magnum, P.I.*," said Pearl. "Tom Selleck gave it to me. The Samuels case?"

"Not a clue."

"That doesn't sound helpful."

Nina moved quickly. "But I'll have him up to speed by end of day."

"All right." Pearl put the pistol back in the holster. "How well do you know Tobias Rattler?"

"Never met him."

Pearl turned to Maslow. "I hope you know what you're doing."

"I do," said Nina.

"Results," said Sydney.

"I know," said Nina.

"I'm not paying him for effort."

Thumps stood up and hitched his pants. "That's right," he said. "You're not."

Thumps was halfway down the block before Maslow caught up with him.

"You can't quit."

"Never took the job."

"Sydney's not that bad. She's just intense."

There were things Thumps needed to do. Check on Cooley. Find Freeway. Talk to Claire. Things more important than a sleazy television show.

"Look, how about I buy you a coffee." Maslow touched his arm. "I owe you that much."

Thumps wasn't sure he could manage another cup of coffee. "Don't owe me a thing."

"And it will give me a chance to tell you about the show, give me a chance to change your mind. You think we could do that?"

Mirrors was across from the Tucker hotel. The café had opened in the spring. Thumps remembered an article in the paper that talked about the bistro being fashioned after a famous coffee house in Uruguay.

"Café Brasilero," Nina told him, as they crossed the street. "In Montevideo."

Thumps had heard of Uruguay, and he was pretty sure he had heard of Montevideo, but Café Brasilero didn't ring any bells.

"Eduardo Galeano?"

"Okay."

"Jesus," said Maslow. "You don't know Eduardo Galeano?"

"Television?"

"He's one of South America's most famous writers. Café Brasilero in Montevideo was his favourite hangout. Don't tell me you've never read *Mirrors*."

"*Mirrors*? Like the café?"

"*Memory of Fire*? *Upside Down*? *The Book of Embraces*?"

Mirrors might have been the new kid in town, but the muntined windows set in an exposed brick wall and the reclaimed wood made it feel as though it had been around for the last hundred years. The interior was dark with soft edges that had been judiciously worn down with a power sander and gently distressed with a logging chain.

"I always wanted to meet Galeano," said Nina, "but he died before I had the chance."

The massive bar at the far end of the bistro appeared to have been lifted out of a nineteenth-century saloon. On the walls, you could still see the bones of faded letters and phantom advertisements lost in the skin of the wood, while overhead, a tin ceiling floated above a mishmash of wood tables and chairs.

"Window seat?" said Nina. "Watch the world go by?"

"Sure."

Mirrors was empty except for two women bent over their laptops, tending to designer coffee cups the size of bathtubs.

"The sheriff said you used to be a cop." Nina took the chair against the wall. "He said we could trust you."

Thumps didn't like having his back to the door. Old habits, old instincts. From where he sat, he couldn't see who came in.

"What do you know about reality shows?"

"Never watched one."

Nina froze for a second. "Never."

"Nope."

"*Survivor? The Bachelor?*"

Thumps smiled. "I've led a sheltered life."

"Do you have a television?"

Thumps nodded. "Somewhere."

The server magically appeared at their table with two menus.

"Coffee," said Thumps.

"Sure," said the young woman. "We have brewed, pour-overs, lattes, cappuccinos, flat whites, straight espresso . . ."

"Black."

"Our special today is a smoked almond mocha macchiato."

"Just black coffee."

"We make a great cortado."

"I'll have the special," said Nina. "And one of those lemon cranberry muffins."

Thumps glanced at the board above the bar that listed all the coffees and teas Mirrors offered. He stopped counting at thirty-two.

"Okay," said Nina, "the first thing you need to know about reality shows is that they're not about reality. They're about entertainment."

Thumps wondered what a Café Zorro was. Or a Guillermo. Something with cream, no doubt, maybe some chocolate.

"But just because *Malice Aforethought* is entertaining doesn't mean it doesn't deal with serious matters." Nina took a large folder out of her purse. "Trudy Samuels."

The surprise was the prices. A double espresso was four dollars. A mocha latte was five.

"The official verdict was 'death through misadventure,' but we think it was murder."

"We?"

"Public opinion," said Nina. "And Trudy's mother. She's agreed to be on the show. She wants justice for her daughter."

The server brought the drinks. The muffin smelled good. Maybe a small piece wouldn't raise his blood sugars that much.

Nina opened the folder. "Copy of the original crime-scene report. Photographs, coroner's report, sheriff's notes. It's long on public relations with the rich and powerful and short on investigative action."

Thumps sat back. "You don't need me."

"Original investigation was uninspired," said Maslow. "You used to be a cop. Must have handled your fair number of homicides."

"Handled suicides, too."

"You weren't involved in the original investigation, so you're impartial."

Thumps wanted to give Maslow the statistics on cold cases, how few of them ever got solved.

"And you're part of this community. People will talk to you."

Nina's drink had a large dollop of whipped cream floating in the cup. It looked like an iceberg in a shipping lane.

"We want you to investigate the case," said Nina. "Take it back to the beginning. Turn it inside out. See what you find."

Thumps leaned back in the chair. "You have any idea what a Café Medici is?"

"No interest in justice?"

"No interest in a television show."

"Do you know how many people watch *Malice Aforethought*?"

The coffee wasn't bad. Smooth. Complex. If anything, it was somewhat better than the coffee at Al's. Not that Thumps was going to share that observation with Alvera. Then again, the coffee at Mirrors cost three times as much.

Nina took out a pen and wrote a figure on the paper place-mat. "This is the daily rate. We'll guarantee a ten-day minimum."

Thumps raised his cup. "Good coffee."

"That girl's death still haunts this community. I can feel it." Nina pushed the folder across the table. "You could help give closure to the living."

"I'm not a cop anymore," said Thumps. "I'm a photographer."

"Unsolved murder. It can eat at you." Maslow signalled the server and slipped into her coat. "But I guess you know that better than most."

Thumps stayed at the table, contemplated the rest of the coffee choices listed on the board, and tried to guess what they might be. Maybe next time he'd try an Egg Coffee. Or a Kopi

Susu. Or a Botz, even though it didn't sound all that appetizing.

Thumps was tempted to leave the file on the table. Instead, he slipped it into his bag. Maybe he'd read it later. Or maybe he wouldn't. Right now there were more important matters that needed his attention.

Given the way his day had gone so far, he'd start with the easy one first.

SIX

When Thumps had been a young cop just starting out, he had worked his fair share of traffic accidents. The Northern California coast was famous for narrow, windy roads that ran out along the ocean and disappeared into dense forests of cedars and giant redwoods. North of Arcata, the 101 quickly turned into a two-lane affair with short passing sections and quick turnouts that no one used. Certainly not the tourists who arrived each summer dragging trailers the size of Nebraska behind them, or the loggers who drove their trucks from the scaling yards to the sawmills with all the courtesy of a tank battalion on manoeuvres, or the expensive people out of Silicon Valley, San Francisco, and Marin County who raced the sixty-three miles from Trinidad Head to Crescent City at speeds approaching terminal velocity in their Caymans, Chirons, and Berlinettas.

Every summer, finalists for the Darwin Awards smashed into trees, plunged off cliffs, and ran into each other as they tried to negotiate a road that had originally been built for pre-war Packards, DeSotos, and Studebakers. The winners would be rushed to local hospitals or straight to the morgue. The losers would be given speeding tickets and court dates. The vehicles would be hauled off to the various tow impounds, body shops, and junkyards.

Then the road would be cleared, and the next qualifying heat would begin.

THUMPS STOOD OUTSIDE Mirrors and waited for his eyes to adjust. The sun wasn't particularly warm, but it was bright. He ran through his to-do list once again. Car, cat, Claire. Of the three, the car was the easiest task, the one that could be accomplished with a minimum of competence and effort, while the cat mystery would sort itself out.

Claire, however, would require interpersonal skills that Thumps had yet to fully master.

And driving to the reservation to find her would require a car. Which he didn't have.

Roxanne hadn't said where they had taken his Volvo, and Thumps had forgotten to ask. In Chinook, cars involved in accidents generally wound up at either High Country Towing or Bingham's Scrap and Salvage. High Country had the towing contract with the county. Bingham's took anything made out of metal. But Thumps was pretty sure he wouldn't find his two-door coup at either location. If Cooley had had anything to say in the matter, the Volvo would have been taken to Stas Black Weasel.

And not because Stas was Blackfoot and therefore family of the extended sort.

He wasn't.

Stas was one hundred percent Russian. Dark hair, blue eyes, a bear of a man covered in hair, with a voice like a trash compactor. He had been a master mechanic with Mercedes-Benz in Stuttgart, Germany. One summer, he had come to Montana to see the Rockies. Angela Black Weasel was working at the Logan Pass Visitor Center in Glacier National Park as an interpretive guide. The two of them met, fell in love, married, and moved to Chinook. Angela got a job with the tribe, and Stas opened Blackfoot Autohaus, a small garage that specialized in luxury imports.

People who didn't know Stas assumed that he had taken Angela's last name because of the European interest in all things Indian, but that hadn't been the case.

"Fukin is good name in Russian," Stas would tell anyone who asked, "but not so good in English. This is true, yes?"

Stas Fukin. Stas Black Weasel. Not that the name really mattered. What was important was that Stas was the best mechanic and body man in a hundred miles.

So if the Volvo was at Blackfoot Autohaus, the car was in good hands and the only question was whether Stas would be there. Technically, the garage was open Monday through Friday from 7:00 to 6:00, but these hours tended to be suggestions, and the actual times of operation fluctuated depending on the season.

Hunting and fishing season.

If you wanted your car repaired at Stas's garage, you didn't call ahead and make an appointment. Stas had a phone, but he tended not to answer it.

"I answer phone," he would explain, "I cannot work on car."

So, you drove to the garage and hoped that Stas was there and not off tramping through the mountains or standing knee-deep in his favourite trout stream.

The bay doors were up. Stas was standing under a car in his white coveralls. There was a BMW sedan and an older Porsche against the fence. The Volvo was not to be seen.

"Come." Stas waved Thumps over. "You must see this."

Thumps hadn't spent much time under cars and had no idea what it was he was supposed to see.

"Catalytic converter," said Stas, touching a metal pod. "Here, muffler."

The converter was damaged. The muffler looked to have been crushed.

"2006 Honda Element EX-P," said Stas. "Very interesting car. Small engine. Big interior. Four-wheel drive. Cute, yes?"

Thumps had seen the occasional Element on the street, and they were cute. In a boxy sort of way.

"Poor acceleration," said Stas. "But this is not stock Honda. Scary lady has it fixed up."

"Scary?"

"Yes," said Stas. "Scary lady has gun here." Stas patted his side. "I think maybe she is Israeli Mossad."

"Sydney Pearl," said Thumps. "This is her car?"

"Motor has been modified," said Stas. "More horse. More displacement. Good suspension. Valves. Voom, voom. You understand?"

"It's been customized," said Thumps. "High performance."

"Yes," said Stas. "Sound system also. Voom, voom."

Most garages Thumps had been in were grease pits. Stas's looked more like a surgery. The tools were in drawers or hanging neatly on the walls. The floor was spotless. Stas's coveralls were spotless.

"This model is four-wheel drive," said Stas. "So, scary lady's friend takes car off road. Too much voom, voom." Stas reached up and gave the muffler a shake. "So I fix this, and car is good as new." Stas paused, looking for the right words. "Your car is different story. *Grustnyy*. You understand this?"

Thumps had no idea what the word meant, but it had the sound of something being crushed underfoot and thrown away.

Stas wiped his hands with a red rag. "Come," he said. "Let us have tea."

Stas's office was cleaner than his garage. There was a framed poster of a 1920s street scene that featured a Mercedes town car just coming into view. Next to it was one of the "Stop the Pipeline" posters. The Mercedes poster was a stylized art deco piece in reds and browns with a cream background. The pipeline poster was bolder and less artistic, with no attempt at subtlety. Cold blacks. Cold whites.

Hanging on the wall next to the pipeline poster was a cowboy hat.

"You bought a cowboy hat?"

Stas turned the kettle on. "Sure. Yes. Why not. Mayor has new program. Everyone is to pretend to be western people."

"The Howdy program."

"Yes. Howdy. Everyone friendly." Stas put the hat on his head. "Howdy! What do you think?"

"Perfect."

The hat was too small for Stas's head.

"I have new words also," said the mechanic. " 'Yoppee,' 'pardner,' 'weacken.' Is this correct?"

"Close enough," said Thumps.

Stas hung the hat back on the hook. "In Russia we have Cossacks. Like cowboys. Also like Indians. But no Howdy program."

Thumps smiled.

"So, there is good news and there is bad news. This is how you say it, yes?"

46

"It is."

"First," said Stas, "Volvo is a good car. Swedish, sure. Better than Lada or Volga piece of shit. Not so good as German, but still good."

"Nice to know."

"Of course, now Volvo is Chinese, and that is maybe not so good," said Stas. "But your car is Swedish car."

"So that's good?"

"Yes. Of course. But the accident. That is not so good." The kettle began whistling. Stas poured the water into two cups. "Peppermint?"

"Peppermint is fine."

"So," said Stas as he handed Thumps one of the cups. "Now we see what is what."

The Volvo was at the back, hiding in the shadow of an old yellow school bus. The front window was gone, and the entire passenger side from the front bumper to the trunk was smashed and scraped.

"Man who runs red light strikes your Volvo here." Stas patted the hood. "Then both cars crash into each other. Boom. Like bomb."

The Volvo was listing badly. One wheel was twisted and bent under the frame, as though the car had broken a leg.

"Man who runs red light driving Chrysler." Stas made a face. "Chrysler. Like Lada. Piece of shit."

The damage was as bad as Thumps had imagined.

"You have insurance, yes?"

"Just comprehensive."

"Ah," said Stas. "Okay. So, good news. The other guy, he is at fault."

Thumps walked the length of the Volvo. How long had he and the car been together? Certainly before Chinook. Even before that deadly summer on the California coast. Now that Thumps thought about it, the Volvo was probably his longest-standing relationship. What did that say about him?

"So Chrysler man must pay for car value. But value is not enough to make repairs." Stas took a slip of paper out of his pocket. "Bad news. Here is cost to make car like new."

Thumps looked at the figure.

"Maybe you friends with car. Like horse, yes? Maybe you want to fix. Maybe you want new horse." Stas sipped his tea. "You tell me as you wish."

"Was Cooley injured?"

"Cooley?" Stas's face broke out into a broad grin. "Cuts. Bruises. Cooley was not happy with Chrysler man."

"Cooley hurt the guy?"

"No, no," said Stas. "Okay, yes, maybe scare him little bit."

"I don't know what I want to do." Thumps put his hand on the trunk. The metal felt cold and dead. "I haven't talked to the insurance company yet."

"Insurance." Stas spat on the ground. "Like big stomach."

"What?"

"Money goes in one end," said Stas. "Shit comes out other end. This is true, yes?"

The sky to the west had turned a cold silver. It was early, but at this time of the year there was always the chance of a storm sneaking in out of the northwest and burying the high plains.

"If I want to get the car fixed, how long will it take?"

"Two weeks," said Stas. "Maybe more. Insurance pay for rental car?"

Thumps shrugged. "I don't know."

"No matter," said Stas. "No rental cars in town. Television people took them all."

"The reality show?"

"Sure," said Stas. "Reality. Bullshit. All the same, yes?"

"Great."

"You know Cooley, yes?"

"Sure."

"He is your friend?"

Thumps nodded, not really knowing where Stas was headed.

"He is my friend as well. He takes me hunting. Moose. Elk. Does not mind that I am Russian man. For him, I am family. You understand?"

"I understand."

"So, you are Cooley's friend, friend of family, and I must find you a car." Stas tossed the rest of his tea on the ground. "You want school bus?"

Thumps looked at the bus next to the Volvo. All four tires

were flat. The hood was up and Thumps could see that the motor had been removed. "That's a joke, right?"

"Yes, of course," said Stas. "Good joke, yes?"

"Excellent," said Thumps.

THE TRUCK WAS an old Dodge step-side with a short bed. Both fenders were dented, and rust had begun to chew its way through the metal.

"Not pretty," said Stas, "but good heart."

"It's fine."

"This is my first vehicle. When Angie and I get married, her father gives me this."

The windshield had several long cracks running through the glass, and the rear bumper was bent, as though someone had backed into an immovable object at speed. At one time the truck had been white, but time and weather had scrubbed it grey.

"You talk to insurance. You make decision on car. Now I have time to fix. Later there is elk, maybe moose."

Thumps took the keys and weighed them. "Cooley at home?"

Stas waved a hand. "Maybe. Maybe not. Cooley has job with television people. They want Indians who look like Indians. You understand?"

"Sure."

"So they hire Cooley. He looks like good movie Indian, yes?"

"Yes."

Malice Aforethought. The money they were offering would cover most of the repairs. It might even buy him a good used car.

"Maybe you can get job as movie Indian," said Stas, his voice matter-of-fact. "Good money in looking like movie Indian. Then maybe you can afford new German car."

"I really appreciate the truck."

"Sure, sure." Stas waved a hand and headed back to the garage. "When you see Cooley, tell him I say howdy."

Thumps looked at the Volvo. He wondered if the car felt deserted, if it knew he was thinking of leaving it to rot in the backyard of a Russian cowboy. Climbing into the cab of Stas's truck seemed like a betrayal, but he did it anyway. Then he set the key in the ignition and pulled the old step-side into gear.

SEVEN

The truck drove like a truck, and it rode like a truck. Thumps could feel every imperfection in the road, along with some that weren't even there. Maybe this was the buckboard and stagecoach experience he had read about in westerns, had seen on late-night television. Still, he was grateful for the transportation. It wasn't a Porsche or a BMW, but then neither was it a beat-to-shit yellow school bus with flat tires and no engine.

Parking in the downtown was always an adventure. Most times, you would have to circle the block, watching for the telltale signs that someone was pulling out of a parking space.

Exhaust fumes. Tail lights. An open trunk.

On the fifth pass, he gave up and pulled into the city lot behind the library with the pay-as-you-go parking ticket dispenser. Maybe things were going to look up later.

He couldn't imagine anyone wanting to steal the Dodge, but he locked it anyway. If the Volvo was a writeoff and he had to replace it, he might think about getting a pickup. There was, Thumps had to admit, a certain ethos to a truck that a Swedish sedan could never hope to match.

A half-ton with mud flaps, a tool box, a gun rack, and one of those pine-tree-shaped air fresheners hanging from the rear-view mirror.

Dolores Cardoza was on the phone with a customer. She motioned for Thumps to take a seat. "That's what a deductible is," she was saying. "That's why they call it a deductible."

Dolores's office seemed to suggest that selling insurance was neither a glamorous nor a profitable occupation. Dark wood panelling, a dropped ceiling with yellowing acoustical tiles, shag carpet that looked like a plowed field, and a dead fern in a bucket.

Evidently the mayor's Howdy program hadn't found its way here yet.

"Yes, the total damage to your kitchen is $4,240." Dolores looked at Thumps and rolled her eyes. "And from that amount we deduct the deductible, which in your case is a thousand dollars."

Thumps had never paid a great deal of attention to the business of insurance. He had house insurance, of course, and car insurance. But he had never considered life insurance or health insurance or a policy that covered disability. He had heard of dancers who insured their legs and singers who insured their voices. Aside from the house and car, the only thing he had of any value was his camera equipment, and that would be covered by his home insurance policy.

Wouldn't it?

"Yes, you can get a policy with no deductible," Dolores was telling her client. "But you have to decide on that when you take out the policy, not when you make a claim."

A coat of paint would do wonders for the office. Take out the shag and put in a nice Berber. Lose the dropped ceiling and get rid of the fern.

"Probably be a week before head office sends you a cheque." Dolores set the phone back on the cradle and turned to Thumps. "I suppose you want money too."

"Sure."

Dolores opened a file. "You only have comprehensive," she said, as though this were a serious misdemeanour. "And we're still a 'fault' state, thank God."

Thumps waited.

"I've seen the police report." Dolores opened a file. "A Mr. Dettmer from Orleans, Massachusetts, ran a red light and smashed into your car, so technically his insurance company is on the hook for any damages to your car or any personal injury you may have suffered."

"Technically?"

"Apparently Mr. Dettmer doesn't have any insurance." Dolores closed the file. "And it seems he's left town. He was supposed to be in court last week but didn't show."

Thumps slumped a bit in the chair. "So I guess I'll cancel my policy."

Dolores's head snapped up. "Why would you do that?"

"I don't have a car."

"But you're going to get your car repaired or find another car."

"Maybe."

"What about a rental?"

"What about it?"

"If you drive a rental, you'll have to have insurance." Dolores leaned forward, as though she were going to reach across the desk and shake some sense into him. "And while you're here, we should talk about the benefits of investing in a whole-life policy."

THE TRUCK WAS where Thumps had left it and, so far as he could tell, no one had tried to steal it. Dolores was right, of course. As long as he was driving Stas's truck or a rental or any car for that matter, he would need insurance.

He was surprised to discover that his cameras and lenses were *not* covered by his homeowner's policy. Because it was professional equipment, he would need an additional rider to protect it from accidental loss or theft, a rider that Dolores was only too happy to sell him.

So there was no coverage for the car. And no coverage on his cameras. Maybe he should reconsider the job with Maslow and *Malice Aforethought*.

Or maybe Stas would trade a framed photograph of a herd of elk in a winter landscape for the school bus.

"Hey, Thumps."

Cooley Small Elk was leaning on the fender of the step-side. The truck was trying its best to stay upright.

"You okay?"

"Fine."

Cooley had a bad cut on his forehead that had required stitches and a dark bruise just below one eye. "Dolores any help?"

Thumps shook his head. "Guy who hit you didn't have insurance."

Cooley stood up. So did the truck.

"Guy ran a red light. Didn't see him coming."

"Drunk?"

"Just stupid."

Cooley made most people uneasy. It wasn't his fault. In spite of his good nature, the man looked foreboding and dangerous, as though he had just stepped off the pages of a James Fenimore Cooper novel. With black hair, black eyes, dark skin that got even darker under the summer sun, Cooley Small Elk would have been the perfect poster boy for Wild West shows and wagon-train massacres.

And he was massive, a large boulder that had just rolled down a mountain and landed with a thud next to where you were standing.

Cooley had always had long hair. But Thumps couldn't remember him wearing it in braids before.

"That for the TV people?"

Cooley tugged on one of the braids. "Feels real strange. Don't think my hair likes being tied up in knots."

"Looks authentic."

Cooley smiled. "You coming tomorrow night?"

"Tomorrow?"

"Big Halloween party at the bookstore," said Cooley. "You're supposed to dress up like people who scare you."

Thumps tried to think of people who scared him.

"Marvin's bringing the big drum," said Cooley. "You want to sit in?"

"Maybe I'll see if Claire wants to come."

Cooley shook his head. "She's gone."

"What?"

"Moses and me stopped by her place, but she wasn't there. Her truck was gone along with the stuff people take with them when they're going somewhere else."

"Where'd she go?"

"No idea. Moses thought she might be at Roxanne's, but she wasn't." Cooley tugged on one braid and then on the other as though he were trying to make sure that his head was even. "She's got relatives in Great Falls, but she's not there either."

"What about Stick?"

"We asked, but he don't know where his mom is. Moses figures that she took off so she could think about things. According to Moses, this is something that women do."

Thumps yawned. He was suddenly tired, as though his blood sugars had dropped when he wasn't looking.

"Moses figures she'll come home when she's ready." Cooley gave each braid another hard yank. "Moses says that, in the end, everyone comes home. Even cats."

EIGHT

Thumps left the truck parked where it was and walked the three blocks to the Aegean. The bookstore was housed in an old Carnegie library that Archimedes Kousoulas had rescued from a developer and turned into what the little Greek liked to call "the best bookstore in the real west."

There was Prairie Lights in Iowa City, Archie would explain to any who would listen, Powell's in Portland, and Elliott Bay in Seattle, so the Midwest and the West Coast were covered. But in the real west, at least according to Archie, the Aegean was it.

"The best bookstore in the real west" wasn't a motto, and the Aegean wasn't just a bookstore. It was more a cultural centre, and given the mayor's Howdy program, Thumps expected the place would be done up like a western saloon or a *Deadwood* brothel or maybe even an army fort.

Today, however, the Aegean looked like a clothing store, smelled like a clothing store, smelled like clothes that had been left in the closet too long or clothes that had been packed away in trunks and drawers along with little sacks of cedar or a generous helping of mothballs.

"Thumps!" Archie popped out from behind a rack of men's suits. "It's about time."

Thumps didn't ask Archie why it was about time. He knew better than that.

"You don't write, you don't call. You're back, what, a week, and you don't stop by until now?"

"Two days."

"What?"

"I've been back two days," said Thumps. "Actually, a day and a half."

Archie normally wore slacks and a shirt to work. Today he was dressed in a pair of baggy grey pants, a light blue shirt with a big pointy collar, and an argyle sweater vest. Along with a pair of two-tone shoes, black and white, that Thumps recognized from old detective movies.

"Okay," said Archie. "So how is Claire? How are you? How was the operation? Tell me everything."

Thumps looked around the bookstore. The books were still there, but they had been pushed back to make way for the clothes.

"What's all this?"

Archie frowned. "Vintage clothing of course." Archie took a suit jacket off the hanger. "Here, try this on."

Before Thumps could object, Archie had the jacket on him and was straightening the shoulders.

"1940s double-breasted." Archie hurried Thumps over to a full-length mirror. "Probably British. Dark blue with chalk stripes. Centre crease pants with cuffs. Flannel instead of wool. Wide lapels. Padded shoulders. All you need is a nice homburg with a petersham band and a pair of lace-up oxfords with a contrasting cap toe and you're set."

Thumps tried to remember the last time he had worn a suit. "I don't need a suit."

"Of course you need a suit," said Archie. "And why buy a new one when you can have the exclusivity of vintage."

"Exclusivity?"

"What? You think you're going to see this suit on anyone else in town?"

"The Aegean is a vintage clothing store?"

Archie waved a hand. "No, of course not. This is temporary. Just until Gabby can get her shop set up."

Thumps tried to pretend he recognized the name.

"Gabriella Santucci?" said Archie. "Used to own a vintage clothing store in Helena? Moved here this spring?"

"Your girlfriend?"

Archie blushed. "She's not my girlfriend. She's a friend. Okay? I'm just helping her get settled."

"Okay."

Archie slipped the jacket off and hung it back on the hanger. "No, it's not okay. That's how rumours get started."

"Okay."

"Would you stop saying 'okay'?"

"It's a nice jacket."

"Of course it's a nice jacket. Gabby has a great eye." Archie turned in a slow circle. "How do I look?"

"Okay."

"Again with the okay."

"You look great."

"Of course I look great."

Thumps checked the bookstore. There were several people wandering the stacks. Several more were lounging in the chairs that Archie had brought in so folks could relax and read. Cynthia Broadbent was manning the register.

Thumps lowered his voice a little. "I was hoping we could talk."

"You want to talk?" Archie tried to look shocked. "Wait. Let me call the media."

"Archie . . ."

Archie's face turned serious. "Is this about Claire?"

"No, it's not about Claire."

"Your car? Your cat?"

Thumps tried to keep the exasperation out of his voice. "How do you know about my cat?"

"That reality show," said Archie. "They hired you, didn't they?"

"No, they didn't hire me." Thumps realized that several of the customers were looking at them. "Could we go someplace *private* and talk?"

"Private," said Archie, as though he had never heard of the concept.

"Like your office."

"Sure," said Archie. "But I can tell you right now, show business is a slippery slope."

The last time Thumps had been in Archie's office, the place had been awash in books. Books on shelves. Books on the floor. Books stacked up on chairs and strung out along the windowsills. Today it was a 1940s movie set. Green metal filing cabinets with brass handles, a wood veneer desk with a matching wood swivel chair, and a black Bakelite phone. On the wall were recruitment posters for World War II and movie posters for *Sergeant York*, *The Best Years of Our Lives*, *Going My Way*, and *For Whom the Bell Tolls*. He had actually seen *Sergeant York* with Claire at one of Archie's movie nights at the Aegean.

Gary Cooper had been the lead.

That was all Thumps could remember about the film.

"Okay." Archie plopped himself down in his chair and put his hands on the desk. "So now you have private."

Thumps sighed. There was little point in trying to dance around the question. "What do you remember about Trudy Samuels?"

"Trudy?"

"And Tobias Rattler."

"I was right." Archie gave Thumps a scolding look. "The reality show."

"I didn't say yes."

"Jesus." Archie made another face. "Thought you were a photographer."

Archie had never been stingy with information. This was the first time Thumps had ever seen the little Greek attempt anything that resembled restraint.

Thumps took a step towards the door. "Look, forget I asked."

"Sit." Archie gestured to the chair in front of his desk. "You talk to someone else, they'll just get it all wrong."

Thumps guessed that the wood and metal chair was from the 1950s. Whatever the era, the chair was uncomfortable as hell.

"The Samuels family started Big Sky Oil around the turn of the century," Archie began. "By the time Buck Samuels took over as patriarch and CEO, the family was filthy rich. He built a big estate out past Randall. Black Stag. Married Mary Scofield, and they had a daughter."

"Trudy."

Archie nodded. "Trudy was about six when her mother died. Then Adele Price showed up. Swept Buck off his feet, if you believe the romantics." Archie took a breath. "Or saw an opportunity and took it, if you side with the cynics."

Thumps wondered which camp Archie was in.

"Not that Buck was any winner. He was cold and aloof.

His only passion was for making money. Adele was beautiful and smart, and I'm guessing that Buck was pleased to have found himself a pliant trophy wife *and* a surrogate mother for his child. But if he thought that, he was wrong. Adele was all spurs and no saddle. Made it her duty to tell people how to live their lives."

"Didn't get along with the daughter?"

"Cinderella had it easy." Archie rubbed his head. "Absent father. Demanding stepmother."

"Sounds like a bad soap opera."

"Without the annoying commercials." Archie paused for a moment. "Trudy had all the problems that wealth can afford. Alcohol. Drugs. Anger management."

"And Rattler?"

Archie cleared his throat. "Our Toby was a loner. Smart and good-looking, but an outsider. No parents, no money. A boy without prospects."

"A rather Victorian concept."

"Alive and well today," said Archie.

Thumps could see it, could see why a girl like Trudy might run to a boy like Toby. He would have been everything her world wasn't. Mysterious, exciting, dangerous. And Thumps also knew just how welcome a kid from the reservation would have been in the world of dinner parties and country clubs.

"They met in high school."

"And got together?"

"Who's telling the story?" Archie went to one of the shelves and took down a book. "This is Trudy."

The picture showed a young woman with light hair and dark eyes. From her expression, you couldn't tell if she was happy or in pain.

"Here's Toby."

Toby's photo was eerily similar to Trudy's. No smile. The same long-distance stare, as though he saw something farther out and away.

"Toby was a foster-home orphan. Trudy was the poor little rich girl. Neither one of them fit in. Except with each other. After they got together, word was that Trudy stopped the drinking and drugs, stopped trying to hurt herself."

Thumps ran through the scenario. "Even so, her parents couldn't have been too happy about Rattler."

"Buck was dead by then, and yes, Adele was furious that her stepdaughter was spending time with a heathen." Archie couldn't help the smile. "She actually used that word. 'Heathen.'"

Thumps let Archie run.

"There was an incident," said Archie. "Happened after a football game. Trudy was attacked. Rattler rescued her and took her home. Adele called the sheriff's office and claimed Toby had tried to rape Trudy."

"Can't imagine Trudy was happy about that."

Archie nodded. "In the end, Trudy moved into town and got an apartment."

The two men sat in Archie's office and listened to the sounds of the town float through the bookstore. Finally Archie stood and put the yearbook back on the shelf.

"With Rattler?"

"Nope," said Archie. "By herself."

Thumps tried to hold his skepticism in check.

"Sure, everyone thought they were lovers, but I think they were just good friends, maybe the only friends either one of them had. Trudy and Toby. Around town, they were known as T & T."

"How old was Trudy when she died?"

"Eighteen and a bit," said Archie.

"So Adele inherited the Samuels fortune?"

"Buck's will was complicated," said Archie. "Last I heard, the case was still in court."

"The devil's in the details."

"Details, my ass," said Archie. "The devil's always in the money."

Thumps remembered someone saying that a good lawyer makes a case drag on for years, while a great lawyer makes it last even longer.

"There was a son. From Adele's first marriage." Archie picked at his sweater vest. "Adele expected to bring the boy with her when she married Buck, but Buck wouldn't budge."

"He wouldn't take the son?"

"Adele had to leave him with a sister," said Archie. "Don't think she ever forgave Buck."

"Shakespeare."

Archie nodded. "All that's missing is a ghost."

"And Rattler?"

"He left," said Archie. "As soon as the coroner's jury came back with their decision, he was gone."

Thumps's butt was beginning to ache. "*Malice Aforethought* wants me to look at the case again. Review the evidence. They're hoping that I can prove that Toby killed Trudy."

"Thought you were a photographer."

"Guy who totalled my car didn't have insurance."

Archie nodded. "So, you going to take the job?"

Thumps shifted in his seat. "I'm still thinking about it."

"Here's something you don't have to think about." Archie held out a flyer. "Halloween party tomorrow night. Everyone is going to dress up as people who scare them."

Thumps looked at the flyer.

"You could come as George Armstrong Custer."

"Custer doesn't scare me."

"Okay," said Archie. "What about Alfredo Balli Trevino?"

Thumps drew a complete blank.

"He was the Mexican doctor who was the inspiration for Thomas Harris's Hannibal Lecter."

"Charming."

"Or Bela Lugosi. I have a vintage tux and a cape that I could let you rent." Archie stood up and fixed his cuffs. "And you should buy that suit. Jobs in television are a dime a dozen, but opportunities this good don't come along every day."

NINE

Thumps hoped he would find Freeway curled up with Pops on his neighbour's porch, but neither the cat nor the large, farty Komondor was anywhere to be seen.

Nor were there any signs of life at Dixie's place.

Virgil Kane's parents hadn't named their son after the Robbie Robertson song, but when Joan Baez made it famous, everyone started calling him "Dixie" and the nickname stuck. Virgil didn't seem to care one way or the other, but Thumps found it a little disconcerting to have to guess whether to call the man by his given name or the one he had acquired through no fault of his own.

Thumps sat in the truck and let it idle. He could hide away in the house with the doors locked and the phone turned off and go through the mail that had accumulated while he had been in Seattle. Maybe there was something in the jumble of letters and flyers and coupons that would cheer him and take his mind off the stumble of modern existence.

He could always organize his refrigerator. Any form of structure usually raised his spirits. Except there was nothing to organize. He'd have to go shopping first before he could hope to impose his will on groceries.

At some point he would have to read the file that Nina Maslow had given him. He didn't expect to find anything, but *Malice Aforethought* was clearly working on the assumption that Trudy Samuels's death was neither an accident nor suicide. It wasn't likely, but maybe Maslow had discovered something that the initial investigation had missed.

Or he could go car shopping. The perfect way to waste what was left of the day.

Thumps took one more look to make sure he hadn't missed his cat hiding in the shadows or laid out with Pops the dog on his neighbour's porch.

Nope.

He pulled the truck into gear and touched the accelerator.

Aside from a beat-to-shit Ford sedan, the Volvo was the only car he had ever owned. The Ford had been second-hand. He had bought the Volvo new. Maybe it was time for another new car. He didn't have the money to make that happen, but there was nothing to say he couldn't look.

He could always lease a car as a way to keep the monthly payments down. Ora Mae Foreman, who owned Wild Rose

Realty, leased her BMW from the dealership in Great Falls, and Ora Mae was a woman who knew what she was doing.

Salgado Motors was owned by Freddy Salgado. The Salgado family had been in Chinook since before the town first appeared on maps. Freddy's great-grandfather had ranched the Ironstone Valley, and his grandfather and father had been in banking, with branches throughout Montana, until they had sold out to Wells Fargo.

Freddy hadn't cared for ranching or banking. He liked cars.

"Dad wanted me to be a doctor, but who wants to spend a life cutting people open when you can work on cars? You got to do what makes you happy."

Thumps had never thought of Freddy as a photography enthusiast, but the man had showed up at Thumps's last show and bought three prints.

"You know Sebastião Salgado?" Freddy had asked him at the reception.

Thumps had several of Salgado's books. "Terrific photographer."

"According to Dad," Freddy told him, "we're distant cousins, so I got to have a couple of photographs on the wall in case someone asks."

"What about Sebastião's photographs?"

"I bought one of his already," said Freddy. "Last time I was in New York. They're expensive. Yours aren't so bad. Besides, it's always good to buy local."

There were five cars on the showroom floor. Thumps wandered through the maze of colours and chrome. Sitting in a corner by itself, roped off from the rest of the cars, was an old Corvette.

"Hey, Mr. DreadfulWater." Freddy Salgado strolled out of his office. "How goes the photography?"

Freddy was a big Elvis fan. A few years back, he had entered an Elvis impersonator contest in Missoula and placed second. There was talk that he was going to try his hand at the big Elvis Festival in Las Vegas, but Thumps didn't know if Freddy had actually gone.

"Heard about your car." Freddy made a sympathetic sound with his lips. "Hell of a thing to lose a classic like that."

"May be able to fix it."

"Sure," said Freddy, "but they're never the same."

Thumps looked at the Corvette.

Freddy gently lay a hand on the roof. "1963 Corvette Sting Ray coupe. First fixed roof Chevrolet ever made. Split rear window. Independent suspension with transverse leaf springs. 360 horsepower L84 327-cubic-inch small-block V8. Rochester mechanical fuel injection. Even has air."

Thumps nodded, even though he didn't understand half of what Freddy had just said.

"Know how many 360s Chevrolet made?" Freddy didn't wait for an answer. "Fewer than three thousand. You a car man, Mr. DreadfulWater?"

"Sure."

"Bought it about eight years back. One of the happiest days of my life. Elvis drove one of these in *Viva Las Vegas*. Not many people know that. And there was a black '63 coupe in *The Dead Pool* with Clint Eastwood, but it was a toy, a remote-control car rigged with a bomb."

"No kidding."

"Only time I drive this baby is during the summer. Rest of the year it stays put, safe and sound here in the showroom."

"Bet it brings in a lot of business."

"Hey," said Freddy, "you ever photograph cars? Not product shots. More art stuff. Black and white. Cars doing things. Cars in unexpected places. Parts of cars."

Thumps knew what to do with a river or a mountain. He couldn't imagine what he would do with a car.

"And nothing with naked women," said Freddy. "That's calendar shlock. I'm talking fine art photography."

"Hadn't thought about it."

"Think about it. I got cars you could use." Freddy opened his arms as though he were expecting a hug. "So, here it is."

"What?"

"The Outback. It's our crossover. The comfort of a sedan, but the carrying capacity of an SUV."

Freddy opened the door and let Thumps slide in behind the wheel.

"What do you think?"

The seat was surprisingly comfortable. There was a power adjustment that moved it forward and back and up and down. The back reclined as well, and there was a button for lumbar support.

"So, am I right in thinking you two are getting married?"

"Married?"

"If it's a secret," said Freddy, "I'm your man."

"Me and Claire?"

"She was in the other day," said Freddy. "Sat right where you're sitting. Figured she sent you in for a second opinion. The Outback is a great choice for a family car."

The interior was two-tone leather, saddle brown and black. Thumps had forgotten how nice a new car smelled.

"Claire was looking at cars?"

"Real concerned about the safety features. Wanted to know about the tethers for the child seats."

"Child seats?"

"I blew it, didn't I?" Freddy looked apologetic. "Look, don't tell her I let it slip."

"When was she in?"

Freddy thought for a moment. "Yesterday. Just so you know, she liked the 2.5 Touring model with the technology package, in Tungsten Metallic. Said she was going to stop by when she got back."

"Did she say where she was going?"

"I asked her if she was looking to trade in her truck."

"Did she mention Seattle?"

"I don't have a Tungsten on the lot," said Freddy. "But there's one in Helena I can bring over, once I have a deposit."

Thumps got out of the car and shut the door. "You ever make it to Vegas?"

"The Elvis thing?" Freddy struck a pose and belted out the opening lines of "All Shook Up." "Naw. It was fun for a while. Get all dressed up like the King. Take the 'Vette for a spin. But I have more fun being me. You know what I mean?"

"Absolutely," said Thumps.

"But there's always time for a comeback." Freddy rolled his shoulders, swivelled his hips, and hit the chorus running. "I still got all the moves."

Thumps watched Freddy do a couple of spins and a groin bump. He liked the man, but now he was going to spend the rest of the day trying to get the damn song out of his head.

TEN

Thumps had planned to work his way through the other dealerships, see all the new cars, lose himself in the enthusiasms of retail therapy, but talking with Freddy had changed all that. Claire had a perfectly good truck. No more than four years old. Try as he might, he couldn't think of a reason she would want to swap it out for a crossover whatnot. Pickups were the vehicle of choice on the reservation. The unpaved roads and dirt tracks were a mouthful of bad teeth that ate up everything else.

And child restraints? Thumps was sure that Claire wasn't pregnant. She was what? Thirty-nine? Forty? At what age did women stop having babies? They had never talked about children. He couldn't imagine her wanting another. Stanley Merchant, her one and only son, had been a big enough pain in the ass to deter any mother from trying again.

Maybe it was the cancer. A new car as a way of imagining a future.

So Claire had left town. Logic said that she had gone back to Seattle for more treatments or more tests. Without telling anyone that she was going. No great surprise. Claire could be self-contained, isolated, inaccessible. Other times she could be gregarious, generous, loving. You could just never count on which Claire was going to arrive on your doorstep.

Or which one was going to turn and walk away.

Thumps wondered if Claire confided in anyone. Certainly not in the men in her life. Not Stick. Not him. But women talked to other women, didn't they? Roxanne Heavy Runner? Beth Mooney? Ora Mae Foreman? Maybe he could ask one of them.

Thumps didn't have a death wish, so Roxanne was out. The secretary for the tribe had all the warmth of a tank and all the patience of a live hand grenade. If he asked about Claire, Roxanne would most likely run him over or blow him up.

Beth Mooney might know, but chances were he'd have to talk to her while she worked on a corpse. Beth doubled as a family doctor and the county coroner. She lived on the top floor of the old Land Titles building. Her medical practice was on the first floor. The basement was the morgue.

Thumps was intimately acquainted with that dank, dark room and its frightening smells. He didn't need a refresher course.

Which left Ora Mae. Thumps doubted that Claire would confide in Ora Mae, but the woman had earned a reputation as a clearing house for realities and rumours. If something was afoot in town, Ora Mae would know. Plus she had a bright, cheery office with windows and no armoured vehicles, fragmentation devices, or dead bodies lurking in the corners. Given the choices, Ora Mae was the clear winner.

As he drove across town, Thumps was forced to ask himself why he was bothering. Claire was perfectly capable of looking after herself. She'd show up when she wanted to show up. Whatever she was doing was, in the end, her business, and none of his own. They weren't married, whatever that meant. They weren't even engaged.

Wild Rose Realty was on Clark Street, and it had its own parking lot. The lot was for customers only, and a large sign warned that imposters would be towed. Thumps pulled in between a late model Mercedes and a gunmetal grey BMW.

So these were the cars property barons were driving.

The realty office was in full Howdy swing. Thumps had no idea where Ora Mae had gotten the thing, but there was a full-size, blow-up longhorn bull standing in the middle of the reception area, as well as several sawhorses with saddles thrown over them. A scene from a cattle roundup was painted on the large window that overlooked the street, and the coffee table had been replaced with hay bales and barn board.

"Howdy."

Thumps tried to remember the receptionist's name and failed. Instead of a nameplate, the woman was wearing a sheriff's badge.

"Hi, is Ora Mae in?"

The woman was grinning. "I reckon she is."

Thumps couldn't tell if the woman was amused or embarrassed.

"Oh. It's just you." Ora Mae was dressed all in black. Tooled cowboy boots, whipcord slacks, a double-breasted cowboy shirt with silver buttons down both sides, a neckerchief, and a Stetson.

"Howdy." Thumps tried to get the grin off his face. "Just moseyed over to say hello. Thought I'd take a gander at all the decorations."

"You park in my lot?" A pair of matched pearl-handled revolvers were strapped around her waist and tied off at her thighs. "The lot's for customers," said Ora Mae. "You a customer?"

Thumps felt the grin fade.

"But you don't have a car." Ora Mae looked somewhat relieved. "Your car was totalled."

"Stas lent me his truck."

Ora Mae's face tightened and she tapped the sides of the holsters. "I love that man, but I hope you didn't park his piece of junk next to my bimmer."

* * *

WONDER OF WONDERS, Thumps found a parking space in the first pass, and when he got back to the realty office, Ora Mae was in a better mood.

"Claire's missing?"

"She's not missing," explained Thumps. "She's just not here."

Ora Mae moved effortlessly from concerned to cautious. "Woman's got the right to be wherever she wants to be."

"Sure."

"You two have a fight?"

"Nope."

"Then it's sweet you're worried," said Ora Mae. "Shows you care."

"She was out at Freddy's yesterday. Looking at cars."

Ora Mae shook her head. "What the two of you should be looking for is a house."

Thumps frowned. "I have a house. Claire has a house."

"That sad sack of a bachelor pad isn't a house," said Ora Mae. "Layout is wrong. Location is terrible. Backyard looks like something out of *The Addams Family*. What you going to do if you have kids?"

Thumps had a quick flashback to Freddy and the Outback and the question of child-seat tethers.

"Claire doesn't want any more kids."

"Doesn't work like that," said Ora Mae. "Just ask my sister."

"Anyway," said Thumps, "I need another car before I need another house."

"Bad investment," said Ora Mae. "That bimmer of mine is a sweet ride, but it's nothing but depreciation on four wheels."

Ora Mae had given him her speech on real estate and the wisdom of parking your money in property any number of times.

"You should talk to Moses Blood," said Ora Mae. "Just found him a condo at Mesa Verde."

As far as Thumps knew, Moses had lived his entire life on the reservation. He had a small house on bottomland along the river. It was a quiet, gentle place where everything moved in slow motion. Thumps couldn't imagine him leaving that world.

"It's a one-month rental," said Ora Mae. "I'm guessing he wants to see what life in the big city is like before he makes a decision."

"Moses?"

"And look at Archie," Ora Mae continued. "Now there's a man who knows his real estate."

"Archie?"

"Bought the old Carnegie library, didn't he? And then he goes and buys the old clothing store."

"Budd's?"

"Course he didn't buy it through an agent, and that's always a mistake. If it had been my listing, I would have gotten Budd a heck of a lot more than Archie paid him."

"What's he going to do with Budd's?"

"He's not saying, but I got him a solid rental fee from those

TV people." Ora Mae pushed the brim of her hat up a bit so Thumps could see her entire face. "Heard a rumour that you were working for that reality show."

"False alarm," said Thumps.

"You turned down *Malice Aforethought* and that nice Ms. Nina Maslow?"

"Guilty."

"Then you're not as dumb as you look." Ora Mae sighed. "Dredging up the past isn't going to settle anything. You remember O.J.?"

People of the State of California v. Orenthal James Simpson had been carried on national television, a *commedia dell'arte* featuring O.J., Marcia Clark, Johnnie Cochran, Mark Fuhrman, Judge Ito, and a supporting cast. In 1995, it had been *the* prime-time drama on television for more than eight months.

"You know anyone *doesn't* think that Simpson did it?"

"The jury?"

"No one likes a smart mouth." Ora Mae's eyes were fierce and dancing. "Point is, people believe what they want to believe. Facts and lies got nothing to do with the truth. The truth is just what you believe it to be, and nothing is going to change that."

"Maybe *Malice Aforethought* will solve the case."

"Were you listening to anything I just said?" Ora Mae slid one of the pistols out of the holster and aimed it at the bull's head. "That poor Samuels girl is dead, and no barrel-of-monkeys TV program is going to fix that."

"The stepmother's going to be on the show."

"Adele Samuels?" Ora Mae twirled the revolver around on her finger and dropped it back into the holster. "Saw her in town yesterday. With her dweeby son."

"Dweeby?"

"Eaton or Evan. Something popular like that."

"Adele's first marriage."

"Woman's a bowl of hard sorrows." Ora Mae patted the bull. "You know, I should have you take a picture of me and Ferdinand."

"Ferdinand?"

"The bull with the delicate ego?" Ora Mae struck a pose. "Tell me I don't look like a black Johnny Cash."

ELEVEN

Maybe Archie was right. The Trudy Samuels story did seem a little Shakespearean.

The dispassionate king.

The narcissistic queen.

The damaged princess.

The abandoned child.

The warrior hero.

Buck, Adele, Trudy, and Eaton or Evan or whatever his name was. And Tobias Rattler. Two dead. Three standing.

Or maybe Ora Mae was right. Just another barrel of monkeys.

Thumps had never understood the logic behind the expression. A barrel would be easy enough to get, but why put monkeys in it? He had watched monkeys at the zoo, and they didn't appear to have the temperament for barrel cramming. And just who was supposed to have the promised fun?

Maybe *Malice Aforethought* knew something about Shakespeare and monkeys that he didn't.

There was a ticket on the windshield of the truck. Thumps saw it at the same time he saw the sign for the fifteen-minute loading zone.

So that's why there had been an available parking space.

Great. Another expense. When he got home, he'd probably find that his stove had thrown a shoe or that his refrigerator had stumbled into a gopher hole and broken a leg. Or that Freeway was waiting for him on the porch with a litter of kittens. Thumps was sure that the cat had been spayed, but the way his day was going, anything was possible.

Maybe Claire *was* pregnant.

Suddenly, a job with a sleazy television show and the payday it promised wasn't as objectionable as it had first appeared.

His house was as he had left it. Quiet and empty. Thumps dropped his bag on the kitchen table and began sorting through the mail that had accumulated while he had been in Seattle. The first sort was easy. All the offers of free credit cards, the flyers for everything from lawn care to home evaluations, the coupons for fried chicken, triple burgers, and all-you-can-drink soda pop, and anything addressed to "resident" went straight into the trash. Thumps had never made an exact count, but he'd guess that the ratio of junk to real mail was probably ten to one.

Today it was more than that.

There was a flyer for cataract surgery and another for the removal of unwanted hair. Both used lasers. Thumps didn't think it was the same laser, but he couldn't say with any certainty that it wasn't.

The legitimate mail wasn't much better. Two bills. One for electricity. One for phone service.

Thumps opened the Pacific Gas and Electric bill. Never a good idea. It was considerably more than the parking ticket. Along with the bill was a facsimile of a handwritten note saying that the company would be adjusting rates to better serve him and his electrical needs.

Thumps spent the next hour organizing his books. They had gotten out of order. Walter Mosley had wound up next to Eden Robinson. Richard Wagamese had slipped in between Alice Munro and Margaret Atwood. He debated rearranging the volumes by genre or by topic or even gender and race, and nationality, even though he understood that all of these categories were social constructions, all of them precarious at best. Some more dangerous than others.

In the end, he settled for the alphabetical solution.

As he always did.

He had gotten as far as the *R*s when he heard someone at the front door. Freeway wouldn't bother ringing the doorbell, and the only person he wanted to see right now was Claire.

"Hi, Mr. DreadfulWater."

Through the screen door, he could see his next-door

neighbour Virgil Kane. With a large piece of pie on a plate and Pops the dog at his side.

"Saw you were home," said Dixie. "Hope I'm not disturbing."

Thumps left the screen door closed. He didn't want company. Maybe Dixie would take the hint.

Dixie held the plate up so Thumps could get a good look at the pie. "Pops is concerned about Freeway."

And maybe he wouldn't.

As soon as the large Komondor heard the cat's name, he began demolishing the front porch with his tail.

"She come home yet?"

Thumps opened the door. Pops padded his way through the kitchen and the living room. Dixie stepped inside and took a long look around the kitchen, as though he were a health inspector who had stumbled upon a suspicious restaurant.

"Not yet."

Pops wandered into the bathroom. Thumps could hear the dog using the toilet as a water bowl.

"I'm real sorry."

"Not your fault," said Thumps, trying to make the absolution sound sincere.

Pops came back into the room with Freeway's blanket in his mouth, as though he had found the missing piece of a puzzle.

"You asked us to look after your kitty," said Dixie, "and now she's gone."

Pops dropped the blanket on the floor and waited expectantly. Thumps reminded himself once again that he should have some treats on hand for when the monster dog came visiting.

A large bone. Half a cow.

"She's gone off before," Thumps lied. "She always comes back."

Dixie put the pie on the table. "I don't know what to tell you. Hope she's not . . . you know."

"Dead?"

The word was a punch in the gentle man's stomach, and Thumps felt bad the moment it cleared his lips. It was a cruel and unnecessary jab, and one that he should have regretted more than he did.

Pops collapsed down on the floor and farted.

"Pops is real broken up," said Dixie, gesturing to the dog. "Depression throws his digestion off."

Thumps tried breathing through his mouth. "Pie looks good."

Dixie's face lit up. "Made it last night. Northern Spy. It's the only apple I use. Except for the one Granny Smith I throw in for sauce."

Thumps tried moving Dixie and the dog towards the door with just the power of his mind. It hadn't worked any of the other times, and it didn't work now.

"Did you see the flyer for our block party?"

"Block party?"

"First annual," said Dixie. "Everyone's bringing a dish. I'm making a cassoulet. Hey, if you have a photo of your cat, we could make up some posters and pass them out. We could even offer a reward."

Thumps felt a little light-headed. He braced himself against a chair. What was that? Low blood sugar? The dog? Beth had warned him about low blood sugar and high blood sugar, how the trick to managing diabetes was balance.

"We better get going." Dixie strolled to the door and stepped onto the porch. Pops heaved himself up and followed. "New episode tonight on the unusual friendships that animals have with other animals. Last week, it was a rabbit and a crow. Pops and Freeway were laughing so hard I thought they would hurt themselves."

Thumps couldn't remember the cat ever being interested in television.

"The pie's a little tart," Dixie called out over his shoulder. "Don't like to use a lot of sugar."

The pie didn't stand a chance, but it still took the better part of an hour before Thumps started to feel better. The only other food in the house was a can of baked beans and a jar of black olives.

The hypoglycemic gourmand.

IT WASN'T MUCH of a meal. The beans were heavy and sweet and the olives had a musty taste. He put the dishes in the sink and stood there waiting for something to happen. He wondered if normal people had such moments, suspected that people with partners, with real jobs, with children, never had the time to consider the question of choice, that for them the crush of life came packaged with all the answers.

Eat.

Kids.

Collapse.

He could drive out to the reservation, check to see if Claire had come home yet. Make sure she was okay. Be available in case she wanted to talk. Sure, it felt a little like stalking, but Claire would recognize good intentions when she saw them.

He could stay home, in case Freeway showed up with tales of fiddles and spoons and laughing dogs.

Or he could just stand at the window and watch the night turn the world black.

The phone kept him from slipping into a deeper depression and conjuring up even more ridiculous metaphors. It could be Archie or the sheriff or a telemarketer, in which case he didn't have to move. The answering machine would manage the call.

And if it was Claire, Thumps could grab the phone and catch her in mid message.

Instead, the voice on the phone was unfamiliar, a young woman by the sound of it, someone who did not have a missing lover or a wrecked car or a lost cat.

"Mr. DreadfulWater."

The voice was crisp and precise. It wasn't Helen Mirren or Judi Dench. But it could have been.

"Gloria Baker-Doyle here. I'm to be your driver tomorrow. Shall we say 8:30? Yes? Well, brilliant."

Thumps waited for the machine to click off in case there was more to the message. But there wasn't. He didn't know anyone named Gloria Baker-Doyle. He hadn't arranged for a pickup. If the woman hadn't used his name, he would have supposed that the call was a wrong number.

Curious.

Thumps looked at the clock. There was always the TV program Dixie had mentioned, the one about unusual animal relationships. Maybe watching how disparate animals got along would give him a few helpful tips that might come in handy when Claire decided to return.

TWELVE

The show had featured a duck and a monkey who were fast friends. The monkey rode on the duck's back, and the monkey gathered seeds and insects and fed them to the duck. But the story didn't have a happy ending. The monkey found a live electrical wire that had fallen down and was electrocuted. The duck tried to save her friend by picking at the wire and was electrocuted as well.

Thumps had turned the show off when the duck began to shake, but by then it was too late.

He didn't sleep well. All night long, the duck kept trying to pick the live wire off the monkey, and there was nothing Thumps could do to stop her. Several times he had had to get up to pee, and each time he put his head down on the pillow, there was that stupid monkey and that stupid duck.

So he was late getting up, and when he got to the kitchen,

he remembered that he hadn't done the shopping. No eggs. No butter. No potatoes. No quinoa. He opened and shut the refrigerator door several times, searching the shelves in the hope that something resembling breakfast would magically appear, warm and ready to eat.

He stepped onto the porch and looked to see if there were any lights on at his neighbour's house. Dixie would probably have a couple of eggs to spare. The problem was the man liked to talk, and Thumps wasn't much of a conversationalist in the morning. Or in the afternoon for that matter.

"Mr. DreadfulWater?"

There was a dark green sedan parked at the curb. The young woman standing next to the car was tall and uniformly slender, top to bottom. Black slacks, leather jacket, short spiky hair the same colour as her pants. More than anything, she reminded Thumps of a Montblanc fountain pen he had seen at an airport gift shop.

"Gloria Baker-Doyle?" said the woman. "I left a message last night?"

So the call hadn't been a wrong number. Or a joke.

"Is there anything I can do to help you get ready?"

Thumps felt somewhat caught out, standing there in a T-shirt and pyjama bottoms. "I'm fine," he said. "What's this about?"

The woman hurried to the porch and handed him an envelope. Inside was a business card. *Fire and Ice Gallery. San Francisco, New York, Amsterdam.* Clipped to the card was a hundred-dollar bill.

"We should probably be away."

On several occasions, when he was a cop in Northern California, Thumps had been offered inducements to look the other way. A speeding ticket, a health violation, a domestic dispute. But no one had given him a business card with money attached and arranged for a livery service and driver as part of the bribe.

Curious.

Thumps checked the envelope for a note. "I take it your job is to deliver me somewhere."

"Quite," said the woman.

His first impulse was to return the envelope and its contents to Gloria Baker-Doyle, retreat into the house, and shut the door. He didn't need more intrigue in his life. He needed someone to feed him. He needed groceries to magically appear. He needed his medical appointment with Beth to be cancelled.

"Will there be food?"

"There will," said Gloria. "Are those pyjama bottoms?"

Thumps closed his eyes. He turned his face to the morning sun and took a deep breath. "I'll get dressed," he said.

THUMPS SAT IN front.

"You can sit in back."

"Like a big shot?"

"Yeah," said Gloria. "Brilliant."

This was Nina Maslow's handiwork. Nothing else made sense. The woman wasn't used to taking no for an answer. Okay, so he would enjoy the ride, her company, and a free breakfast.

And then he would go grocery shopping.

Gloria kept her eyes on the road ahead and both hands on the wheel. "I understand you used to be a policeman."

The Audi had a power passenger seat. Thumps tried several positions until he got comfortable. "I was."

"Did you enjoy the work?"

"Enjoy" wasn't the word Thumps would have used for police work. Most of the time the job had been dull and routine. The rest of the time it had been unpleasant.

"Me uncle's a policeman," said Gloria. "Scotland Yard."

The car was remarkably quiet. His Volvo hadn't been all that good at keeping road noise at bay. In the Audi, you could drive through the world without having to listen to it go by.

"Do you know why Scotland Yard is called Scotland Yard?"

"I don't."

"The original location of the Metropolitan Police Service in London was at 4 Whitehall Place. It had a rear entrance on a street called Great Scotland Yard, and over time that entrance became the public entrance, and police services became known as Scotland Yard."

"Gloria Baker-Doyle," Thumps said, thinking out loud. "English?"

"Scottish, actually," said Gloria. "Me great-great-grandfather was Arthur Conan Doyle."

Thumps stopped playing with the lumbar support button. "Really?"

"No," said Gloria, without the hint of a smile, "but a great many people are keen to make the connection."

"So you're not a consulting detective."

"Solicitor," said Gloria. "Or I will be as soon as I finish my last year of recognized training."

Thumps realized he had been caught out.

Gloria was way ahead of him. "It's the clothes, yeah?"

And the hair, Thumps wanted to tell her. And the black eyeshadow. And the stud in your nose. And the row of piercings in both ears. And the tattoo on your neck.

"Me dad is on me all the time." Gloria tapped her fingers on the wheel. "'What's wrong with heels?' he says. 'What's wrong with a dress?'"

"So, you're going to be a lawyer?" said Thumps, moving the conversation back to safe ground. "You have a specialty or something?"

Gloria had a nice smile. "Celebrities," she said.

Thumps smiled back. "So this is . . . fieldwork?"

"Something like that." Gloria passed a slow-moving truck. "You know what celebrities have in common?"

"Lots of money?"

"Risk," said Baker-Doyle. "Every time an actor takes on a role, every time a soccer player steps onto the pitch, every time a singer opens his mouth, they're vulnerable." Gloria sounded almost sympathetic. "Average career for a celebrity in any field is about six years." She gave Thumps a quick glance to see if he was listening. "Men manage better than women, but I shouldn't have to tell you that. And that's if they don't get injured or wind up involved in a scandal or say something stupid that goes viral. My job is to manage and limit that risk. It's not a noble calling, but it's fun, and I don't have to hit home runs or pretend I'm a bloody hobbit."

Once you were east of Chinook and looking for food, the only choice was Shadow Ranch. About ten years back, Vernon Rockland had arrived in town and bought the Anderson ranch on the eastern slope. A summer retreat, he told everyone.

"This is Nina Maslow's idea, isn't it?"

Then, when no one was paying attention, Rockland turned the property into a sprawling upscale country club complete with hotel and golf course, along with a family water park, tennis courts, riding stables, and a skeet-shooting range.

"We going to Shadow Ranch?"

"We are," said Gloria. "But I'll wager you knew that as soon as we left town."

Rockland had hosted several of Thumps's photo shows, had even bought a couple of the larger landscapes.

Gloria turned off the main road and began winding her way up to the resort. "When you're finished, come out front and I'll take you home."

"What are you going to do?"

"Hear they have a fancy women's store in the hotel." Gloria stopped the car in front of the double glass doors and winked at him. "Promised me dad I'd try to find a tiara and a pair of glass slippers."

THE MAÎTRE D' perched at the entrance to the dining room was a large man, bald, with a full beard and round glasses that made him look like a barn owl.

"Ah, Mr. DreadfulWater. There you are."

Thumps gave a quick nod. "Here I am."

The man tucked a leather-bound menu under one arm, glided past the breakfast buffet, and wound his way between the tables.

Nina Maslow was nowhere to be seen.

"Thumps!"

Calder Banks was sitting at a corner booth by the window. He stood in one fluid motion and tossed his napkin carelessly on the table as though it were a prop in a scene. The man was dressed in chocolate slacks, a vanilla shirt, and a caramel jacket. At a distance, he looked like an ice cream bar on a stick.

"Thanks for coming."

"Your dollar."

Calder's laugh sounded like a shotgun going off in a closet. "My variation on the business card scene in *American Psycho*."

"Sure."

"Christian Bale? Reese Witherspoon?"

Thumps had had the breakfast buffet at Shadow Ranch before. The bacon and sausages were okay provided you got to them before the heat turned them into jerky, but the eggs were always a disappointment.

"Order off the menu," said Banks, reading Thumps's mind. "That way everything is fresh." Calder put a thin folder on the table and slid it to Thumps. "I think you'll want to see this."

Thumps recognized the name on the folder. It was his.

Inside the folder was a four-page document, an outline of his life in bullet points. Childhood, high school records, military service, university, his career as a cop. The last page was a summary of the Obsidian Murders.

"Nina does really good background work," said Calder. "She's one of the best in the business."

So Maslow knew about that case, knew about Anna Tripp and her daughter, Callie, knew how badly he had failed them.

"Nina says you turned us down," said Calder.

Thumps closed the folder and opened the breakfast menu.

"And you're probably thinking I invited you here to try to change your mind."

The à la carte offerings weren't extensive, and by the time you added in a cup of coffee and juice, the cost of ham and eggs was the same as the full buffet with its fruit-and-cheese plate and dessert bar.

"Because that's what I would think."

The smart money was on the buffet. Quantity, economy, all you can eat. Who could argue with that? It was one of the narratives that had made America great.

And fat.

"But it's not." Calder paused for effect. "I'll be honest with you."

Thumps had never cared for the phrase, had always assumed that anyone who felt compelled to tell you he was being honest wasn't.

"I wanted to give you a heads-up."

In the morning light, Thumps could see why Banks was the face of *Malice Aforethought*. Rugged good looks, brilliant white teeth arranged in his mouth like a string of cocktail marshmallows, skin that glowed as though he had been waxed and buffed to a high shine. Everything about the man was crisp and clean and under warranty as though someone had just broken the seal and lifted him out of the carton.

"What do you know about show business?"

Thumps couldn't resist.

"'There's no business like show business.'"

Calder's shotgun laugh rattled through the room. "*Annie Get Your Gun*. 1946. Ethel Merman and Ray Middleton. Betty Hutton and Howard Keel starred in the film version."

Thumps sipped his coffee. It was his own fault. Now the song was playing in his head.

"What you need to know about show business is that the shelf life of an actor is shorter than warm yogurt. You start off as a nobody and wind up as a nobody. You know the old joke?"

Thumps was trying to think of the missing word from the second verse.

"Who's Calder Banks? Get me Calder Banks. Get me someone like Calder Banks. Who's Calder Banks?"

Smile. Thumps remembered. That's what show-business people do.

"We're not going to solve the case. Hell, we never solve cases. We rehash the forensic evidence. We point fingers. We embarrass people. We back the visuals with mood music." Calder leaned back. "You see what I'm saying?"

Thumps wasn't sure if Calder knew what he was saying.

Calder's face softened. "Three years ago I had the lead in a new cop drama. *The Streets of San Francisco*."

Thumps remembered an old show by the same name. It had starred Karl Malden as a veteran cop with Michael Douglas as his young sidekick.

"A remake of the 1970s original," said Calder. "The new show was going to be a mega-hit."

The food arrived. The sausage was dry. The eggs were hard. Thumps poked them with his fork and gave up.

"Then the show was cancelled." Calder slowly buttered his toast. "That had been my big chance."

Thumps wanted to tell Banks to forget about eggs and stick with the fruit and the yogurt.

"Now I'm doing reality shows and hoping that I'll get another shot."

"I hear *Malice Aforethought* is a big hit."

"Do you know how many reality shows are out there?"

Thumps wondered if there was a situation in which he and Banks might be friends.

"Like blackheads on a teenager's face."

Probably not.

"What'd you think of Sydney Pearl?"

"Different."

"The gun," said Calder. "Right? You know Tom Selleck gave it to her? And that unopened bottle of Lagavulin 21? Goes for just under five hundred dollars. Story there, too. And ask her about the Element. Everything Pearl has is a story."

Thumps could feel his energy flagging. He should probably check his blood sugars.

Calder gestured at the eggs. "How's your food?"

"Sad."

"I understand you're a photographer." Calder signed the bill and waved the server over. "Landscape mostly?"

Thumps nodded.

"Do you know the gallery? Fire and Ice? They specialized in landscape, nature, and environmental photography."

Thumps knew the gallery well. Each time he had gone to San Francisco for a law enforcement conference, he would stop in to see the current exhibition. Kilian Schönberger, Max Rive, Atif Saeed, William Lau, V. Tony Hauser.

"Owners are friends of mine. Peter and Ileus Kanakis. Use my name. They're always looking for new talent." Calder stood up and straightened his jacket. "Have you stopped to ask yourself why Nina wants you to investigate the Samuels case? Because that lady doesn't do anything without a reason." Calder's glow darkened. "Watch your back. For some reason, you appear to be on her agenda."

Thumps sat at the table and enjoyed the sunlight coming in through the side window. He considered wandering over to the buffet to see what was available at the dessert bar. He wasn't going to get anything. It was more curiosity.

Fire and Ice Gallery.

He had to admit that Calder had gotten his attention. On Maslow's agenda? What was that supposed to mean? Banks had made it sound like a threat.

Curious.

It would have taken time and effort for Maslow to put together the background check, and Thumps could come up with only one reason why she would have gone to the effort.

Trudy Samuels.

Somehow or other, Maslow thought he was connected to that case. He didn't see how, but it might be prudent to read the police report on Samuels's death and review the forensics. Just for the hell of it. See if anything jumped out at him. If nothing else, it would give him something to do while he waited for Claire to call, while he waited for his cat to come home.

How much trouble could it be?

THIRTEEN

Gloria Baker-Doyle was waiting by the Audi. Thumps wondered if she had had a chance to do any shopping.

"Where to now, m'lord?"

"Home, I guess," he said.

Gloria held up a black lump of plastic. "Care to drive?"

Thumps could see where Gloria Baker-Doyle could be an easy person to like.

"I would."

"There was an old truck parked at your place."

"A loaner," said Thumps. "My car is in worse shape."

"Brilliant," said Gloria.

It took Thumps several minutes to adjust the seat and the mirrors and to figure out the Audi's controls.

"The ignition is electronic," said Gloria. "All you do is push this button. And you don't actually shift."

"I don't?"

"It's electronic as well."

Thumps touched a small button on the dash and immediately felt cool air rise out of the seat beneath him.

"The seats are heated," said Gloria. "And they're air conditioned as well."

"Does it drive itself?"

"Not quite," said Gloria, "but it does have adaptive cruise control and blind-spot monitoring."

The Volvo had a manual gearbox, air conditioning, and a radio, but it was still a car. So far as Thumps could tell, the Audi was a computer.

"Do I have to log in?"

"Brilliant," said Gloria.

Thumps took the long way back to Chinook, along the river with its rock outcroppings and hairpin turns. The car didn't flinch, stayed flat and level as it hugged the road and bolted down the straight sections.

"You drive like me dad."

Thumps wasn't sure if this was a compliment or a criticism, and he didn't ask.

"You find your tiara?"

Gloria grinned. "Naw. But I did find a blinding nose ring."

Thumps slowed as they hit the city limits and took his time rolling through the downtown in case he saw someone he knew. He circled the block several times before he pulled up in front of the old Land Titles building.

Gloria looked at the two-storey red brick. "What's here?"

"My doctor's office," said Thumps. "And the county morgue."

"One stop shopping, yeah?"

"Yeah," said Thumps. "Brilliant."

The Land Titles building was one of a handful of historic buildings in Chinook. It had been built in 1893 and had been the site of land transactions, lawsuits, fist fights, and gun battles. In 1902, ranchers and farmers had come to blows over a water dispute and blazed away at each other until both sides ran out of ammunition.

"You want me to wait?" Gloria played with a spike of hair.

"For what?"

"In case you don't come out."

In 1910, the old Land Titles building was replaced by a new Land Titles building, and the two-storey, red brick edifice with its arched windows, checkerboard banding, and granite sills was sold at public auction. By the time Beth Mooney and Ora Mae Foreman bought the building, it had been a brothel, a billiard parlour, a restaurant, a lawyer's office, and a men's club.

Gloria handed him a card. "If you need me," she said, "call this number."

"And you'll come running?"

"James Taylor," said Gloria. "Like the song, yeah?"

Thumps stood at the front door and considered the new keypad and intercom that Beth had had installed at the start of the summer. Before, the building had had a one-button intercom that serviced all three floors. Now there were three buttons. The first buzzed the second floor. This is where Beth lived, where Thumps could count on a comfortable sofa, a cup of tea, and a cookie.

The second buzzed the first floor. This is where Beth had her medical practice. The space wasn't as nice as the second floor and the wood chairs were hard, but it had the benefit of being on the same level as the front door and made for an easy escape if an escape was necessary.

The third button buzzed the basement, where Beth maintained the morgue, where she performed autopsies and stored dead bodies.

Thumps liked the new keypad. Now he didn't have to guess. He could press the button for the second floor or for the first floor, and if Beth didn't answer, he'd just come back another time. With the floors organized, he saw no reason or need to risk the third button.

So he didn't.

Beth was probably in her office on the first floor, waiting for him. But he pressed the button for the second floor, hoping he'd get lucky.

"Yes?"

Sometimes optimism was rewarded. "It's me."

"Basement."

"What?"

"Just kidding. Come on up."

Beth was waiting for him when he got to the top of the stairs. She was smiling and looked much too pleased with herself.

"Not funny."

"Sure it was," she said.

The last time Thumps had been in Beth's apartment, the walls had been painted a medium taupe. Now they were a soft yellow. There was a new rug on the floor and a new sofa that looked to have been made out of a couple of recliners.

Beth stood in the middle of the room and waited for Thumps to say something.

"Place looks great."

Beth cocked her head. "You're going to have to do better than that."

"My car's totalled," said Thumps, hoping to change the subject and elicit a little sympathy. "And I think my cat's dead."

"Freeway?"

"I came home and she was . . ." Thumps let the sentence fragment dangle in space.

"She's really dead?"

Thumps shrugged.

"So what you mean is . . . she's missing."

Thumps shrugged again.

"Stop shrugging and sit down."

Thumps tried the sofa. He was right. Recliners.

"It's from Norway," said Beth, "and it's expensive, so you better say something nice."

Thumps adjusted the one side until he found a comfortable position.

"How's Claire?"

Thumps had been hoping that Beth wasn't going to ask that question. Claire's health was Claire's business. She had made that quite clear.

"Okay."

"That's it? Okay?"

"Okay's good."

Beth rolled her eyes. "Okay, then let's talk about you." She sat down at the kitchen table, put on her reading glasses, and opened a folder. "This is you." She held up a page. "And this is your blood chemistry results. You know what they tell me?"

Thumps checked to see if the sofa had a lumbar support. "I'm cured?"

Beth snorted. "Have you been watching your diet?"

"Absolutely."

Beth went back to reading and making small sympathetic noises. "Okay, then I'm going to take you off the pills."

"Great." Thumps tried not to sound too pleased, but the pills had been expensive, and remembering to take them all the time had been annoying.

Beth looked at him over the top of the glasses. "We're going to have to put you on insulin."

Thumps stopped playing with the recliner sofa and sat up straight.

"Insulin? Like with a needle?"

"Normally your pancreas makes insulin." Beth paused and softened her voice. "But yours isn't doing that anymore. So, yes, with a needle."

"Aren't there other pills we can try?"

"I've already sent a prescription over to the pharmacy. You can pick it up any time."

"What if I cut out the ice cream?"

"This isn't *Let's Make a Deal*." Beth closed the folder and set her glasses on the table. "This is serious. Did you ever read that brochure on diabetes I gave you?"

Thumps tried to remember if he had ever seen a brochure on diabetes.

"Sure."

"The part about blindness, stroke, organ failure, and amputations?"

Thumps brought the recliner back to a full and upright position. "So I have to inject myself with insulin?"

"Yes."

"Once a week?"

"With every meal."

Thumps knew a joke when he heard one. "Not funny."

"The pharmacy will give you a booklet and a chart that

explains carbohydrate counting and how to gauge the amount of insulin you'll need in each injection."

"You were kidding about after every meal."

"But in the end, insulin is an art rather than a math formula." Beth leaned back in the chair. "If you exercise after a meal, you'll need to take less insulin. If you plan to sack out on the sofa and watch TV, you'll need more. There's the chance that your body will still produce insulin from time to time, and that can throw things off."

"Every meal?"

"In the end, you're going to have to get attuned to your body and what high and low blood sugars feel like. It will be a little tricky at first."

"Am I dying?"

"Yes," said Beth, "and the insulin is going to help to keep you alive."

"The sofa isn't all that comfortable. I liked the old one better."

"I'm sorry." Beth nodded. "I know this isn't good news."

"You and Ora Mae back together?"

"You really want to go there?" Beth's face darkened into a storm front. "It's not my fault you're diabetic."

Okay. He was sorry he had brought Ora Mae up. That had been unkind. Beth was right. It wasn't her fault he was diabetic. It was a disease after all, not some form of punishment or retribution.

Thumps was at the door when Beth stopped him.

"Tell Claire I'm here if she wants to talk."

"Sure."

"The needles are not a big deal," she said. "You'll get used to them."

"Sure."

"But I'm really sorry about your cat."

FOURTEEN

Thumps stood on the sidewalk in front of the old Land Titles building and considered the possibilities. To his left was Chinook Pharmacy and the exciting new diabetic regime. To his right was Al's and a late breakfast. He hadn't eaten much at Shadow Ranch, and he was hungry. If he was lucky, he could sneak in before the lunch crowd arrived.

The decision was an easy one. The pharmacy could wait.

There was only one other person in the café. A woman in a hooded windbreaker several sizes too big. She was at the counter hunched over a plate of food and a cup of coffee.

Not a regular.

That happened every so often. A tourist would get lost and wander in, or someone passing through town had heard about the café and decided to give it a try.

In spite of its uninspiring interior.

Most good eateries had their own personality. Al's had smells. Grease and damp wool, strong coffee and sweat combined to form currents and eddies that ran through the café like tides, and Thumps imagined that the main sensation people who walked in off the street for the first time had was that of being shoved underwater.

Thumps was already on his favourite stool, waiting for Al to bring the pot, before he realized who she was.

"Mr. DreadfulWater."

Sydney Pearl. *Malice Aforethought.*

"Al and I were just talking about you."

Al was standing at the grill, a steel spatula in her hand. She didn't look happy to see him.

Pearl pushed the hood off her head. "I understand you had breakfast with Calder."

"At Shadow Ranch?" shouted Al. "Some people might consider that collaborating with the enemy."

"I told her it wasn't your idea," said Pearl. "Don't think she believed me."

Thumps had hoped for a quiet sanctuary, a place where he could contemplate his failing health and feel sorry for himself, a place where he could drown his sorrows in crispy hash browns and scrambled eggs.

Al waved the spatula at him. "Good thing I'm a generous and forgiving person."

Pearl had a waffle in front of her. Along with two large sausages.

"A waffle?" Thumps stared at Al. "You only make waffles and sausages for people you like."

"Sydney's going to put me in the show."

"Are those honey garlic pork sausages?"

"Colour," said Pearl. "We try to involve local people in the show."

"Is that real maple syrup?"

"Don't be a baby." Al brought the pot and filled his cup. "I don't make you waffles because you're diabetic."

"So did Calder cry on your shoulder?" Pearl stayed bent over her food.

Thumps pointed his lips at the grill. "Scrambled eggs, hash browns, multi-grain toast, and salsa. Please?"

Al wiped her hands on her apron. "Oh, so infidelity makes you hungry?"

Pearl pulled the hood off her head. "Did he tell you that *Malice Aforethought* was his big chance to get back into the game?"

"Is it?"

"Yes," said Pearl. "And no. Calder's got the looks and the camera likes him. He's long on the visuals, but he's short on the talent. If this were a dramatic series, he'd be the guy they kill off in the first episode."

"But it's not."

"Nope," said Pearl. "It's reality TV. Calder doesn't have to act, he just has to narrate."

"And he's got a good voice."

Pearl cut a piece off the waffle. "For Calder, reality TV is as good as it gets. He just doesn't know it."

"And you've told him this?"

Pearl smiled. "Do I look like I care?"

Al took longer than usual with his breakfast. She was known to get grumpy if her regulars ate somewhere else. But Thumps hadn't really eaten at Shadow Ranch. He hoped she didn't know about Mirrors.

"Here's your breakfast," she said. "I cut back on the potatoes and eggs, seeing as you've already eaten."

"I didn't eat anything." Thumps sagged on the stool for effect. "My blood sugars are dropping fast."

Al kept the pot on her hip. "Jimmy said he saw you coming out of that new joint across from the Tucker."

Okay. So she knew about Mirrors as well.

"*Malice Aforethought* is network prime time," said Pearl. "Hard to get to the top. Harder to stay there."

Thumps dumped the salsa over his eggs.

"We have eight episodes in the can." Pearl settled her forearms on the counter. "They've been okay, enough salaciousness, innuendo, and violence to keep the audience awake. But for the last two episodes, we need something stronger."

The low light in Al's wasn't doing Sydney Pearl any favours. In the gloom of the café, she looked gaunt. Her hair was thin and limp, the skin around her eyes slate grey and desert dry.

Thumps wondered if she was still packing the .38.

"Have you reconsidered our offer?"

And there it was, staring him in the face. Thumps mentally kicked himself. He should have seen it sooner.

"You need Rattler."

Pearl tilted her head to one side. There was a faint rash on the side of her neck that started below her ear and disappeared under the jacket.

"And you don't have him."

Pearl went back to her waffle.

Thumps turned on the stool. "What's it cost to bring your cast and crew to Chinook?"

"It's expensive."

"And you wouldn't have made that commitment unless all the pieces were in place."

"What's your point, Mr. DreadfulWater?"

Thumps ran through the various scenarios and came up with the same answer. "What you have is a cold case. You want it to be a murder, but right now you have zip. Buck Samuels is dead. Sheriff Tull is dead. No witnesses. All you really have is a rich family, an angry stepmother, and a dead girl."

Pearl closed her eyes.

"And Tobias Rattler. Reservation bad boy. Famous novelist. Was he Trudy's lover? Did he kill her? Did he cause her to commit suicide? How am I doing?"

"Please," said Pearl. "Continue."

"The only way the show works is if you can fabricate a confrontation between Adele Samuels and Rattler."

"Mr. Rattler agreed to be on the show." Pearl turned on her stool. "He signed a contract."

"But now he's decided that he doesn't want to do it?"

"Three days ago."

Thumps spooned the last of the salsa out of the container. There were a number of ways for Pearl and *Malice Aforethought* to have come to this impasse. But there was only one that made sense.

"Because you lied to him."

Pearl's poker face was impressive. She picked up her coffee cup as though she were examining it for cracks.

"That's not very friendly."

Thumps saw his mistake. "No, not you. Nina Maslow. Maslow told him that *Malice Aforethought* just wanted to interview him about Trudy Samuels. What did she tell him? A documentary? A memorial? A tribute? A short conversation with Calder? Remembering Trudy? Something like that?"

"For an ex-cop," said Pearl, "you'd make a decent producer."

"But what Maslow really planned to do was to spring Adele Samuels on him. A surprise. He'd be on set chatting with Calder and then Samuels would arrive and accuse him of murdering Trudy. You wanted to embarrass him, suggest that he killed the girl. The Jerry Springer moment. Two dogs in a box. How am I doing?"

"It's a little gauche, but you've managed the plot quite well."

"And Rattler found out about your little plan."

"So it seems."

"A slaughterhouse with nothing to slaughter."

"You should have stopped at 'two dogs in a box.'"

Thumps tried to see all the possibilities at once and came up short. "What I don't understand is what you expect me to do. You don't want me to investigate the case. The only thing that makes sense is you're hoping I can talk Rattler into being on the show."

"We want you to do both."

Thumps could feel it. There was something he was missing. "I don't know Rattler. He doesn't know me."

"Do you know the difference between legality and justice?"

"Sure," said Thumps. "And I also know the difference between truth and lies."

"No need for cynicism, Mr. DreadfulWater," said Pearl. "It doesn't become you."

"There is nothing to suggest that Rattler had anything to do with what happened to Trudy Samuels."

"Mrs. Samuels believes he did."

"Emmitt Tull looked at him hard," said Thumps, "and Rattler was never even charged."

"Legal versus justice," said Pearl. "Surely you know the two are not the same."

"Which brings us back to my question," said Thumps.

"My job is to make sure this program is a success." Pearl kept her voice calm and even. "And I only have two more shows to make that happen."

"And if the last two episodes are terrific?"

Pearl finished up the waffle. "Network picks up the option for another year. Fame and fortune."

"And if they don't?"

"In order to survive in this business, you have to be a hopeless optimist or a high-functioning sociopath." Pearl pushed the rest of her waffle to where Thumps could reach it. "We have a production meeting at 3:00. Why don't you stop in, see what we're doing. Maybe you'll discover that we have mutual interests."

Thumps tried to imagine what those interests might be. "So which one are you?"

"Me?"

"Optimist or sociopath?"

Pearl dropped a twenty on the counter, pulled her hood up over her head, and pushed off the stool. "Who the fuck cares?"

Thumps didn't realize that Al was standing in front of him until he looked up from his coffee.

"I like her," Al said. "She's tough and she's smart."

"She has a gun."

"Hell," said Al, "I have a gun."

"So you're going to be a TV star."

"You're not getting off that easy."

Thumps held up his hands. "I didn't ask to go to Mirrors, and I didn't ask to go to Shadow Ranch."

"That's what the Nazis said."

"The Nazis said they were following orders."

"Same thing." Al looked at his plate. "Something wrong with my hash browns?"

"No." Thumps sighed. "Just tired."

Al filled his cup to the top. "Okay," she said. "Seeing as you lost your car and your cat, and can't find Claire, and the diabetes has gotten worse, I'll cut you some slack."

Thumps sat up with a start. "What about my diabetes?"

"Having to shoot up with insulin after every meal is not the end of the world."

"Jesus."

"What?" said Al. "It was a secret?"

Thumps closed his eyes and breathed deeply. "You really going to be in that show?"

Al threw the dish towel over her shoulder. "Why not? Looks like fun. I get to stand around just like I do here, except I get paid better. And I don't have to clean up after."

"Maybe they'll shoot a scene here in the café." Thumps slipped a ten under his plate. "You could be Chinook's new celebrity destination. Might even win the mayor's Howdy award."

Al's eyes brightened. "There's an award?"

"Hell if I know," said Thumps.

Al leaned against the cash register and folded her arms across her chest. "Isn't it time for you to stick yourself with a needle?"

Thumps slung his bag over his shoulder. "Coffee at Mirrors was pretty good."

"Yippee." Al twirled the dish towel around her head like a lariat as she walked back to the grill. "Yippee."

FIFTEEN

The front windows of the Chinook Pharmacy had been transformed into a Plains Indian panorama with tipis stretched out along a river as far as the eye could see. There was a herd of buffalo in the foreground, with the sun just coming up on the horizon.

It wasn't Albert Bierstadt, but it could have been.

Inside, the pharmacy was done up to look like a western jail, the kind of jail anyone who had seen *Rio Bravo* or *A Fistful of Dollars* would recognize. Someone had built a miniature cell out of trellis panels and painted the whole thing dark grey so that the cedar slats looked like iron bars. Taped to the walls were wanted posters that featured most of Chinook's prominent citizens. There was a poster for Archie "the Kid" Kousoulas and one for Beth "Shotgun" Mooney, dead or alive, five thousand dollars each.

"Howdy, Mr. DreadfulWater."

Normally Chintak Rawat would be dressed in his starched white pharmacy jacket. But today he was dressed in leather chaps, a western shirt, and a ten-gallon hat that reminded Thumps of sailing ships and flying nuns.

"You're looking mighty grim," said Rawat, and he took his six-gun out of its holster and spun it around on a finger. "I reckon you and me got a score to settle."

There was a large poster behind Rawat that said "Gun Fights Available on Request."

"Gun fights?"

"Oh, yes," said Rawat, dropping John Wayne from his voice. "A great deal of western fun. Perhaps you would like to try to best me."

Thumps chuckled. "A gun fight? Me and you?"

"I am quite quick," said Rawat. "Already I have bested Mr. Archie and Mr. Cooley."

Rawat had arrived from Toronto about seven years back and bought the drugstore from Harry Lomax when Harry retired and moved to the Oregon coast. Biblical admonishments to treat your neighbour as yourself aside, Rawat had not had an easy time of it, cultural diversity being an alien concept in this part of the civilized world.

But the cost of gas and the time it took to drive to Great Falls or Helena to get their drugs finally convinced folks to do what generosity and compassion could not.

"Alas, the sheriff is quicker than he looks."

"You and Duke?"

Rawat held out a holster and a single pistol. "Prepare to slap leather."

What the hell. Thumps strapped the holster around his waist and tied the holster off at his thigh. Rawat stalked out from behind the counter.

"I mean to kill you in one minute, Ned," said Rawat, getting back into character. "Or see you hanged in Fort Smith at Judge Parker's convenience. Which'll it be?"

Thumps waited for Rawat to make the first move.

"No, no," said Rawat, breaking character. "You're supposed to say, 'I call that bold talk for a one-eyed fat man.'"

"What?"

"*True Grit*," said Rawat. "John Wayne, Glen Campbell, Kim Darby, Robert Duvall. The remake with Jeff Bridges and Matt Damon was not as much fun."

Rawat let his hand hover just above the butt of the pistol. Thumps felt a jolt of excitement course through his body. Rawat was right. This was fun.

Both men moved at the same time.

The explosion was unexpected, as was the slight recoil of the pistol.

"Jesus!"

"That was very close," said Rawat. "I think we have killed each other."

"What the hell was that?"

"Oh dear," said Rawat. "Yes, I forgot to mention that these are movie prop guns with special blanks. Very authentic. Available online from Los Angeles."

Thumps waited for his heart rate to return to normal. "You might want to warn people ahead of time."

Rawat stepped back behind the counter and took off his hat. "Dr. Beth has sent in a new prescription," he said, the cowboy gone for the moment. "It appears that the initial medical protocol was not as effective as expected."

"She says I need to be on insulin."

"Yes," said Rawat. "That is exactly what she is saying."

"And that means a needle?" Maybe Thumps had misunderstood what Beth had said.

"Oh, yes," said Rawat. "This means many needles. Are you testing your blood sugar levels on a regular basis?"

"So I have to keep testing my blood even with the insulin?"

"This is accurate," said Rawat. "You have a small needle for testing the blood, which you already do, and now you need a larger needle for introducing the insulin into the body."

"Larger?"

"Has Dr. Beth shown you the proper procedure?"

"No."

"And has she discussed with you the possible side effects and the potential for infection?"

Thumps realized he was only hearing every other word. "She hasn't."

"It is really quite simple."

Rawat opened a box containing a zipped case that looked as though it would hold glasses. Inside was a long tubular device that could have been a fountain pen but wasn't.

"This is the injector," said Rawat. "You twist it like this. Then you insert the vial of insulin like this. Then you peel the protective cover off the needle and screw it on the end of the injector."

Thumps looked at the needle. Rawat was right. It was larger than the lancet he used to draw blood for testing.

Rawat held the injector up so Thumps could see what he was doing. "You dial in the amount of insulin you need like this, lift your shirt and pinch a roll of fat at your waist, insert the needle into the fat, and depress the plunger."

Thumps needed to sit down somewhere and put his head between his legs.

"And has Dr. Beth mentioned the possibility of hitting nerves with the needle?"

Thumps shook his head.

"Then I will say no more about it."

Rawat took his time explaining the ins and outs of insulin use.

"It is not an exact science," he said. "There are all sorts of variables in insulin use. For instance, you must ask yourself, 'Am I overweight?'"

No, Thumps thought to himself, *that is not a question I want to ask.*

"Another question is, 'How much do I exercise and when?'"

"You mean like at a gym?"

"Yes, of course at a gym," said Rawat, "but exercise can also come in other forms. For instance, does your work provide a high, a moderate, or a low amount of physical activity?"

Thumps wasn't liking where this was headed.

"And of course, we must ask ourselves the most difficult question of all." Rawat paused to see if Thumps wanted to come up with the answer himself.

"Diet?"

"Exactly so," said Rawat. "Of course, knowing what one should do and doing it are not always the same thing."

The bill for the insulin, the injector, and the needles was a shock, like the gun going off in his hand.

Rawat put the cowboy hat back on his head and set it at a rakish angle. "Are you gonna do something?" he said. "Or just stand there and bleed?"

"What?"

"*Tombstone,*" said Rawat. "1993, with Kurt Russell, Val Kilmer, and Sam Elliott."

Thumps looked at the bill again. "So how are sick people who don't have a lot of money supposed to get well?"

"Yes," said Rawat, "this will appear to be a conundrum until you understand that the well-being of the individual is not the primary concern of health-care corporations."

"Great."

"So I shall say no more about it."

THE SIDEWALKS WERE empty. The air had turned dark silver, and there were cold clouds on the horizon. Snow in the mountains by evening. Thumps had arrived in Chinook on a day like this. The Volvo had broken down on the outskirts of town, and he had been forced to wait for the car to be repaired.

What was it now? Five years? Six years since that summer on the Northern California coast when bodies began showing up on the beaches around Arcata and Trinidad Head. Ten people in all. Five women, four men. One child. There had been little similarity. Not in age or occupation. Some of the victims had been local. Others had been passing through on vacation. Each body left just above the high tide mark with a small piece of obsidian in their mouths, something you wouldn't find on a beach, something the killer brought with him.

Anna Tripp and her daughter, Callie.

Thumps had been away at a forensics conference in San Diego. By the time he returned, there was nothing left of the life he had had. So he resigned his position, packed the Volvo, and headed east.

He didn't remember deciding to stay in Chinook. He just had. And each fall, when the geese passed overhead on their way out of Canada, headed south, Thumps would imagine going, would imagine getting back on the road and leaving everything behind once again.

He guessed that it was people who held you in place. Wives, husbands, lovers, children, friends. Or perhaps it was a landscape, the light in the morning, the sky at night. Or maybe it was simply having nowhere else to go.

But right now he wasn't going anywhere. At least he wasn't going to be driving. The truck Stas had lent him was parked at home. Not a long walk, but there was nothing waiting for him there save the silence of an empty house.

SIXTEEN

Thumps was sure that attending a production meeting was a waste of time, and he stopped short of Budd's to reconsider. Ironstone Jewelry was having a sale on diamond pendants, and the Natural Gourmet had a special on herbal teas. Thumps took his time looking in the windows of both stores to see if there was anything he might need.

There wasn't.

Nor did he need to be sucked into the Pearl and Maslow quagmire of prime-time justice and small-screen entertainment. There had been the first shoe, the hint that he had a vested interest in the Samuels case, and Thumps suspected that it wouldn't be long before the second one hit the floor.

Gloria Baker-Doyle and Nina Maslow were standing next to the espresso machine. Their faces reminded Thumps of tired mothers in supermarkets trying to manage unruly children.

"Mr. DreadfulWater." Maslow rearranged her face. It wasn't a smile exactly. "There you are."

"Here I am."

Gloria gestured to the machine. "You know anything about espresso machines, yeah?"

"Still not working?"

"We found the portafilter," said Nina, "but now it won't turn on."

"Is it plugged in?"

Both Nina and Gloria reprised their market-mommy faces.

"And you've flipped the switch?" said Thumps, pushing his luck further than good sense would recommend.

Nina gave Gloria a weary look. "Why didn't we think of that?"

"Because we're girls," said Gloria.

"Maybe the breaker is blown." Thumps waited. "It's an old building. The circuit might not be able to handle the load."

Maslow rubbed her hands together. "Is this how guys talk when they get together?"

Thumps smiled. And kept his mouth shut.

"So we're looking for a breaker box?"

"Probably a fuse box."

"Brilliant," said Gloria. "I've always wanted to see a fuse box."

The fuse box was in a closet under the staircase, and the news wasn't good. Someone or several someones had, over the years, tried to renovate the electrical circuitry without changing the size of the service. The wiring looked as though it had been teased with a comb.

"It's a sixty-amp service," said Thumps. "It should be at least a hundred amps."

"How exciting," said Gloria.

"So," said Nina, "we're blowing the circuit every time we try to turn the machine on."

"Probably."

"Can it be fixed?"

"Sure," said Thumps. "All you have to do is pull out all the wiring, put in a new service, and you're good to go."

Maslow grunted something under her breath. "And if we don't want to do that?"

"Find a free circuit that won't overload."

"Is this your first production meeting, Mr. DreadfulWater?" Nina headed up the stairs without waiting for an answer. "You're going to love it."

The second floor of Budd's was in the process of being turned into a set, a rustic log room with enormous windows that opened onto nothing. Thumps didn't know where *Malice Aforethought* had found the carved wood furniture, the heavy draperies, and the thick oriental carpets, but the effect was startling.

Daniel Boone comes to Downton Abbey.

Sydney Pearl was sitting on a high-back sofa, a script in her hand. "What do you think?"

"Elaborate."

"Black Stag," said Pearl. "It's the living room of the Samuels's estate. Nina worked from photographs."

"Clever."

"Was that sarcasm?" Pearl put the script to one side. "Or appreciation?"

"I've always found it somewhat grotesque."

Thumps turned to find an older woman standing at the staircase. She was dressed in a dark blue cashmere suit with a pale white brooch on a lapel.

"Buck saw it as rugged elegance."

Thumps had never seen the woman before, but he didn't need an introduction to know who she was.

Pearl was off the sofa and across the set. "Mrs. Samuels," she said. "It's good of you to join us. You know Nina, of course."

Thumps saw no point in trying to guess a woman's age. It was an enterprise for fools. Adele Samuels could have been fifty, but simple math put her in her late sixties.

Samuels looked right at Thumps. "This isn't Rattler."

Adele Samuels was slender and ram-rod straight, with soft hair the colour of silver foil and blue-grey eyes that reminded Thumps of a fall blizzard.

"No," said Nina. "This is Thumps DreadfulWater. He's going to help us with the investigation."

"You're Indian." Samuels's lips curled up at the edges.

"I am."

"Blackfoot? Cree?"

"Cherokee."

Samuels didn't try to soften her voice. "Do you know Mr. Rattler?"

"I don't."

"I see," said Samuels, dismissing Thumps and turning her attention to Maslow. "I thought we had an understanding."

Maslow nodded. "We do."

"Rattler is to be on the show," said Samuels, "but now I hear that he doesn't intend to appear."

"He'll be here."

"Because there's no point in talking to some Cherokee who doesn't know anything," said Samuels.

Maslow let the complaint slide off her back. "Is your son going to be joining us?"

"Finding a parking space," said Samuels. "He'll be here shortly."

"Ethan, isn't it?" said Nina.

"It is," said Samuels, turning from one woman to the other. "He's to be with me on set when we confront Mr. Rattler."

"What have I missed?"

The man who came puffing up the stairs was younger than Thumps. He was plump, with thinning hair and thinner lips. His face was damp. There were dark blotches under his arms and across his chest as though he had just come from the gym. Or a long run.

"Hi," said the man. "I'm Ethan Price."

"Adele's son," said Pearl.

"That's right." Ethan had a nice open smile that he must have gotten from his father. "For better, for worse."

"So, we're here." Samuels's mouth made a sound like a steel trap snapping shut. "You said you needed to go over some of the material."

"Just a few questions," said Nina.

"Let's not take too long," said Adele. "I have things to do."

"We're happy to help," said Ethan.

"Great," said Maslow. "First of all, I'd like to get a feel for the geography."

"Geography?"

"In a manner of speaking," said Maslow. "For instance, at the time of her death, Trudy didn't live with you."

"At the time of her murder," Adele corrected. "And no, she didn't live with us. She lived in town."

"And the drive from town to your place would take, what? Half an hour?"

"I can make it in twenty-two minutes." Ethan smiled and shook his head. "So long as you don't get nailed in Randall."

"What does any of this have to do with anything?"

"It's okay, Mom," said Ethan. "They need all the background they can get."

"After Trudy moved off the estate," said Nina, "did she ever come back?"

"For what?" said Adele.

"A visit," said Maslow. "To pick up stuff she might have forgotten. To talk to you about how her life was going."

"No," said Adele. "We didn't talk."

"I'd see her at school," said Ethan. "We'd say hello."

"So neither of you knew what was happening in her life once she left Black Stag."

Adele sat up even straighter. "Of course we knew. It's a small community, Ms. Maslow. People see things. People talk."

"Did you ever talk to Mr. Rattler?"

Adele bristled. "Why would I talk to him?"

"Just checking," said Maslow. "For instance, you might have wanted to warn him off your stepdaughter."

"Trudy did what she wanted to do," said Adele. "She didn't listen to anyone except herself. She was spoiled, and she was selfish."

"We knew she was hanging out with Rattler," said Ethan. "But there was nothing much we could do about it."

"Did she happen to call you the night she died?"

"Ms. Maslow," said Adele. "Trudy and I didn't talk. She was a drunk, and yes, she did drugs. She was not a pleasant person to be around. But she didn't deserve to die the way she did."

"Actually," said Ethan, "she was off alcohol and drugs the last year or so."

"Drunks are good at hiding what they are," said Adele. "Buck was an expert."

Thumps stood quietly and watched the two women move

back and forth along the baseline. It was like watching a slow-motion tennis match. With knives.

"So you never met Mr. Rattler?"

Ethan jumped in. "He brought Trudy home one night. She was drunk."

"Was he?"

"Drunk?"

"Yes."

"No," said Ethan. "I don't think so."

"That was when I called the sheriff," said Adele.

"Because?"

"What would you do if someone like Rattler brought your daughter home drunk with her dress torn?"

"I'd probably call the police," said Nina.

"I would certainly hope so," said Adele. "Are we finished?"

Maslow looked at Pearl. "One last question. You testified at the coroner's jury that you believed that Tobias Rattler was responsible for your stepdaughter's death."

"I did."

"There's nothing in the record to support that conclusion."

"Why are you asking me these questions?"

Maslow softened her voice. "These are questions our viewers are going to ask."

"Not everything got into the record," said Ethan. "A couple of days before Trudy died, she went back to the drinking and drugs. I saw her at school. She was a mess."

"Any reason why?"

"Something happened with her and Rattler," said Ethan. "What I heard was that Rattler had dumped her and that she was furious."

"She had a temper," said Adele. "There is no denying that."

"But you don't think she might have committed suicide."

"You don't commit suicide when you're angry," said Adele. "I can tell you that."

Maslow stood up. "I think that does it."

"That's it?" said Ethan. "Shouldn't we go over what we're going to say on camera?"

Nina shook her head. "No. We want that to be spontaneous. We want it to be organic. I'll have a schedule shortly. On the day of the shoot, we'll pick you up and bring the both of you here to the set."

"Just make sure Rattler is here."

"He will be," said Maslow.

Adele Samuels paused at the staircase. "You know, you could have found a place with an elevator. I don't think that would have been too much to ask."

Thumps waited until Mrs. Samuels and Ethan had made their way to the first floor.

"What's going on?"

Nina shrugged. "What do you mean?"

"You don't have a show," said Thumps. "What you have is a bunch of what-ifs that don't add up to anything."

"Actually," said Pearl, "we have a great deal more than supposition and conjecture."

"We do," said Maslow.

There it was again. The feeling that he was missing a piece to the puzzle, a feeling that Maslow and Pearl knew more than they were saying.

"Rattler is never going to be on the show," said Thumps. "There's no reason for him to come."

"That's your job, Mr. DreadfulWater," said Pearl. "Find Mr. Rattler. Talk to him. I'm sure you'll find a way."

"And," said Maslow, "thanks for the help with the espresso machine."

SEVENTEEN

Ora Mae peered at Thumps over the top of her glasses. "Well, here's a ton of trouble."

The realty office was quiet. The big longhorn and the bales of hay had been moved to a corner of the room, away from the workstations.

"Don't be dumping your grumbly self all over my brand-new carpet."

"That condo that Moses is renting," said Thumps. "I need the address."

Ora Mae pressed her fingertips to her lips. "You ever hear of doctor-patient privilege?"

"You're not a doctor."

"And you're not a patient."

Thumps could hear the exasperation in his voice. "Of course I'm not a patient."

"How's Claire?" said Ora Mae. "I haven't seen her since you two got back."

"Claire's fine," said Thumps. "Moses?"

"I hear the operation was a success."

"The address?"

"Is there a problem with the condo?"

"How should I know? I don't even know where it is."

"This is serious shit, DreadfulWater," said Ora Mae. "I can't be giving away addresses to just any cowboy who walks in off the street."

"I'm an Indian."

"And I'm a black woman in a white town," said Ora Mae, "so don't be playing the race card with me."

"Moses is a friend. I'm worried that he might be in trouble."

"That nice old man?"

"And I need your help."

Ora Mae picked up a pen. "You been by Beth's lately?"

Thumps glanced at the bag of diabetic supplies on the floor by his leg. "Yes."

"What colour are the walls?"

"What?"

"The walls. In the living room. What colour are they?"

"I don't know. Yellow, I think."

"Light or dark?"

"Ora Mae . . ."

"Light or dark?"

"Light."

"Damn." Ora Mae shook her head. "That woman just can't get past yellow. She ask about me?"

"Absolutely," said Thumps. "Yes, she did."

"Good thing you don't lie for a living," said Ora Mae. "You'd be butt poor and begging."

Thumps was not about to get between the two women. They'd work it out, or they wouldn't. Nothing waiting for him there but misery and blunt-force trauma.

"You two might think about talking to each other."

Ora Mae screwed her lips into a knot. "You don't do helpful any better."

"Could I please just have the address?"

"You want to tell me why giving you that sweet old man's address is so important?"

"It would take too long."

Ora Mae settled back in her chair. "Short version."

There were certainly other ways to find out where the condo was. But they would all take more time and effort than he wanted to spend.

"*Malice Aforethought.*"

"That's disgusting," said Ora Mae. "You think you could get me on the show?"

"What?"

"Lesbian real-estate agent." Ora Mae patted her hair. "Dark secrets of the housing market. They do shit like that."

Thumps rubbed his forehead. "I'll put your name in."

Ora Mae peeled a green sticky off the pad. "You tell anyone where you got this and you'll be looking over your shoulder the rest of your life."

"Okay."

Ora Mae tapped a long, manicured finger against her chest. "You don't want to be annoying this woman."

Thumps couldn't think of a single woman he wanted to annoy.

Ora Mae sat up straight and turned her face so that it caught the light from the window. "And when you talk to those TV people, make sure you tell them just how photogenic I am."

THE CONDO COMPLEX was on the other side of the river, and Thumps made the mistake of thinking that a walk on a lovely fall day would be invigorating. It wasn't. By the time he found the address, he was tired. He should have gone home first and picked up the truck.

Now he'd have to walk back.

Mesa Verde was a cluster of condominium units that were done up to look like the Anasazi cliff dwellings in southwestern Colorado.

With only limited success.

Instead of adobe, the exterior was cinder block with a spray-on acrylic resin stucco finish that was already beginning to lift off around some of the windowsills and door frames. There were dark stains down the side of the condos where the eavestroughs had leaked, and the concrete walkways had started to crack and buckle from the hard plains winters.

Thumps should have asked Ora Mae what these units cost. Not that he was going to buy one any time soon. But depending on price, Mesa Verde might make him feel better about the condition of his own house.

Number 49 was facing the river and promised to have a nice view. Thumps pressed the doorbell and was greeted with the American national anthem.

Another thing that needed to be fixed.

"Hey, Thumps."

Cooley Small Elk was standing in the doorway, a neat trick for a man who was bigger than the frame.

"Moses said you'd find us soon enough."

"So Moses is here?"

"He said it's because you're such a good detective."

"I need to talk to him."

"Yep." Cooley stepped to one side. It was like rolling a large boulder from the entrance to a cave. "We've been expecting you."

The interior of the condo was standard apartment fare. Sheetrock walls, textured ceilings, low-pile industrial carpeting and engineered hardwood flooring, vinyl mouldings and baseboards.

Moses Blood was standing at the kitchen table, sorting

through the pieces of a jigsaw puzzle. "It's supposed to be a colony of puffins," said Moses. "One thousand pieces."

"So you actually rented a condo?"

"There's a pool," said Moses, "and a gym where you can ride a bicycle that doesn't go anywhere."

"Don't forget the Ping-Pong table," said Cooley.

"Cooley," said Moses, "get your uncle a glass of water. And some of those chocolate cookies."

Thumps couldn't imagine Moses leaving the reservation and his place on the river. "You're moving into town?"

Moses picked up a piece and tried to wedge it into a corner. "Why would I do that?"

"Then why did you rent a condo?"

"He didn't."

The man was Thumps's age, tall with short black hair and sad eyes. He was set at an angle, bent over slightly at the waist, as though he had stood against a strong wind too long.

"Tobias Rattler," said the man.

Rattler's hand was soft and gentle. Thumps was tempted to squeeze it to make sure that the man was real.

"I asked Moses to rent a condo for me so I wouldn't have to deal with the media."

"We're helping Toby keep a low profile," said Cooley.

"Yes," said Moses. "That spy movie we saw had a place just like this."

"A safe house," said Cooley.

"That's right," said Moses. "It's where the hero hides to recuperate from his wounds and to figure out who betrayed him."

"Toby's got this place for a whole month," said Cooley. "Plenty of time to solve the case. And the pool is great."

"You feel like a walk, Mr. DreadfulWater?" said Rattler. "Wouldn't mind stretching my legs."

"That's a good idea." Moses tried another piece that didn't fit. "Cooley and I are going to work on the puzzle, and then he's going to show me how to use the elliptical trainer."

"But we can't spend too much time working out," said Cooley. "There's a new TV series on tonight that's supposed to be real scary."

"They got a lot of scary shows on television." Moses made a face. "White people sure like to be frightened."

"Vampires and zombies," said Cooley. "In the old days, it was just cowboys and Indians."

"That's right," said Moses. "But these days, the cowboys are mostly gone, and we're not as daunting as we used to be."

Cooley put a huge hand on Thumps's shoulder. "If you had a white jacket and a stethoscope, you could go to Archie's party as a doctor."

"Yes," said Moses, "that would certainly terrify me."

Rattler slipped into his jacket and put on his shoes. "We can talk along the way," he said. "I imagine you have a question or two."

EIGHTEEN

The river path quickly left the condominiums behind, and by the time Thumps and Rattler reached the first bend, all signs of settlement and civilization had slipped away. The Ironstone snaked its way through the valley, sharp and dark, cutting into the land, drifting past the cottonwoods already stripped of most of their leaves. Magpies scuttled about in the wolf willow, and crows slouched in the trees, yelling insults at the intrusion into their world.

"I love the country," said Rattler, "but I live in cities. Do you know why?"

"The traffic?"

Rattler laughed. "You ever live in a big city?"

Thumps had visited places such as San Francisco and Denver, Toronto, and New York. But he had always lived in smaller towns. Central California, the Northwest Coast, the High Plains. Towns like Chinook. All of them, just like Chinook.

"Nope."

"One's not any better than the other," said Rattler. "They're just different."

"You were raised on the reservation."

Rattler nodded. "On and off. Reservation's worse than a small town. If you want to be invisible."

"And you wanted to be invisible?"

Rattler kicked at a stone and sent it scuttling into the prairie grass. "You know the difference between a celebrity and a writer?"

Thumps wondered how many more days like this were left before the first storms came down from the north and buried the high plains. Before the cold took over the world. Maybe he'd go away this year. Somewhere warm. He'd always wanted to see Hawaii or maybe Australia. The seasons were flipped at the bottom of the world. Winter was summer, and summer was winter.

"Trudy Samuels," said Rattler so softly that Thumps could have mistaken the sound for the wind in the trees.

"You were friends."

"The best." Rattler began walking again, moving stiffly like a thin bird wading in water. "We met in high school. Two loners trying to stay out of the way of the world."

Thumps remembered his high school years. Not with any great fondness. "Almost impossible."

"Bad boy Indian. Rich white girl." Rattler paused and then continued. "Mother died when she was young. Cinderella stepmother. Father's death messed her up good. You can do the math."

"Sounds like the plot for a bad novel."

Rattler chuckled. "It is the plot for a bad novel."

Thumps zipped up his jacket. He should have worn something warmer. "Can't imagine Adele was happy with the relationship."

"Not sure anything makes that woman happy," said Rattler. "It wasn't Trudy. And it sure as hell wasn't me."

Thumps watched his shadow. It stretched out in front of him as though it were trying to get away. Or maybe it was just trying to find someplace warm.

"Trudy ever try to kill herself?" Thumps hadn't wanted to ask the question, had hoped that Rattler would have come to it on his own.

"Not when I knew her. Maybe before." Rattler ran a hand through his hair. "Don't you want to know if I killed her?"

Thumps didn't say anything.

"When they found Trudy's body, Adele yelled murder as loud as she could."

"But you were cleared."

"Not quite the same, is it?"

No, thought Thumps, it's not.

"I didn't kill her," said Rattler, "and I don't think she committed suicide."

"What's left?"

"But that's not what you want to know, is it?" Rattler rubbed his hands together and stuffed them in his pockets. "You want to know why I'm here. Why I came back. After all this time."

Thumps tried to think of all the reasons that would have brought Rattler back to Chinook and could only come up with one.

"Moses asked you?"

"Never knew my parents. I bounced around foster homes. Reservation, off reservation. Sometimes I stayed for a while, other times I ran away. Moses found me on the side of the road. I was trying to hitchhike to Paris."

"France?"

"I had seen pictures of the city in a book," said Rattler. "It looked nice."

Thumps remembered the first time he had seen a picture of the Golden Gate Bridge. His mother had brought a magazine home from work. The bridge was on the cover.

"Anyway, he took me to his place. Fed me. Gave me a place to sleep." Rattler started laughing to himself. "Next morning, he drove me into town. We stopped at the library and looked Paris up in an atlas."

Thumps smiled.

"We followed the roads with our fingers to Minneapolis,

through Chicago, and all the way to New York and the Atlantic Ocean." Rattler took a deep breath. "And then we got back in his truck and went home."

"And you stayed."

"Moses didn't mind that I was invisible."

The sun sank in behind a ridge. If they didn't turn around in the next little bit, they'd be walking back in the dark.

"Moses thinks I left because of Trudy." Rattler made a clicking noise with his mouth. "That I left because she died."

"But you didn't?"

"I was never going to stay." Rattler turned his face into the buffeting wind and the dying light. "There was nothing for me here."

The river was in shadows now and the cottonwoods were settling in for the night. Thumps had forgotten how quiet the land could be.

"So," he said, as he walked alongside the taller man, "what *is* the difference between a celebrity and a writer?"

NINETEEN

Thumps didn't know how far he and Rattler had walked. Certainly farther than he had intended. Evening had caught them before they turned around, and by the time they got back to the condo, Thumps could feel his knees.

And his feet.

"Sydney Pearl says you agreed to be on the show."

"I thought it was going to be a documentary."

"Then you discovered it was *Malice Aforethought*."

"Surprise, surprise," said Rattler.

"And you backed out."

"I did. They weren't real happy."

"Maslow and Pearl want me to talk you into doing the show."

"They paying you?"

"That's the idea."

"But you're wondering why I'm here." Rattler kicked at

another stone. "If I wasn't going to do the show, why come back to Chinook. Why not just stay in Barcelona?"

"Barcelona?"

"Amazing city," said Rattler. "The Basilica of the Sagrada Familia is stunning."

"And now here you are."

Rattler's face softened. "Here I am."

THUMPS HAD HOPED to catch a ride home, but Moses and Cooley had already left for the reservation to catch the TV series of the undead and the living dead. He wondered if Moses had had a chance to try out the elliptical trainer, wondered what the old man thought about running in place and getting nowhere.

The old Dodge was waiting for him at the curb when he limped onto his porch, a mocking reminder of exactly why cars had been invented. He tried to recall the last time he had been on an extended trek. The hike up to Blackfoot Falls when he had gone looking for Stanley Merchant, Claire's son? Stick had been a suspect in a murder case, and Thumps had tried to find him before the damn fool fell off a cliff or got himself shot by the police. Had it been that long?

Thumps didn't expect to find Freeway waiting for him. And she wasn't. The house was as empty and cold as when he had left it. He checked the message machine.

Nothing.

The folder that Nina Maslow had given him was on the table. Maybe there was something in the crime-scene descriptions, officer interviews, photographs, and forensic reports that would provide answers, but he doubted it. And before he could even think about tackling the report and its dull, plodding prose, he needed to get something to eat. How long had it been since his last meal? Shadow Ranch? Al's? Not since late morning? What had happened to lunch? Where was dinner?

Wherever dinner was, he suddenly realized that it wasn't going to be here.

He still hadn't gone shopping. The cupboard was bare. The refrigerator was empty. The easy answer would be to jump in the truck and go to the new giant-squirrel fast-food joint the sheriff had recommended. Not an appealing idea. Golden arches, red-headed girls, giant squirrels. There was a reason they called it fast food.

The Halloween party.

Thumps had been to any number of events at the Aegean, and in every case, there had been food. Some very nice food, as he recalled. And if he left right away, he might get there before it was all gone.

He tried Claire's home phone.

Answering machine.

He tried her cell.

Then he grabbed his jacket and his hat.

* * *

THE WINDOWS OF the Aegean were ablaze as though the old library had been set on fire. As he stepped out of the truck, he heard the big drum. The Clay Pigeons. No mistaking Marvin Soop's voice. Singing an intertribal? At a Halloween party? How had Archie managed that?

Thumps stood on the sidewalk and reconsidered his decision. When he had been safe at home, the promise of free food had sounded appealing. Now that he was faced with the reality of having to talk to other people, of having to socialize with friends and strangers alike, the plan had lost much of its attraction.

There was still time to escape. He could get back in the truck, stop at Skippy's for takeout, and spend the evening at the kitchen table, reading the file. Maybe the police reports were bristling with gripping prose. Maybe fast food had improved when he wasn't looking.

Or he could slip into the bookstore, raid the food tables, and run to the safety of the drum. No one would bother him there, and he could lose himself in the voices of the other men.

The Clay Pigeons were a fluid group. Sometimes the drum consisted of four singers. Other times the Pigeons would field a dozen men. Thumps had been to powwows where some of the better-known drum groups—Red Bull, Black Lodge, Old Agency Singers—would wear matching shirts and leather vests. The Pigeons generally went with an assortment of jeans and mismatched T-shirts, but tonight the eight men around the buffalo hide drum were dressed in black suits and black shirts.

"Thumps!" Archie popped out of the crowd like a trapdoor spider. "Where's your costume?"

The food tables were at the back of the bookstore. Thumps could see a chunk of something juicy under a heat lamp.

"You just came for the food, didn't you?"

"Is that a roast?"

"Look at that," said Archie. "Even the Clay Pigeons got dressed up."

Thumps looked over at Marvin. "Who are they supposed to be?"

"Energy extraction corporations," said Archie. "Marvin's ExxonMobil. Wutty is Royal Dutch Shell. Russell is British Petroleum. Jimmy is Saudi Aramco."

"Energy extraction corporations?"

"They're supposed to be an oil slick." Archie began dragging Thumps through the crowd. "If you had bought that suit, you could have come as Gazprom."

It was a roast. Al was standing behind the table, carving off slices.

"Well, look who came for the free food."

Archie handed Thumps a plate. "See," he said, "even Alvera got dressed up."

Al looked the same as she always did. Thumps tried to imagine who she was supposed to be and came up empty.

"Jack the Ripper." Al waved her carving knife at Thumps. "No one knows what she looked like."

Thumps was reasonably certain that Jack the Ripper had been a he.

"Maybe he was," said Al. "And maybe he wasn't."

"Wouldn't mind a couple of slices."

"Not sure the food's for people who don't dress up."

"Is there horseradish?"

In addition to the roast, there was potato salad and a platter of tomatoes with fresh basil, multi-grain rolls from the Fjord Bakery and a variety of desserts from Lucille's. The "cauldron of blood" was raspberry juice with a little lemon juice added for bite. Mirrors had donated the coffee. Even Morris Dumbo had shown up for the party with several boxes of day-old doughnuts.

Archie had set up tables at the back of the store for seniors and anyone else who was too tired to stand.

"That includes diabetics," said Archie. "And you can eat with your new friends."

Gloria Baker-Doyle and Calder Banks were at a table in the corner. Gloria was wearing a ratty straw-blond wig and a pair of blue plastic-rimmed glasses. Calder was wearing a tweed jacket with a white shirt and tie.

Thumps wondered if Gloria had dressed up as Sydney Pearl. He could see where Pearl would be scary. Calder's outfit felt a little old-fashioned, not the sort of thing that a twenty-first-century television star would choose to wear.

"Ted Bundy," said Calder. "I auditioned for the part but Michael Reilly Burke beat me out."

Gloria tried to suppress a yawn and failed. "Sorry."

"Long day?"

"There are no short days on set," said Calder. "Or many short nights for that matter."

"They're not here," said Gloria, reading his mind. "Boss Pearl is busy in her dungeon torturing the shooting schedule, and Mistress Maslow is on location, trying to figure out the angles."

"On location?"

"Where the murder took place," said Gloria. "Brilliant, yeah?"

"By herself?" Thumps tried to picture Maslow wandering Belly Butte at night. "She's a big girl," said Calder.

"She wanted to get a feel for the landscape," said Gloria. "I volunteered to go with her, but she wanted to go alone."

"No chance she'll run into wild Indians." Calder's voice was edged with hope. "Is there?"

"She should have been back by now." Gloria glanced around the room. "I've tried calling, but she's not picking up."

"She's missing good food and a fun party." Calder gestured towards the drum. "How come all the songs sound the same?"

Thumps was on his way back to Al and the roast when he remembered that he was diabetic and that he was going to have to come to terms with the concept of moderation and mealtime insulin. The injector was in his bag, but he had no idea how much to take. What was the ratio of insulin to roast beef? Had the potato salad been a good idea? He was pretty sure that the tomatoes were okay, but he had serious doubts about the chocolate brownie.

And the lemon tart.

He should have paid more attention to the details when he was at the pharmacy.

Thumps locked the bathroom door behind him. Rawat had hinted that insulin usage was as much an art as a science. The injector looked more fearsome now that it was out in the open, now that he was faced with the reality of the disease. He had no idea if he should slip the needle in slowly or just jam it home and be done with it. He wasn't keen on either option. Maybe he could stab himself through his shirt. It might cushion the blow and make it not feel so . . . medical, might give it the appearance of a casual afterthought, something that he could forget immediately.

The needle made a soft popping sound as it broke the skin, but it didn't really hurt. A pleasant surprise. Okay, this might not be as bad as he had feared, even though his heart was racing. Thumps leaned on the bathroom sink and stared in the mirror. He wondered if you could look at someone and tell that they were sick or that they were dying.

Probably not. What good could come of that knowledge?

The party was in full swing now. Marvin had started a round dance, and all the thieves and gangsters and swindlers and serial killers and genocidal maniacs were holding hands, two-stepping their way around the bookstore in a giant serpentining circle, a variation of a conga line that reminded Thumps of a scene from *The Addams Family* movie. Raul Julia, Anjelica Huston, Christopher Lloyd. 1991. God, but that had been a funny film. "Don't torture yourself, Gomez," Huston tells Julia. "That's my job."

"Thumps."

Cooley looked as though he had dressed in the dark. The navy suit didn't fit quite right. The white shirt was twisted to one side and the bright blue tie had wandered off over one shoulder. The Donald Trump mask was pretty good, and it wasn't until Cooley turned around that Thumps realized what had happened.

"The mask is too hot to wear," said Cooley, "so I put everything on backwards. That way I can talk to you and scare everyone behind me."

Moses was wearing a tight blond wig, with a little rouge added to each cheek.

"Just as well," said Cooley. "When I had the mask on over my face, I had thoughts of groping women and not paying my bills."

"We should join the dancers," said Moses. "Marvin and the boys sound real good tonight."

"Moses wanted to come as Margaret Thatcher."

Moses licked his lips. "The Iron Lady."

"But since I was coming as Donald Trump," said Cooley, "he settled for Hillary Clinton."

"You know," said Moses, "pretending to be a woman is not as hard as being one."

Thumps watched Donald Trump and Hillary Clinton join the round dance. He was tempted, but he was also tired. He worked his way around the perimeter of the store until he was standing at the front door.

Gloria and Calder were still at the table, talking about something over coffee. Archie and Gabby Santucci were moving through the stacks with the rest of the dancers, the whole community in motion. Thumps had already looked for Claire several times, in case she had come in without his noticing.

She hadn't.

But he looked one last time, before he opened the door and slipped into the night.

TWENTY

It was the insulin.

No other explanation.

By the time he got home, he was wide awake. Tomorrow he'd have to stop in at the pharmacy and talk to Rawat about other possible side effects of the drug and what he could do about them.

Maybe give the fast draw another try.

The file was where he had left it. Thumps had never enjoyed reading crime-scene reports, didn't know any cop who did. They weren't written to entertain. They were official documents, the language clumsy and stilted, facts and statements stacked up like cordwood for a long winter.

Whoever had taken the crime-scene photographs had used a strobe, and the flash had washed away any trace of humanity.

Trudy's corpse could have been a prop in a horror movie. Or a mannequin in a department store window.

Death was never pretty. And it was never kind.

A young girl dead in the middle of nowhere.

As far as he could tell, there was nothing in the file to suggest that the police hadn't done a thorough job investigating Trudy's death, nothing to indicate that they had missed something. Nothing to indicate that there was anything to find.

Thumps went through the file again, page by page, line by line. Trudy Samuels had been found at the bottom of Belly Butte. Her car was parked at the top. The injuries to her body were consistent with a fall. There was no suicide note.

If this was all Nina Maslow had, *Malice Aforethought* was wasting its time. Which didn't make sense. Maslow wasn't stupid, and she wasn't sloppy. The file Calder had shown him had been a summary of his life, an outline, and the only way she could have put that together was if she had a larger and more complete file. So where was her complete file on Samuels? All he had in front of him was the police report. Where was Maslow's research work on the case?

Thumps went through the file again, but he knew he was wasting his time. If Maslow had discovered something about the case, something that suggested foul play, it wasn't here.

That night Thumps lay in bed, never quite asleep, never quite awake, his dreams bright and frantic, like lightning strikes in a storm. Claire lying on a beach, Anna and Callie falling down a mountain, Trudy and Tobias happily married with three kids.

Nina Maslow in bed next to him.

No sense to any of it. Just flash and blast and the long, dark silences in between. It was well after nine when Thumps finally gave up, got out of bed, and stumbled into the shower. He stood under the water and tried to wash away the exhaustion with a bar of soap that smelled like vanilla. He couldn't stay here all day, he knew that, but there he remained until the water ran cold and the banging began.

Someone was at the front door.

Cooley would have just let himself in. Claire would have rung the doorbell. Dixie would have stood on the porch until Thumps noticed him. Archie would be banging *and* shouting.

Which left only one person.

"Howdy," said the sheriff, without any hint of humour. "You just get out of bed? No wonder the country is in the shitter."

"I was in the shower."

Duke was holding two cups of coffee in a carry tray. "You smell like an ice cream cone."

Thumps could feel his hair begin to drip. "I'm going to get dressed."

"Hell of an idea," said Duke.

"There's nothing to eat unless you like dry cat food."

"You mind stepping on it?" Duke put the carry tray on the table. "Some of us have jobs."

Thumps closed the door to the bedroom. The sheriff arriving

at his house first thing in the morning was never a good beginning to his day. When the man arrived with coffee, it generally meant that Duke wanted a favour. Or worse, help with a problem.

Thumps found his jeans. He checked his shirt. Still good. "Coffee's not going to do it," he shouted, as he rummaged in his dresser for a clean pair of socks. "If you want to talk, you're going to have to buy me breakfast."

Duke grunted something that sounded distinctly unpleasant.

Thumps took his time buttoning his shirt and deciding whether to wear runners or boots. He settled on boots. By the time he got back to the kitchen, the sheriff was pacing the floor like a herd of buffalo on a game trail.

"Finally."

"I have to deal with my car." Thumps stood in the middle of the kitchen and tried to imagine that he was an immovable object. "I have to go grocery shopping."

"Drink your coffee," said the irresistible force.

"And I have to eat."

Duke reached into his pocket and came out with a lump of something folded up in a paper wrapper. "Breakfast."

Grease stains had already begun to appear on the wrapper. Thumps could smell overcooked beef and burnt onions.

"You're kidding."

"You can eat it in the car."

"I'm not going anywhere."

"Don't make me arrest you," said Hockney.

"For what?"

"For being a pain in the ass." Hockney grabbed Thumps's jacket from the back of the chair and tossed it to him. "Saddle up, Kemosabe."

"You have any idea what 'Kemosabe' means?"

"Nope," said Duke.

"So where are we going?"

"It's a surprise."

"I don't like surprises."

"How about that." Duke held the door open with his foot. "Neither do I."

It was a breakfast wrap of some sort, fatty and awash in melted cheese. Thumps held it away from his lap.

"This isn't breakfast."

"I got you the deluxe version."

"I can't eat this."

Duke kept his eyes on the road. "There's a candy bar in the glovebox."

"I'm diabetic."

"Then eat the wrap."

Thumps had hoped that, wherever the sheriff was taking him, it would be in town and that whatever Duke had in mind would be simple and short-lived.

It wasn't.

Duke left town on the fly, and by the time Thumps had

finished the wrap, the sheriff had turned off the highway onto the old lease road that ran out across the prairies all the way to the mountains.

"We going to Canada?"

"Don't get grease on my seat."

"'Cause I didn't bring my passport."

There were no clouds. Against the thin blue sky, the mountains looked hard and exact. As though someone had sharpened them for the coming winter. As they came over a low rise and Thumps saw the landscape open up in front of them, he realized where they were headed.

"Belly Butte?"

The track to the top of the butte was narrow and deeply rutted, and the sheriff had to straddle the runnels left by the rains and ease his way over the heavy rocks that rose out of the ground like the spine of some prehistoric beast.

Amazingly, there were four other cars that had also made the climb and were waiting for them. Beth Mooney's station wagon was parked close to the edge of the butte. Lance Packard was parked farther back. Duke's deputy was standing by his cruiser, a pair of binoculars around his neck, a roll of crime-scene tape in his hand, and a coil of climbing rope over his shoulder.

A white Toyota was parked next to Sydney Pearl's Honda.

"I need your eyes," said the sheriff, as he parked the SUV.

"No, you don't," said Thumps. "You have Lance and Beth."

"Just shut up and pay attention."

Beth was waiting for them and she wasn't particularly happy. "About time."

Duke nodded in Thumps's direction. "I had to stop and feed him."

"He tried to poison me with fast food."

Beth frowned. "You're not supposed to eat that crap."

Duke pulled his hat down tight on his head. "Could we save the medical moaning for later and get on with it?"

Below, at the base of the butte, was a body. Thumps couldn't tell who it was from here, but he was willing to take a guess.

"Shit."

"Shit is right," said Duke.

"Nina Maslow?"

The sheriff turned to him. "Why would you say that?"

"Maslow wasn't at Archie's party," said Thumps. "She came out here for a site visit."

"At night?"

"That's what I heard."

"I hate to interrupt the chit-chat." Beth held up her camera. "But I need the body photographed and brought up."

Thumps didn't like what he was thinking. "You brought me out here to help you carry a body."

"Not me," said Duke. "You and Lance."

"No way."

"We can't drive down," said the sheriff. "And you are a photographer."

"It's got to be two hundred feet," said Thumps. "And I didn't bring my camera."

"More like three hundred," said Beth. "There's a trail over there, but it's steep, so you big, strong men get to go."

"No can do," said the sheriff. "I have to interview the witness."

"You have a witness?"

Duke waved a hand at Lance's cruiser. "Guy who called it in."

Thumps squinted into the high glare. In the shadows of the back seat, leaning against the door of the police car, was Tobias Rattler.

Beth handed Thumps her cellphone. "You can take pictures with this."

"A phone?"

"You do know how to work it?"

"Who takes photos with a phone?"

"Okay." Beth took the phone back. "Looks like we all get to go."

"Be careful." Duke strolled over to the cruiser. "Three hundred feet. And I hear it's steep."

TWENTY-ONE

The trail from the top of Belly Butte to the prairie floor was a run of steep switchbacks, and as Thumps made each of the sharp turns, the dirt and small stones sliding out from under his feet like fresh snow, he imagined he was on skis, working his way down a world-cup slalom course.

"Enjoy yourself now." Beth slid along right behind him. "Coming up won't be as much fun."

Nina Maslow lay at the bottom of the scree field. One arm was bent at a nasty angle and her face had been badly cut by the rocks.

Beth pushed her way past Thumps and Lance Packard. "Stay put," she said, "until I get a good look."

"Hell of a fall," said Lance. "I'll bet you really pick up speed."

Thumps watched Beth walk the perimeter slowly in a

counter-clockwise pattern, using her cellphone to snap pictures. Then she stepped in and squatted down next to the body.

"Forensics 101," she shouted back to Thumps and Lance. "Who wants to go first?"

"Lance," said Thumps, volunteering the deputy.

Lance turned bright red as though he had been asked by his mother if he was sexually active.

"Injuries consistent with a fall." Lance put the binoculars to his eyes and scanned the side of the butte. "I can see slide marks. Could have lost her footing and fell."

"Okay," said Beth, "let's hear from Tweedledee."

Thumps stared at the body. When he was a cop, he had never gotten used to dealing with the dead. Most times he hadn't known the deceased. Nina Maslow he knew. Yesterday, she had been alive and well, and now she wasn't. Thumps tried to make sense of seeing her like this, and couldn't.

"Maybe."

"Maybe?" Beth put her hands on her hips and waited. "You want to elaborate?"

"Nope," said Thumps.

Beth nodded. "Your turn, Tweedledum."

Lance blushed again, but not as much. "That's a nasty head wound."

"Yes, it is," said Beth.

"She could have got it from the fall," said Lance, picking his way through the sentence as though it were a minefield.

"But we'll know more when we get her back to my parlour, won't we?" Beth stood up and took another picture.

Lance brightened. "Forensics, right?"

Thumps looked at the top of the butte. It was a long, hard fall. The top part was sloped, but then the side of the butte dropped away and it was a straight plunge to the bottom.

Beth shaded her eyes with her hands. "But first we have to carry her back to the top."

"We?"

"You and Lance," said Beth. "I'm just the pretty face."

If going down Belly Butte had felt like a ski hill at St. Moritz, coming up was more akin to scaling the Matterhorn.

With a body bag.

Lance took one end and Thumps took the other. Every so often, they would stop to catch their breath.

"You want to know how much farther?"

The weather was chilly, but Thumps's shirt was soaked with sweat and his shoulders ached. "No."

"Me neither," said Lance.

The sheriff and Beth's station wagon were waiting for them when they got to the top. Rattler was out of Lance's cruiser, a twist of coloured paper in one hand.

Thumps set his end down. "Are those flowers?"

"Yellow roses." Duke dropped the tailgate of the station wagon. "Took you long enough."

Thumps bent over and put his hands on his knees. Lance

stood up straight, trying to pretend that the hike up hadn't bothered him at all.

"You counting cars?" Duke hitched his pants.

"I am."

"Beth's station wagon," said Hockney. "Lance's cruiser. My official vehicle."

"The Toyota's mine," said Rattler. "A rental."

"Which leaves the Honda."

"Car's registered to a Sydney Pearl," said Lance. "I checked the registration."

"So," said Thumps, "we got the right number of cars and the right number of bodies."

"Damn," said Duke. "I hate it when two plus two turns out to be four."

The organization was impressive. Five cars. Six people.

Beth drove Maslow's body in the back of the station wagon to the Land Titles building. Lance headed into Chinook by himself.

That left three cars and three people.

"I called Stas," said the sheriff. "He's going to tow the Toyota and the Honda to the impound."

"Thought High Country had the contract with the county."

"They do," said the sheriff, "but Mr. Rattler here, in consideration for our limited budget and to show his good faith in the matter, has volunteered to pay for the tow of both cars."

"That's me," said Rattler. "Mr. Volunteer."

"How about I drive the Honda into town?"

"It's part of a crime scene," said Duke. "You don't get to test drive a crime scene."

Thumps looked out towards the mountains. Clouds had begun to sneak in behind the peaks.

"I suppose I'm a person of interest," said Rattler. "Because I found the body and called it in?"

"Yep," said Duke. "That would do it."

Thumps rubbed his eyes. He was tired and he was hungry. "What I don't understand is why you dragged me out of bed and brought me up here against my will?"

"I fed you breakfast."

"That wasn't breakfast." Thumps could hear his stomach begin to rumble. "And then you forced me to carry a dead body up the side of a cliff."

"Lance did most of the work," said Duke.

"The sheriff's right," said Rattler. "The deputy did have the heavy end."

"I still don't see why you needed me. You have Maslow's body. You have the guy who found her."

"All true," said Duke.

"You have his statement."

The sheriff rubbed his hands together. "Going to be cold tonight."

"You don't have a statement?"

"Nope," said the sheriff. "No statement."

Rattler shrugged.

"He's under arrest?"

"Nope," said the sheriff. "Not unless finding a murder victim is a crime."

"He must have said something."

"Not a word," said Duke. "When Lance arrived on the scene, Rattler told him he'd only talk to one person."

"I did say that." Rattler smiled and started for the edge of the butte.

"Where the hell you think you're going?"

Rattler held the flowers up over his head and kept walking.

It took Thumps a beat to realize who that person was. "Shit."

"Exactly my sentiment," said the sheriff. "The world-famous novelist will only talk to you."

Thumps took a deep breath and let the air seep out the sides of his mouth. "And that's why you hauled me out here. To question him."

"Hell, DreadfulWater," said Duke, as he climbed into his cruiser, "why else would I have bought you breakfast?"

Rattler stood at the edge of the butte, quiet and still, and as Thumps watched, he let the flowers fall from his hand and float out into the bright prairie sky.

TWENTY-TWO

The morning's drama had been a four-act farce with no intermission, and the drive back to Chinook gave Thumps time to review his role in the production.

Act one. The sheriff drags him out of his house.

Act two. The sheriff tries to poison him with a bacon-fat wrap.

Act three. The sheriff forces him to carry a dead body up the side of a mountain.

Act four. The sheriff coerces him into grilling the man who found the body.

Friday to the sheriff's Robinson Crusoe. He was going to have to get a better agent.

This was not the first time that Hockney had abused their friendship, and it probably would not be the last. Most times, Thumps let it slide.

"Where we going?"

"My office."

This was not one of those times.

"Not happening," said Thumps.

"What?"

"Not happening. I'm not going back to your office."

"DreadfulWater . . ."

"I'm hungry," said Thumps. "I think my blood sugars are dropping."

Duke tried to impersonate a pipe bomb. "City's not buying you another breakfast."

"I can't work on an empty stomach."

"Now that you mention it," said Rattler, "I'm hungry too."

The sheriff gripped the wheel a little tighter. "Does this look like a food truck?"

"Al's," said Thumps. "I want to eat at Al's."

"That's a great idea," said Rattler. "Haven't seen Alvera in years."

"You're a suspect," said Duke. "Suspects don't get breakfast."

"I thought I was a person of interest," said Rattler. "How about we talk over food and coffee?"

"I have coffee at the office."

Thumps turned to Rattler. "No, he doesn't."

Duke kept his eyes on the road. "You know, one of these days, you're going to hurt my feelings."

"Low blood sugar is no laughing matter," offered Rattler. "Breakfast may constitute a medical emergency."

"As a diabetic," said Thumps quickly, before the momentum disappeared, "I need to eat at regular intervals."

"Jesus," said Duke. "Are you two engaged?"

"Al's," said Thumps. "I'll only talk at Al's."

"Christ, DreadfulWater, you're not the person of interest! The guy in the back seat is the person of interest!"

"And this person of interest will only talk to DreadfulWater." Rattler yawned and closed his eyes. "At Al's."

Al had a run of plywood booths along the far wall. Not that any of the regulars ever used them. The booths were tourist seating and to be avoided at all costs. In the first place, they were uncomfortable as hell, wood benches instead of a padded stool, and secondly, if you sat in a booth, it meant you were a world away from the coffee pot. Al seldom came out from behind the counter, so if you were in a booth and wanted a refill, you had to get up and bring your cup to Al.

All the booths were empty. As they generally were. The sheriff led the way to the last plywood box at the back and arranged the trio so that Thumps sat across from Rattler and the sheriff sat next to Thumps.

Thumps wasn't all that happy with the arrangement. "How come I have to be on the inside?"

"So you can't run off," said Duke. "And this way, we can both see Mr. Rattler's face."

"You boys want to move a little closer together?" Al was

standing behind the counter with a cellphone. "That way I can get you all in."

"Morning, Alvera," said Duke.

"Can probably get good money for the shot." Al spread her hands out as though she were creating a banner headline. "Locals Sit in Booth."

"Police business," said Hockney, trying to make his voice sound official.

"And my counter's not good enough for *police* business?" Al dropped the phone into her apron. "You think I'm going to walk all the way over there?"

"Just leave everything on the counter," said Duke, "and we'll come and get it."

Al frowned, and then her face brightened. "Tobias Rattler. Is that you?"

"Hello, Ms. Couteau."

Al came around the end of the counter with the coffee pot. "Never figured I'd see you again."

"Never figured I'd come back."

Al filled Rattler's cup.

Duke slid his cup over. "I'd like some coffee."

Al ignored the sheriff. "Duke giving you a hard time?"

"No, ma'am," said Rattler.

Thumps pushed his cup next to Duke's. "Coffee?"

Al turned to Duke. "Is Toby under arrest?"

The sheriff sagged a little in his seat. "Not yet."

"This about that Maslow woman?"

"Police business," said Duke.

Al filled the sheriff's cup only to the halfway mark. "Wutty said he saw you at the giant squirrel this morning."

Duke jerked a thumb at Thumps. "That was for him."

"No, it wasn't."

"Shadow Ranch, Mirrors, and now Skippy's?" Al set the pot down on the table with a bang. "Are you *trying* to piss me off?"

"No."

"'Cause you're doing a real good job."

Rattler held up a hand. "Actually, Thumps and the sheriff are trying to figure out what happened to Trudy Samuels."

Al relaxed her shoulders a bit. "Well, it's about time. Emmitt Tull couldn't find his butt if he shoved both hands in his back pockets."

"Maybe some fried eggs and sausage," said Rattler. "With hash browns."

Al nodded. "And I suppose you two want your usual?"

"Please," said Thumps.

"Yes," said the sheriff.

Al pointed the pot at Duke. "You want your eggs burnt?"

"He's not under arrest."

"Just keep that in mind."

Thumps waited until Al had made her way back to the grill. The woman was known for keen eyes and even keener ears.

"You know, I used to work here," said Rattler.

"Here?"

"High school. Washing dishes."

"Good to know." Duke slapped Thumps on the shoulder. "Okay," he said, "it's your show."

Thumps wasn't sure if the whack was supposed to encourage or injure. Maybe a little of both.

"The sheriff wants to know all about your morning."

"Yes, he does," said Duke.

Rattler sipped at his coffee. "You mean, what was I doing out at Belly Butte?"

"Yes," said Thumps. "Why don't we start there."

Rattler folded his arms and leaned back. "Nostalgia."

Duke leaned forward. "Nostalgia?"

"It's where Trudy died."

"Hence the flowers?"

"Hence," said Rattler.

"So, this morning you picked up a bunch of roses and went out to Belly Butte? Because that's where Trudy died?"

"Got the flowers yesterday afternoon."

"And when you got there, you just happened to run into a dead body?"

Rattler rubbed the side of his neck. "What are the odds?"

"How about I just arrest you for being a pain in the ass?" said Duke.

"I heard that!" Al shouted from the grill.

"Jesus," whispered the sheriff. "Is there a microphone under the table?"

Rattler cut his sausages into pieces and tore the toast into smaller pieces. "I got to the butte at around eight. I saw the Honda. I looked around, saw Maslow's body, and called you."

"Golly," said Duke. "Well, that clears everything up."

Thumps raised his cup to see if he could get Al's attention. "Except for the coincidence."

"Yes," said the sheriff, "there's that."

Rattler stopped a yawn. "And you two don't believe in coincidences."

"Trudy Samuels is found dead at the bottom of Belly Butte," said Duke. "And then Nina Maslow is found dead at the bottom of Belly Butte."

"And you think that I'm the common denominator."

"You *are* the common denominator," said the sheriff.

Rattler pushed his plate to the side.

"You going to arrest me?"

"Nope."

Toby slid out of the booth. "Okay?"

"Okay." The sheriff slid out with him.

"You going to walk me out?"

"Nope."

"You going to tell me not to leave town?"

Duke turned to Thumps. "Why didn't I think of that?"

Thumps ran a forkful of potato through the ketchup. "It must have slipped your mind."

Rattler threw his jacket over a shoulder. "You two ever think about taking it on the road? Cheech Marin and Tommy Chong made a fortune."

The sheriff took over Rattler's side of the booth.

Thumps stayed where he was. "You can see the door from there."

"I can," said the sheriff.

"In case Rattler comes running back and wants to confess?"

"As a law officer, I have to be ready for anything."

Thumps used a piece of toast to mop up his plate. "Cheech and Chong?"

"Well," said Duke, "here's another fine mess you've got yourself into."

"That's Laurel and Hardy," said Thumps. "And it's 'another fine mess you've got *me* into.'"

"Either way," said the sheriff, "it's your mess-fortune and none of my own."

Al appeared out of nowhere. "And do my little doggies want more coffee?"

"Please," said the sheriff.

"Yes, ma'am," said Thumps.

"So, have you two figured it out yet?"

"Which 'it' are we talking about?" said the sheriff.

"The murders," said Al. "Pretty obvious if you ask me."

Thumps pushed his cup close to the pot in case Al was distracted and in danger of forgetting. "Samuels and Maslow?"

Al put the pot down and held up three fingers. "Samuels, Samuels, and Maslow."

"Buck?"

Al filled the cups. "Sure," she said. "Adele killed them all."

"Adele Samuels?"

"Ask the sheriff," said Al. "Emmitt Tull let her slide on Buck, and look what happened."

"Emmitt was a decent cop," said Duke in a low voice without much conviction. "He was just rigid."

Al headed back to the grill. "First Buck. Then Trudy. And now Maslow," she called back over her shoulder. "All you two geniuses got to do is connect the dots."

Duke stared at his half-filled cup and waited, but Thumps knew that Al wasn't going to return any time soon.

"You want to give it a try?"

"What?" said Duke.

"Connect the dots."

"Hell, DreadfulWater," said the sheriff, "I was a kid when Trudy died."

"But you've seen the file."

"Emmitt Tull was my uncle." Duke's face tightened. "Trudy Samuels was Chinook's big unsolved mystery."

The sheriff reached across and helped himself to one of

Thumps's sausages. "Buck Samuels died of a heart attack. Man had a wonky heart. Already had two attacks. No real surprise when he keeled over."

"Where'd he die?"

"At home," said Hockney. "Adele called the fire department, but he was dead by the time they got there."

"Rumours?"

"Sure," said the sheriff. "Adele switched his medication out for sugar pills. Or Buck had a heart attack, and she stood around and watched him die before she called for help. Or Adele was having an affair and broke Buck's heart."

"Or he just had a heart attack and died."

"Or that."

"Okay," said Thumps. "Trudy Samuels."

"Pretty girl," said Duke. "In and out of trouble."

"Drugs and alcohol?"

"All that," said the sheriff. "And speeding tickets."

"Speeding tickets?"

"Soon as she turned sixteen, Trudy bought herself a Corvette. I was probably thirteen at the time. Hell of a car. Word was she racked up a ton of speeding tickets. There's a trap in Randall. Trudy would get nailed there at least once a week."

"She ever lose her licence?"

"Nope," said Duke. "Rumour was the citations got fixed."

"Samuels's money."

"Way things worked back then."

"Doesn't sound like a happy kid."

"No," said the sheriff, "don't think she was."

Thumps tried to find a soft spot on the bench. "Tobias Rattler?"

"Him I didn't know at all." Duke looked off at the back wall. "But Emmitt and my dad used to talk. You know how kids are."

"They listen to stuff they're not supposed to listen to."

"Adult stuff was always the best," said Hockney. "There was an incident. Happened after a football game. Best I can figure it, Trudy Samuels was attacked. Behind the bleachers."

"Rattler?"

"Trudy said no. Said Rattler saved her. Ran the guy off."

"But?"

"But then Rattler made the mistake of taking Trudy home, and when Adele saw Trudy and her torn dress in the company of one Tobias Rattler . . ."

"She went ballistic?"

"Evidently," said Duke. "Rattler was older. Rattler was Indian. Adele insisted that Emmitt charge Rattler with rape. That's when Trudy moved off the estate. Got a place in town."

"With Rattler?"

"Nope," said the sheriff. "The two of them hung around together all the time. Maybe they were lovers. Maybe they weren't."

"And when Trudy was found dead?"

"Adele screamed murder. Wanted Rattler arrested and hanged, not particularly in that order."

"But there was nothing to say that it was murder and nothing to tie Rattler to Trudy's death."

"Nope," said the sheriff. "The case had the town dancing for a couple of months, and when the music stopped, Rattler left."

"So what's *Malice Aforethought*'s angle?"

"No idea," said Duke. "Okay, it's your turn."

"For what?"

"Try to connect the dots."

"I don't know shit about the case."

"Sure," said Hockney. "That's your advantage."

"I don't want a turn."

"I can make the parking ticket I gave you go away."

Thumps put his cup down. "*You* gave me that ticket?"

"How about we play *Law & Order*?" said Duke. "You can be the sleazy defence, and I'll be the righteous prosecutor."

"You gave me a ticket?"

"Take your best shot."

Thumps leaned up against the corner of the booth. "All right. When Buck died, was there an autopsy?"

"No. Family doctor signed the death warrant, and Adele had Buck's body cremated."

"Quickly?"

"Within the week."

"The attack on Trudy. Behind the bleachers. I'm assuming there was a police report?"

"Yes," said the sheriff, "and no."

"Not helpful."

"It was Adele who called it in," said Duke. "Emmitt tried to get a statement from Trudy, but she said she didn't know who had attacked her."

"Except she was sure it wasn't Rattler."

"Yes," said the sheriff. "She was sure of that."

Thumps tried to do the math in his head. "When did the attack happen?"

Duke thought for a moment. "Trudy would have been a junior in high school."

"Adele's son, Ethan, would have been living on the estate at the time."

Duke smiled. "DreadfulWater, you have one suspicious mind."

"Buck is dead. Adele moves her son in on top of Trudy. I don't suppose the two of them got along."

"Sibling rivalry?"

"Maybe," said Thumps. "Or maybe Ethan was angry at all the advantages Trudy had received while he was off in the wilderness."

"Are you asking if Emmitt raised that question?"

"Would you know?"

Duke shook his head. "Nothing in the file that says he did."

"So, if Ethan was the one who attacked Trudy behind the bleachers, why wouldn't she tell the world?"

"No reason she wouldn't."

Thumps looked at his empty cup. "And then a year and a half later, Trudy winds up at the bottom of Belly Butte."

"You got any more dots to connect?"

"Forget the dots," said Thumps. "It would be nice to have a motive."

"That's 'cause you're looking at it all wrong." Al had snuck up on them with the coffee pot. "Motive is the oldest one in the world."

"Sex?"

"That's the oldest profession," said Thumps, extending his own cup.

"Money." Al filled both cups. "Adele killed Buck and Trudy and tried to frame Toby so no one would notice."

Duke shook his head. "You don't think Emmitt would have looked at that?"

"Either one of you ever read Buck's will?" Al gave each man a knowing glance. "And what about Nina Maslow?"

Duke moved his cup out of Al's reach in case she tried to take it back. "You think that Nina Maslow found out that Adele killed her husband and her stepdaughter and that Adele killed Maslow?"

"Sure," said Al. "All the pieces fit. *Malice Aforethought* comes to town. The case is resurrected. And suddenly, Nina Maslow winds up dead at the bottom of the same butte as Trudy. You two believe in coincidences?"

"Nope."

"Me neither."

"Simple as pie." Al scraped the plates and stacked them.

"Maslow discovered something, and that something got her killed."

"You got to stop watching so much television, Alvera," said the sheriff.

"Human nature," she called out as she disappeared into the back room with the plates. "Nothing but human nature."

Thumps remembered his insulin kit. Now that he had eaten, he was going to have to give himself a shot, but he had no idea how much to take. He didn't want to lift his shirt here at the table. Was he supposed to go into the bathroom each time and hide out in one of the stalls?

"You know anything about insulin injection?"

The sheriff pulled his face out of his coffee cup. "You're not thinking about sticking yourself here. At the table?"

"No."

"'Cause that would be a little gross."

Thumps slid the kit back into his jacket. "So, what do you think?"

"You mean did Maslow discover something about Trudy's death that got her killed?"

"You have to admit," said Thumps, "it's a tempting thought."

"And it would suggest that whoever killed Samuels also killed Maslow." Duke set the cup down. "Course that still leaves the other question."

"What did Maslow discover?"

"No," said the sheriff. "Which of us is supposed to be Cheech?"

TWENTY-THREE

Thumps had never thought much about the plywood booths in Al's, but after the sheriff left to return to his office and ride herd on the mayor's Howdy program, Thumps discovered that the booth he was sitting in felt like a little sanctuary. It was dark. It was private. It was quiet.

"This ain't a hotel."

Al was back with the coffee pot.

"I'm thinking."

"Word gets out that I let people lounge about in my booths, and I'll be knee deep in ear wire."

"Ear wire?"

"You know," said Al. "Kids with laptops and wires hanging out of their ears. The ones who can nurse one of those latte things and a blueberry lemon muffin until closing."

"You don't serve lattes," said Thumps. "Or muffins."

"You better believe it."

"They all go to Mirrors."

"No sense taking any chances."

Thumps held out his cup, and Al filled it.

"So, Toby worked for you?"

"Washed dishes," said Al. "Cleaned the place."

Al generally wasn't stingy with information. Most times she was only too eager to share.

"And?"

"Man's entitled to his privacy."

Thumps wanted to remind Al about her willingness to share his medical information with the world. "Since when?"

Al snaked her eyes and sharpened her lips. "Sarcasm is the hobgoblin of little minds."

"Consistency," said Thumps. "A *foolish consistency* is the hob-goblin of little minds."

Al wiped her hands on the towel. "You helping the sheriff or you working for that TV program?"

"Neither," said Thumps.

"So what were you two discussing?"

"Sheriff's business," said Thumps. "Duke and I were just having a hypothetical discussion."

Al cocked her head to one side like an owl looking at a mouse. "How about I make you a hypothetical breakfast next time you come in?"

Thumps felt the rush of air and heard the front door bang.

"Good," said the sheriff, "you're still here."

Thumps looked up at Al. "You need to put in a back door."

Al shrugged. "Looks as though you're about to enjoy another one of those hypothetical discussions."

"Come on, DreadfulWater," said Duke. "I haven't got all day."

"I have to go home."

"I'll take you there."

"You will?"

"Absolutely," said the sheriff. "Right after we make one little stop."

THERE WERE ALL sorts of places Thumps could imagine the sheriff taking him. His first guess was the county morgue in the basement of the old Land Titles building. Beth would have Nina Maslow's body on her stainless steel table by now, might have even started the autopsy. If that were the case, Thumps would have plenty of warning and time enough to come up with a good excuse to pass on Beth's creepy dungeon.

Or Duke could be taking him back to his office. The only thing of any danger there was the sheriff's coffee, and Thumps had enough experience and good sense to steer clear of the old percolator.

They had already been out to Belly Butte. Thumps didn't think the sheriff was going to return to the scene of the crime so soon, but anything was possible.

Instead, Hockney pulled his cruiser into the no-parking zone in front of the Tucker hotel.

"Citizen could get a traffic citation parking here," said Thumps. "I hear the sheriff is a real stickler for minor infractions."

"Cheech," said the sheriff. "You can be Cheech."

THE TUCKER WAS the boutique hotel in Chinook. Construction began in 1875, and it opened a year later, just as George Armstrong Custer was riding into the Little Bighorn Valley. In 1890, the top floor burned down, compliments of a hotel guest and an oil lamp. By the end of World War I, the hotel had closed, and over the next half-century the building was used as a hospital, a warehouse, a library, and a roller-skating rink.

A community group had been showing art films in the lobby every Friday and Saturday night when a construction conglomerate out of Los Angeles bought the place and turned it back into a hotel.

Thumps followed the sheriff through the lobby. "I'm guessing you're not buying me lunch."

"I just bought you breakfast."

"No, you didn't. Rattler bought me breakfast. He paid for your breakfast as well."

"Same thing," said the sheriff.

"And seeing as Rattler is a person of interest," said Thumps, pushing his luck, "his buying you breakfast could be construed as bribery of a public official."

Duke's grunt was a shotgun shell being jacked into a 12-gauge pump. "How's your car?"

"How's the Howdy program going?"

The sheriff pressed the button for the third floor.

"What's on the third floor?"

Duke wasn't known for his smiles, and this one didn't disappoint. "Rooms," said the sheriff. "I hear the third floor is lousy with rooms."

The door to 326 was open. Sydney Pearl and Calder Banks were sitting on the sofa. Gloria Baker-Doyle was relaxed in an easy chair.

"Nina Maslow's room?"

"Don't know that I'd hire her decorator."

The room had been trashed. Drawers had been pulled out. File boxes had been dumped out on the floor. The refrigerator and the cupboards had been emptied and the contents left in a pile.

"Sheriff."

Duke tipped his hat. "Ms. Pearl."

"Bedroom's the same," said Pearl.

"You found it like this?"

Pearl shook her head. "Calder did."

Duke turned to Banks. "And you called it in?"

Calder looked uncomfortable. "Actually, I called Sydney."

The sheriff hooded his eyes. "Because she's the sheriff?"

"Well . . . no . . . I mean she's my boss . . . and Nina . . ."

"Is dead," said Duke, finishing the sentence for him.

Gloria got out of the chair. "Calder and I came over here to retrieve Nina's files. Yeah."

"Together?"

"Yes," said Gloria. "We found the suite like this."

Duke walked the room, slowly, stepping over the cereal boxes and the cartons of takeout. "Do you know if anything is missing?"

Gloria looked at Pearl.

"Don't look at Ms. Pearl," said Duke. "She's not the one who'll throw you in jail if I don't like your answers."

"Don't know," said Pearl. "We'll have to go through everything."

"There was a map of the area," said Gloria. "It was on the wall. It's gone."

Duke pushed a water bottle out of the way with his foot. "What kind of map?"

"You know," said Gloria. "One with roads on it."

"A road map?"

"Yeah." Gloria held her hands out. "It was right here. Had all sorts of marks on it. Lines, circles, notes."

"You remember what those marks were exactly?"

Gloria shook her head. "Nah. Just marks."

"A box," said Pearl. "Her research for the remaining shows."

Hockney did a slow sweep of the room. "And it's missing."

"It would appear," said Pearl.

Thumps knew what the sheriff's next question was going to be.

"Hypothetically speaking," said Hockney, "why would someone take a road map and a box of research?"

Thumps hadn't expected anyone to answer the question, and no one did.

Duke looked over at Thumps. "Well, I guess that settles everything."

"What the sheriff means," said Thumps, "is that all of you have contaminated a possible crime scene. If you have removed anything, he would like you to leave it on the table or face charges of obstruction. Furthermore, he would like you to stop touching things and get out of the room as quickly as possible."

"We want to help," said Pearl. "Nina was family."

"And you can," said Thumps, "by letting law enforcement do its job."

Thumps could see that Pearl was not used to taking orders. The woman stood in the middle of the room, looking for an argument.

"All right," she said at last. "But I expect to be kept informed as to the progress of the investigation."

Duke touched the brim of his hat. "Howdy," he said.

Thumps walked the trio out the door and shut it behind them.

"'Furthermore'?" said Duke.

"I thought I was rather succinct," said Thumps.

"You ever talk like that when you were a cop?"

"Can't remember."

Duke looked around the room. "Made a mess of the place."

"They did."

The sheriff took off his hat and made himself comfortable on the sofa. "Option one is a burglar with a fetish for research files and road maps, so let's go with option two."

"Someone kills Maslow and steals her files."

"Which would mean that there was something in the files."

"Trudy Samuels?"

"That's the easy answer."

"And if that's the right answer," said Thumps, "it could mean that Samuels's death wasn't an accident or suicide. Could mean that whoever killed Trudy also killed Nina."

Duke sank into the cushions. "Big leap."

"What else could be in the files that would get Maslow dead?"

"That's the better question," said the sheriff. "And we're probably not going to find out sitting here."

"You're going to take me home?"

"Sorry," said Duke, "but I got a crime scene to secure and process."

"I have to walk?"

"It's a nice day," said the sheriff, "and a brisk stroll will help you work off breakfast."

TWENTY-FOUR

The no-parking zone in front of the hotel was getting crowded. The sheriff's cruiser was still there. The green Audi was idling right behind it.

"Mr. DreadfulWater." Gloria Baker-Doyle hurried around the car and opened the back door. "Could we have a moment of your time?"

"Is that the royal plural?"

"Very good," said Gloria, "but no. It's the regular plural."

Sydney Pearl was sitting in the back seat. "Please join me," she said. "We need to talk."

"Is it about Nina Maslow?"

"It is."

"Then you should talk to the sheriff."

"I plan to do that."

"Then you don't need to talk to me."

"Ride with me, Mr. DreadfulWater," said Pearl. "Where's the harm in that?"

Thumps could think of any number of reasons not to get into the car. Common sense was at the top of the list.

"And I think we can help each other."

"You mean as in I help you and you help me?"

"Exactly."

"The helping me part," said Thumps. "You want to give me a hint?"

"Maslow's file on the Obsidian Murders," said Pearl. "Is that the kind of help that might interest you?"

THE OLD ROAD followed the Ironstone as far as Siksika Rapids, where a section had washed out in a spring flood and never been repaired. Gloria pulled into the makeshift turnaround and parked the car.

Pearl got out of the Audi. "I grew up in Queens. We didn't have this much space. We didn't have rapids."

Gloria had a camera in her hand. "I'll leave you two to talk. Can you get to the river from here?"

Thumps had photographed the rapids years ago. He tried to remember if there had been a trail or if he had had to bushwhack his way through the brush. "To the right. It's probably overgrown."

Gloria gave the camera a wave. "Nothing that will stop a producer."

Thumps watched Baker-Doyle push her way into the willows and disappear. "Gloria's a producer now? That was fast."

"Show business is fast."

Thumps wondered if Gloria had found the path. The only sound he could hear was the river racing over the rocks.

"You don't like me," said Pearl. "And that's fine. In my business, liking someone is generally unwise."

For the first time, Thumps heard something in the woman's voice that didn't have edges and angles.

"You were friends with Maslow."

Pearl's eyes glistened. "What did I just say?"

The wolf willows and scrub had grown up along the bank. Thumps could hear the rapids, but he couldn't see the water. The last time he had come to this section of the Ironstone, there had been a large boulder in the middle of the rapids that had cut the river in half. He wondered if it was still there or if it had been swept away in the spring flood.

Pearl shoved her hands in the pockets of her jacket. "Warhol and Basquiat. Lennon and McCartney. Burns and Allen."

"Thelma and Louise?"

Pearl's laugh was soft and sad.

"The Obsidian Murders?"

"Manners," said Pearl. "Ladies first."

"Okay," said Thumps. "Ladies first."

Pearl walked back to the car and leaned against the door. "Nina and I met in Los Angeles. A prime-time drama. Would have set us up for years."

"But?"

"Show folded before we got to principal photography," said Pearl. "We did a couple of smaller projects together. Mostly successful. And then Nina got the idea for *Malice Aforethought*."

Thumps waited.

"Nina was a genius at research. She'd shake trees just to see what fell out. And she had a gift for knowing what an audience wanted."

"So Maslow called the shots on which story the show did."

Pearl rubbed her hands to keep them warm. "Nina would come up with the ideas, with the stories, and then she'd show me the litter."

"And you'd pick the best-looking puppies."

"The two of us would pick the puppies."

"You had a formula?"

"More a feeling," said Pearl. "First and foremost, the story had to be unsolved. Second, there had to be something about the story that gave it a sparkle."

"Poor little rich girl killed by famous novelist."

"Three, it had to be a story that we had a chance to solve."

Thumps smiled. "You actually solve cases?"

"Sometimes," said Pearl. "Nina solved a cold case in Alabama. DNA evidence. But the guy responsible had died in prison a year earlier."

"Impressive."

"She could see patterns in the evidence. She could hear discrepancies in the court records. She was amazing with raw data. There was another case in Ohio where a sitting congressman had been involved in a hit-and-run of two little girls. Nina saw the clue in a crime-scene photograph. Broke the case open."

"And Trudy Samuels?"

"She was looking at a number of angles."

Thumps tried to imagine what Maslow would have seen from the available evidence. "So Trudy Samuels, accidental death, wouldn't get out of the puppy box."

"No."

"But Trudy Samuels, poor little rich girl commits suicide because she is dumped by famous novelist would?"

"Not a lot of sparkle, but it could work," said Pearl. "*Driven to suicide* is the way we would frame it. Responsibility instead of guilt."

"Or Trudy is drunk and abusive. Rattler hits her. Bad luck."

"Not a lot going for it."

"How about Rattler wants to marry Trudy for her money, but she tells him to get lost, so he kills her in a fit of rage?"

"Better. Any other ideas?"

"Sure," said Thumps. "Adele Samuels and/or her son kill

Trudy. To inherit the money and because Trudy is a major embarrassment. Adele hated her. Ethan was jealous. People get killed for less."

"Bravo, Mr. DreadfulWater," said Pearl. "Nina was right about you."

It took a beat for Thumps to hear the implication.

"The Samuels case doesn't meet your criteria." Thumps turned the possibilities over in his mind. "It's too weak, too many ways for it to fall flat."

"It wasn't my first choice."

"And yet you decided to do it anyway."

Pearl waited as a teacher might wait for her star student to finish the equation.

"But the Obsidian Murders *is* good television."

"No, Mr. DreadfulWater," said Pearl. "It's not good television. It's great television."

"And Maslow knew I was involved in that case."

"A little disingenuous, don't you think?" said Pearl. "According to Nina, you are the Obsidian Murders."

"Christ."

"I told you," said Pearl, "Nina planned ahead."

"You're going to do an episode on that case."

"The premiere episode for next season."

Thumps hadn't seen it coming, hadn't even considered the possibility. Maslow knew that the Samuels case was weak. The only draw was the manufactured confrontation between an angry stepmother and a famous literary figure. But the real reason Maslow and Pearl had come to Chinook was to find him, to enlist him in the investigation. Maslow knew he wouldn't say no, especially if she had uncovered evidence that gave new life to the Obsidian Murders case.

"What exactly did she have?"

"An excellent question." Pearl's face hardened and her eyes lost their sparkle. "Which is why we're here. I'd like to propose a collaboration. You and me."

"You want me to find out what happened to Nina."

"I do."

"In exchange for?"

"You already know the answer to that, Mr. DreadfulWater."

"Maslow had a file on the Obsidian Murders. I find out what happened, and I get the file."

"That makes it sound like blackmail," said Pearl. "I'd rather see our arrangement as an amicable exchange."

"Why should I trust you?"

"Here's what I know: the Samuels case was never all that strong, but Nina found something that had her animated, something she was quite excited about, something new."

"A break in the case?"

"I think so."

"But she didn't say?"

"Nina liked to be secretive," said Pearl. "And thorough. She'd wait until all the pieces were in place before she would move."

"But you don't have Nina's files anymore, do you?" Thumps watched Pearl's face. "The Samuels file. The file on the Obsidian Murders. Other files as well?"

Pearl put her arms over her head and stretched. "Four files in all," she said. "The Samuels case, the Obsidian Murders, and the files we were considering for the last episode of the season."

"Two files for the last episode?"

"We hadn't decided which one to do yet. Nina wanted the Vegas story. I wanted the killings in Key West."

"You know, whoever took those files has probably destroyed them by now."

"Maybe. Maybe not." Pearl looked past Thumps as though she could see something in the distance. "I don't believe Nina's death was an accident. Neither does the sheriff. Someone killed her. Find that person, and maybe you find the files. Find the files and you get what Nina had on the Obsidian Murders."

"That's a lot of maybes."

Pearl made a quick gesture with her hand. "It is what it is."

Thumps heard a sound behind him.

"Back too early?" Gloria sang out, as she burst out of the willows.

"Not at all," said Pearl. "Mr. DreadfulWater and I have had a productive talk."

"Brilliant," said Gloria. "I got some lovely shots of the water. There's a giant rock in the middle of the river. Looks like a dinosaur egg."

So it was still there. With the way everything else in his life was shifting, Thumps found the enduring presence of a large boulder in a dark river strangely comforting.

"So, you two have everything settled? Yeah?"

Pearl opened the back door and got in. "The sheriff is a friend of yours, is he not?"

"He's the sheriff," said Thumps.

"Then I'd appreciate it if you would tell him that I'd like to have my car back."

"It's part of a crime scene."

"I'm fond of that car," said Pearl. "I only let Maslow use it because she was too cheap to buy a car of her own."

"I'll mention it."

"I don't want to have to shoot him," said Pearl.

"Right," said Gloria. "So, where to now?"

"Anywhere Mr. DreadfulWater wants to go," said Pearl.

Thumps watched the thin clouds float along the horizon and waited for inspiration to find him. When it didn't, he slid into the car and closed the door.

TWENTY-FIVE

Pearl waited until they had pulled up in front of the old Land Titles building before she dropped the other shoe.

"Oh," she said, as though it were an afterthought, "I'll also count on you to convince Mr. Rattler to be on the show."

"Not my circus," said Thumps, getting out of the car. "Not my monkeys."

Pearl held the door open. "It's the clowns you have to worry about."

Thumps had stood at the front door to the old Land Titles building on any number of occasions, but this was the first time he had ever found the door open.

"Hello."

He stood on the stoop, pressed each of the three buttons in order, and waited for a reply. And then he pressed them again.

Nothing.

Not good. Thumps couldn't imagine Beth leaving the front door open like that.

"Hello."

"Basement!"

It was Beth's voice, even though it sounded faint and far away. She also sounded irritated. Probably not the best time to ask for a favour.

"It's me."

"Basement!"

Thumps hated Beth's basement. It wasn't any worse than some of the other morgues he had had to endure, and it wasn't any better. Morgues had several things in common. They were cold and dank. They all had a pale stink of human decay. They all featured professional psychopaths who got paid to cut up bodies.

Thumps had expected to find Beth standing at her stainless steel table, sorting through the remains of Nina Maslow. Instead, the table was bare and Beth was on her hands and knees by the side of her desk, a plastic bucket at her side.

"No stupid jokes."

"I wasn't going to make any."

Beth looked up. Her glasses had slid down her nose, and her hair was rattled. "Don't just stand there."

Thumps tried to figure out exactly what Beth was doing on the floor of her basement with a plastic bucket. Nothing immediately came to mind.

"Go around to the other side of the desk and stomp your feet."

"Is this some kind of coroner joke?"

"Damn it, DreadfulWater, just do it."

Thumps got as far as the corner when something flew out from under the desk, slammed into his leg, and went careening around the room, bouncing off the walls and the cabinets.

"Jesus!"

Beth got to her feet, the plastic bucket at the ready. "You're not much help."

"What the hell was that?"

"A squirrel," said Beth.

"A squirrel?"

"Rats with good PR," said Beth. "Don't know how it got in, but I've been trying to chase it out the front door for the last hour."

"And?"

"Evidently," said Beth, "the stupid thing doesn't know how to climb stairs."

"Thought squirrels could climb anything."

"Now I'm trying to catch it."

"I could borrow Duke's gun and shoot it."

Beth froze him with a glare. "If I wanted to shoot it, I wouldn't be crawling around on the floor with a bucket."

Thumps looked around. "Where'd he go?"

"I'm worried that it's a female and that she has a nest somewhere."

"Little squirrels are cute."

"Look under the cabinet."

"But they can also be vicious."

Beth held up the bucket. "That's what this is for. You drive the squirrel to me, and I'll catch her."

"Good plan," said Thumps.

"Was that sarcasm?"

"Yes," said Thumps. "It was."

"The cabinet?"

"I'm not going to put my hand under the cabinet."

"Here," said Beth. "Use this."

Thumps got on his hands and knees and looked under the cabinet. Nothing. Then he shoved the broom handle under the cabinet and wiggled it around. Nothing.

"I don't think she's here."

"Hell." Beth put the bucket down. "Help me move the cabinet."

Behind the cabinet was a small hole in the stone wall.

"That look large enough for a squirrel to get through?"

"'When you have eliminated the impossible, whatever remains, however improbable, must be the truth,'" said Thumps, letting the solemnity of his voice fill the room. "Sherlock Holmes."

"Kill the squirrel," said Beth. "Elmer Fudd."

"All you have to do is put a patch over the hole."

Beth went to her desk and sat down. "Why are you here?"

"To help you catch a squirrel?"

"Ora Mae send you?"

"No."

"Then the sheriff has conned you into helping him again."

"Duke's a friend."

"I haven't started the autopsy yet." Beth opened a drawer and took out a file. "But it would appear that Belly Butte is an accident-prone zone."

"As in Samuels and now Maslow."

"As in." Beth took out a second file. This one was yellow with age, the edges bent and frayed. "Quite the coincidence, don't you think?"

Thumps pulled up the hard metal chair that Beth kept in the basement to discourage visitors from staying too long. "And?"

"You know anyone who believes in coincidences?"

"Nope."

"Me neither." Beth opened the older of the two files. "Trudy Samuels. Female. Eighteen. One hundred and fifteen pounds. Body found at Belly Butte."

"Was she dead before she went over the edge of the butte?"

"How should I know?"

"So you weren't the coroner then?"

"Just how old do you think I am?"

Thumps held up his hands. "A joke."

Beth resettled her glasses. "Here's the interesting part: there was never an autopsy."

"No autopsy?"

"Not a proper one," said Beth. "The coroner, some guy named Wiseman, did a drive-by examination. He didn't open the body. He didn't check any of the organs or the stomach contents. There was no collection of samples and no examination of the head and brain."

"Photographs?"

"Not many. Seven to be exact." Beth laid the photographs out. "These are of the body at the crime scene. These are of the body in the morgue."

"Why'd they photograph her hands?"

"No idea."

"What are those marks on her palm?"

"No idea."

"They look like thin scratches."

"Could be injuries from the fall." Beth picked up the photograph. "Look at her nails."

"Because?"

Beth shook her head. "I suppose you chew your nails."

Thumps instinctively tucked his fingers into his palms. "I keep them trimmed."

"With your teeth?" Beth used a pencil to touch each of Trudy's nails. "She took care of her nails."

"Okay."

"Do you see any damage?"

"Not much."

"That's right," said Beth. "The nails are intact."

"As though she made no effort to save herself."

"Or she couldn't." Beth put the photograph back in the file. "Wiseman made a note that the body showed signs of trauma that might not be associated with the trauma of falling down the side of Belly Butte."

"As in?"

"He doesn't say."

"And Maslow?"

Beth opened the second file. "Nina Maslow. Female. Thirty-one. One hundred and thirty pounds. Body found at Belly Butte."

"Thought you said you haven't done the autopsy yet."

"True," said Beth, "but I've done the Wiseman drive-by."

"And you want me to look at the body?"

"Is that a problem?"

"Didn't you take photographs?"

"I did."

"Let's look at the photographs."

Beth opened the stainless steel cabinet. Cold air spilled into the room, along with the sickening sweetness of decay. Thumps began breathing through his mouth.

"Bruises, cuts, and abrasions consistent with a fall." Beth waved a hand over the body. "But look at this."

Thumps found himself wishing that the squirrel would make an encore appearance.

Beth turned Maslow's head to the side. Just behind the right ear was a nasty-looking wound.

"Most of the other injuries are superficial or at least not life-threatening."

"Could have got the wound from the fall," said Thumps. "Could have hit a rock on the way down."

"Could have," said Beth. "And her hands?"

Maslow's nails were blunt but trimmed and cared for.

"Clear-coat nail polish," said Beth. "Gets a professional manicure now and then."

"Same as Trudy?"

"Maybe."

"How deep is the head wound?"

"Won't know until I open her up," said Beth, "but I expect to find that it's what killed her."

"But it won't tell us why."

"No," said Beth. "That's your job."

"That's the sheriff's job," said Thumps.

Beth pushed Maslow's body back into the cabinet. "You think I can just glue a piece of plywood over the hole?"

"Might want to use concrete filler," said Thumps. "Squirrels can chew their way through wood."

Many of the cops Thumps had worked with had been able to draw a line between the living and the dead. When they looked at a corpse, all they saw was a corpse, an inanimate object that had little relationship to a living person. This was an essential skill for the kind of work that first responders did, a skill he had never learned.

Trudy Samuels's folder was still open on the desk.

"When you do the autopsy on Maslow," he said, "maybe you could reference it against what we know about Trudy."

"You mean such as look for similarities?" said Beth. "Now why didn't I think of that?"

"I used to be a cop."

"Is this where you say, 'Elementary, my dear Watson'?"

"That comes later," said Thumps. "When we solve the case."

"How about we catch the squirrel first?" Beth closed both files and put them back in the drawer. "I think your chance of success is going to be better with the rat."

TWENTY-SIX

The walk home, under a glowering sky, didn't improve his mood. There was nothing that so described a life without purpose, Thumps told himself, as spending an afternoon chasing a squirrel around a morgue. With each block he walked, the more the rodent became a metaphor for all those things he had lost and the things that he had not been able to find.

The house was dark. Not a single light in a single window to welcome him home. So this was how self-pity felt. Not so different from depression.

"Mr. DreadfulWater." Dixie and Pops were on the porch in the shadows. "Guess what?" Pops began pounding his tail against the wood railing as though he were beating out a drum roll. "Pops and I have found your cat."

"Freeway?"

"That's the good news."

Thumps waited a moment. "There's bad news?"

"Not exactly bad news," said Dixie. "It's more like complicated news."

"Okay."

Dixie looked at Pops as though he was hoping the dog would step in and explain the situation.

"There's a real nice family four streets over. Blue house with white trim. The Passangs. Dorjee and Tenzin. From Tibet. They have three kids. I forgot their names, but they look to be great kids."

Pops heaved himself to his feet, waddled over, and leaned against Thumps's leg.

Dixie took a deep breath. "That's where your cat is. With the Passangs."

Pops farted.

Thumps held his breath for as long as he could. "Freeway is with another family?"

"Yeah," said Dixie. "They thought she was a stray, so they took her in."

"She's not a stray."

"Sure," said Dixie. "I know that. But they didn't."

"Blue house with white trim? Four blocks over?"

"They've been taking good care of her. They even took her to the vet."

"The vet?"

"To get her spayed."

Pops folded himself into a warm lump at Thumps's feet.

"Freeway's been spayed."

"Yeah," said Dixie, "that was unfortunate."

"They spayed her again?"

"The vet said it wasn't a problem."

"Jesus."

"When Pops and I found her, I told the Passangs about you and how you had to go to Seattle and how I was supposed to look after the cat and how she had disappeared and how we didn't know where she went."

"I'll go by in the morning and pick her up."

Dixie shifted from one foot to the other. "Yeah," he said, "see, that's the complicated part. They don't want to give the cat back."

"She's my cat."

"Course she is," said Dixie. "But you have to look at it from their point of view. They did pay to have her spayed, and their kids are real attached."

Pops stood up and wandered over to Dixie, the flatulence trailing off the dog like a ground fog.

"And your kitty seems to like it there."

"I'll go talk to them."

"I told them you'd stop by," said Dixie. "They work all day, so the best time is around supper. After that they're busy putting the kids to bed."

Thumps could feel his body sag just a little.

"But this is good news," said Dixie. "The cat's alive. And she's happy."

THE SELECTION AT the Cash and Carry wasn't as good as at Albertsons, but the discount grocery was open. Thumps eased the truck into a parking space and tried to remember what he needed.

Everything.

Milk, bread, butter, meat, cheese, vegetables. He'd pick up a box of those chocolate-coated cookies and maybe some ice cream. It was a well-known fact that depression responded to sugar. Sure, it was a temporary fix. The high and then the low. And sure, as a diabetic, sugar was the last thing he needed.

In any quantity.

When he got to the frozen-food section, he looked at the nutritional chart of several different ice creams to see if the sugar content was as bad as he suspected.

It was.

Fruit. Okay, he'd be smart and get fruit instead. He knew there was sugar in fruit, but grapes, thankfully, didn't have that information stamped on the skin. He could look up the sugar in grapes in the little book on carbohydrate counting that had come with his diabetes supplies.

If he wanted to.

He had been somewhat abrupt with Dixie, and he'd have to

apologize to the man for his poor behaviour. Freeway wasn't his neighbour's problem. Thumps wasn't sure there was a problem at all. Freeway had always gone where she wanted to go and did what she wanted to do. Thumps had fed her, had given her a place to live, had even provided a warm lap for the cat when she was in the mood for a lap. But he didn't own her, had no claim to her other than the friendship they shared.

Now she was with another family. A family with kids. Thumps wouldn't have thought that Freeway would have liked kids. Not that he had ever asked the cat about children. Not that she had ever expressed an opinion.

So. No Claire. No car. And now, no cat. There was a pattern here, one that Thumps wasn't sure he wanted to contemplate. As he walked the aisles, he was struck by the realization that, as it were, he had little left to lose.

If he had anything at all.

"Howdy, buckaree."

Stas and Angie Black Weasel and their three kids materialized from behind a display of bottled water.

"Buckaroo, honey," said Angie.

"Yes," said Stas. "Buckaroo. Because you are man, yes?"

"No, honey," said Angie. "Buckaroo is for male and female."

"Yes," said Stas. "Gender politics. What a great country."

"How are you, Thumps?" Angie's face looked as though it had just come back from a funeral.

"Fine."

"You remember Mikhail and the twins. Lucy. Koko." Angie touched the head of each child in turn.

"We're getting a dog," said Mikhail.

"Maybe there is dog," said Stas.

"You said we'd get a dog," Lucy and Koko said in unison and began spinning around as though standing still had been too much to bear.

"Yes," said Stas, "yes, maybe there is dog. But small dog."

"Big dog!" shouted the kids together.

"You don't have children, do you?" Angie was holding on to Mikhail's jacket with one hand.

"Dog, dog, dog, dog, dog, dog . . ." Mikhail and his sisters marched around their parents, whacking Stas and Angie on the thighs with their hands.

"Have you talked with Claire?"

"When?"

"Then I shouldn't say anything," said Angie.

"Like what?"

"Come on, kids," said Angie. "Let's get some ice cream."

"Ice cream!"

Thumps watched Angie chase after the kids.

"Children," said Stas, leaning on the cart. "You must get some. Then you must get dog."

Thumps tried to imagine a family. Anna Tripp. He tried

to remember Anna's face when she was happy, and Callie's laughter when she was tickled. That memory was slipping away, leaving his body like blood flowing out of a wound.

"What about car?" said Stas. "You keep horse? You shoot horse?"

Thumps put a bag of unbleached flour into his cart. "Don't know."

"Okay," said Stas, "time for dog."

"A dog?"

"Angie say dog opens heart. Makes you forget sorrows."

"She says that, does she?"

"Yes," said Stas. "Also say same thing about children. And chocolate."

THUMPS TOOK HIS time walking the aisles. Now that he was here, there was no point in rushing. Nothing waiting for him at home. Maybe a dog wasn't a terrible idea. They could go on photography trips together, take walks along the river. He could watch television with the dog on his lap. Roughhouse with the dog on the floor.

A medium-sized female. Molly. Coco. Muffy.

He made a detour down the pet food aisle and contemplated the array of wet and dry food and doggy treats that came in an assortment of disquieting flavours and combinations.

Chicken and brown rice. Lamb and barley. Coq au vin with

beets. Alligator chips and beer biscuits. Strawberry licorice chews and emu bars.

By the time Thumps got to the meat section, he had sorted his way through various breeds, trying to come up with the perfect dog. A lab perhaps or a retriever or one of those poodle mixes he had heard about.

By the time he reached the eggs and butter, he had gotten past the romance and moved on to dog reality. Biweekly nail clippings. Teeth brushing. Obedience training. Vet bills. Warm doggy poop in plastic sacks.

Thumps waited in line with his cart. Stas was two checkouts over. Angie unloaded the cart while Stas wrestled with his son. The two girls pulled gum and candy off the displays by the register and tried to hide them under the broccoli and behind the squash.

Family life. Thumps couldn't help but smile. Noisy, animated, with lots of laughing and shouting and crying. There were probably quiet moments as well, when the kids were asleep and the parents had a moment to catch their breath.

Angie pushed the cart out to the parking lot with her son hanging off the front end by one hand like an unwieldly hood ornament, while Stas brought up the rear, rocking from side to side, his daughters wrapped around his legs like a pair of counterweights.

Thumps stacked the groceries on the belt. Maybe, he told himself, when you considered the alternatives, lonely and depressed wasn't so bad after all.

TWENTY-SEVEN

Thumps took his time putting the groceries away. Milk and juice on the top shelf. Butter and cheese in the door. Eggs, chicken, and sausages on the bottom shelf. Lettuce and tomatoes in the crisper.

The bread went into the freezer, the crackers and the dry pasta into the cupboards. Bananas on the counter in a bowl. He set the green bottle of olive oil next to the stove, alongside the jar of coarse ground pepper with its distinctive red cap.

The play of colours and the organization of shapes made him feel as though he were back in control of his world. Each time he opened the refrigerator door, the whole kitchen felt festive and structured.

On any other evening, Freeway would have been waiting for him, turning figure eights around his ankles, demanding to be fed or petted or both. It was a different house without the cat. Thumps checked the pet door. It was working just fine. If Freeway wanted to come home, she could. Her water bowl was full, and there was dry food in her dish.

What had Dixie said? Four streets over? His neighbour must have meant to the south. To the north, the neighbourhood only ran for two blocks before it hit the railroad tracks. And the house? Blue with white trim? If Thumps was lucky, he might be able to spot Freeway through a window.

As he walked down the street, he imagined that the cat had been kidnapped and was being held against her will and that he would rescue her and bring her home. Thumps wondered if this impulse was hard-wired into the gender, the male need to save something. He suspected it had more to do with ego and control, much less admirable traits.

Still, if he had to swim the moat and scale the battlements to save the cat, he would.

Thumps was in luck. There was only one house on the fourth block that was blue with white trim. He had always snorted at the TV crime dramas where forensics would find a piece of a plant or a lump of dirt or an enzyme in a sample of water that could only be found in one place. He had never recalled police work being that easy.

Still, here was the house, the only one on the street with the proper colour combination, so perhaps there was some truth to the cliché.

The lights were on and the curtains were open, so Thumps

could see in. He walked the far side of the street, just a guy out for an evening stroll. Nothing to worry about. Up the street he went and then back down. By the third circuit, he had run out of reasons why he was walking the same block over and over. He didn't think anyone would ask, but there was the chance that someone would feel uncomfortable with a tall Indian roaming the neighbourhood.

Thumps could see into the house itself, could see the kids moving in the living room with the television, could catch glimpses of the mother and father.

But no cat.

Maybe it was the wrong block or the wrong house. Thumps turned around at the top of the street, crossed over so that he was closer to the windows. He slowed down this time, came to a stop, actually bent down, pretending to tie his shoe.

Pathetic.

And then there she was. Freeway. As though by magic. Sitting on the back of the sofa, looking out into the night. Thumps was sure she could see him, but if she did, the cat gave no sign of recognition. She didn't press against the glass or paw at the window. Thumps wanted to wave, to mouth her name, to pat his thigh to bring her to him.

Instead, he stayed in his crouch, tying his shoe over and over again until one of the children lifted Freeway high in the air and ran off with her, while another set of hands pulled the curtains closed.

Later that night, when he was sure everyone was asleep, he walked the four blocks back to the blue house with the white trim and left the bag of cat food on the porch, along with Freeway's favourite toy.

Then he walked home in the dark by himself and began making the phone calls.

TWENTY-EIGHT

Thumps was up bright and early the next morning. It was time, he told himself, as he stood in front of the bathroom mirror, to be decisive. It was time to make decisions.

The decision to give up Freeway had been difficult, but the cat herself had taken the first step. Thumps had simply agreed. His life wasn't one that easily included pets. He wasn't home all that much, and his two-month absence, when he was in Seattle with Claire, had finally convinced the cat to look elsewhere for companionship. A family with children had, at first glance, seemed a wrong decision for an anti-social cat, but in fact, as it turned out, Freeway hadn't been anti-social at all.

She had simply been lonely.

Now it was time to make decisions about the other unre-
solved issues in his life, and first up on the to-do list he had
created the night before was Nina Maslow.

The Tucker hotel came with two restaurants. The Mother
Lode, which catered to elegant and expensive dining, and the
Quick Claim, which handled breakfast, lunch, and late-night
coffee. Sydney Pearl was sitting in a booth at the back of the
Claim. On any other day, he might have been surprised to run
into her like this, but this was where he had asked her to meet
him, and here she was.

What Thumps had not expected were the other two people
at the table. Calder Banks and Gloria Baker-Doyle.

What the hell. Had Pearl sent out a general invitation? He
looked around just in case Adele Samuels, her son, Ethan, and
Duke Hockney were lurking in the shadows.

"Mr. DreadfulWater."

"Ms. Pearl."

"I'm guessing you wanted to meet with me privately."

"That was the idea."

"Problem is," said Pearl, "there's not much about TV that's
private. I asked Calder and Gloria to attend in case they can
answer questions I can't."

"You'll find us quite helpful," said Gloria.

"I must admit," said Pearl, "I was intrigued by your phone
message."

Thumps slid into the booth next to Gloria.

"Meet me for breakfast," Pearl intoned in a low, deep voice. "I've solved Nina's murder."

Thumps was sure he didn't sound like that. "I didn't say I had solved her murder."

Pearl wagged a finger at him. "That was the intimation."

"I said that I had some ideas as to what happened to Nina Maslow."

"And Trudy Samuels?"

"Maybe."

"And you expect me to pay you for *ideas* and *maybes*?"

"I do."

"Quite exciting," said Gloria. "May I be your side stick?"

"Kick," said Calder. "Sidekick."

"Brilliant."

"I'm listening," said Pearl.

"Let's play twenty questions," said Thumps.

Pearl grinned. "The 1940s radio show or the 1950s television show?"

Calder frowned. "There was a television show called *Twenty Questions*?"

"*A Christmas Carol*," said Gloria. "They play a version of twenty questions called 'Yes and No' in the Dickens story."

"First question," said Thumps. "How many shows has *Malice Aforethought* completed?"

"Not counting the Samuels episode," said Pearl, "we've done forty-three."

Thumps wrote the number on the paper placemat. "You said that Maslow actually was able to solve three of these?"

"Two," said Pearl. "The fourth episode and the twenty-third."

Thumps did a fast calculation. "So if we were evaluating the show in terms of its success rate in solving cases, the ratio would be less than 5 percent."

"Actually," said Gloria, "it would be right at 4.65 percent."

Thumps checked his figures.

"Always liked math," said Gloria.

Pearl held up her hands in surrender. "Thank heavens we're not in the business of solving cases."

"But you are," said Thumps. "That's the promise of the show."

Calder brightened. "You mean, where I say, 'Welcome to *Malice Aforethought*, where we investigate the most heinous of unsolved crimes and bring the perpetrators to justice,' at the start of each show?"

"You ever been to a carnival sideshow?" Pearl arranged the silverware in front of her. "Cobra Girl, Frog Baby, the Two-Headed Bear Boy? It's all hype."

"But Maslow actually wanted to solve each and every case, didn't she?"

Pearl cocked her head to one side. "Nina could be somewhat driven."

"The two cases that she solved," said Thumps, "they weren't very strong, were they?"

"You mean in terms of network potential? Awash in graphic sexuality and gratuitous violence?"

"Yes."

"No," said Pearl. "I argued against them."

"But?"

"I trusted her."

Calder came to life. "What has any of this to do with Nina?"

"Trudy Samuels," said Thumps. "How strong was Trudy Samuels?"

Pearl rearranged the silverware. Thumps didn't bother waiting.

"It was weak," he offered. "In fact, I'm guessing it was probably the weakest of all the possibilities."

"Your point, Mr. DreadfulWater?"

"Nina solved the case." Gloria could barely contain herself. "That's it, isn't it? Brilliant. She solved the case."

Thumps waited for Pearl to confirm what he already knew.

"Very good, Mr. DreadfulWater." Pearl's voice was not congratulatory.

"When?"

"Two days, two weeks, a month. I really don't know."

"And?"

"She didn't share the details with me," said Pearl.

Calder shook his head. "Nina liked surprises. We knew she had something, but she wouldn't give us the script points until the day of the shoot. Believed it kept the interaction fresh and real."

"And if the show solves the case . . ."

"Yes, Mr. DreadfulWater," said Pearl, "that is the gold standard of reality programming."

"Is that what got her killed?" Gloria looked around the table. "I mean we're all thinking that, right? I mean, no one thinks that Nina fell off a cliff."

"What do you think, Mr. DreadfulWater?"

Thumps leaned forward. "I'll need Maslow's files."

"Her files?" Calder frowned. "They were stolen. Someone broke into her room and took them. They're gone."

"That's right," said Gloria.

Thumps watched Pearl's face. It didn't change, and he hadn't expected that it would.

"Her files," he said. "All of them."

Pearl tried to look bored. "Surely you're not accusing me of breaking into Nina's room and taking her files?"

Calder slowly turned to Pearl. "No," he said. "He thinks you have copies."

"Does he?"

"He does," said Thumps.

"That's an intriguing theory," said Pearl.

"Not a theory," said Thumps. "The program is too important to have only one copy of the research for the shows. There's no way Nina would allow that to happen. There has to be at least two copies of everything. If I were guessing, I'd expect that there are at least three."

Pearl slowly spread her hands out on the table, palms down. "Actually," she said, "there are four. Two hard copies. One was stolen. I have one."

"Digital?" asked Gloria.

"One is at the office in Los Angeles," said Pearl. "The fourth is stored at a cyber facility in Utah."

"Shit," said Banks. "Now that's paranoid."

"Prudent," said Pearl. "Stick with acting, Calder. Leave the logistics to me."

"You can give me yours or you can make me a copy of the files. A complete copy. Your choice."

"And if I say no."

"Deal's off," said Thumps. "I walk."

"How will you know if I've given you everything?"

"I'll know."

"All right," said Pearl. "I'll give you everything but the file on the Obsidian Murders."

"No."

"Sorry," said Pearl, "but if I give you that file, there's nothing to keep you from walking."

"How do I know you even have the file?" said Thumps. "How do I know that there's anything in it of value? Trust cuts both ways."

"Let's be clear, Mr. DreadfulWater," said Pearl. "I don't trust you, and you don't trust me. But Nina trusted you, and I trusted her. You have my word on the file."

Thumps took a moment. "All right," he said. "Deal."

Sydney Pearl pushed her glasses up on her nose. "Find out who killed Nina, Mr. DreadfulWater. Don't let me down."

Thumps slid out of the booth.

"See," said Pearl. "We're all friends."

THUMPS HAD PARKED the truck in the no-parking zone in front of the hotel. Since Duke was going to fix the one ticket, he might as well fix two. But there was no citation on the windshield. A good omen. And the day had come in warm and windless. Maybe things were looking up.

Or maybe this was just the calm before the storm arrived, the moment before all hell broke loose.

TWENTY-NINE

Thumps pointed the truck west, left Chinook behind, and followed the road as it rose up onto Little Horn Plateau, an area of high plains that stretched north and south along the Ironstone River. The fall sun was at his back, and it lit up the tablelands, red and yellow and dark green. Aspens, larches, lodgepole pines and firs, all brilliant and glowing under a steel-blue sky, a landscape painted in oil with a knife.

Thumps slowed the truck when he got to Randall, just in case the speed trap was still in operation. Randall wasn't really a town, more a turn in the road with a grocery store, a gas station, two bars, and a motel that looked like something from a Hitchcock movie.

The patrol car was sitting in the shade of a large roadside billboard. "Executive Lots" the billboard proclaimed. "Your Piece of the Old West." Thumps had no idea where these lots might be. There was nothing around Randall but flat land and scrub brush. Maybe the guy in the cruiser knew.

Not that Thumps was going to stop and ask.

Black Stag, the Samuels estate, was on the northern edge of the Little Horn Plateau. Buck Samuels had chosen the site carefully. The log mansion he had built was rumoured to resemble the hotels that the Canadian Pacific had built in the Rockies at places such as Banff and Lake Louise, and the Prince of Wales Hotel in Waterton Lakes National Park, which had been built by the Great Northern Railway, though not on the same scale.

Thumps had left a message on Adele's phone, so he wasn't sure that she would see him, but he figured it would be harder to turn him away if he showed up on her doorstep than if he asked permission from a distance.

Buck had thrown up a stone wall that ran out for about ten feet on either side of a set of iron gates that had been sculpted to look like two bull elk with their antlers locked in combat. A bit melodramatic, and so far as Thumps could tell, the gates and the walls were useless. Anyone could simply step round the walls and keep going. But if you had a car, you were obliged to stop at the stainless steel intercom box and press the button.

Thumps decided to keep it formal.

"Thumps DreadfulWater," he said to the box. "For Mrs. Adele Samuels."

Thumps waited for someone to answer. Instead, there was a sharp sound and the gates slowly swung open.

Okay, Thumps thought to himself, that'll work.

The road to the house didn't run straight. It followed the contour of the land, dipping down between rock outcroppings and riding high on the back of the ridgeline.

Thumps had seen any number of log houses but nothing like this. The logs Buck had used were enormous. Thumps didn't know his trees all that well, but he guessed these were old-growth western red-cedar logs chosen and cut to Buck's specifications.

So far as Thumps could tell, it had taken the better part of a forest to build the house.

Adele Samuels was waiting for him when he pulled up in front of the log mansion. She was dressed in jeans and a plaid shirt, as though she were on her way to the barn to toss hay around.

"Mr. DreadfulWater."

The sheriff had a way of touching the brim of his hat to let folks know that he was in charge. Thumps gave it a try.

"Yes, ma'am."

"Intriguing phone message."

"I hoped that you would consent to see me."

"Is that right?"

"It is," said Thumps.

"You read any of Robert Parker's western novels?" Adele was standing at an angle, her arms folded across her chest. "Because you're beginning to sound like Marshal Virgil Cole and Deputy Marshal Everett Hitch all rolled into one."

Ethan Price appeared behind his mother.

"Morning, Mr. DreadfulWater."

"You're a smart man," said Adele, "showing up here like this. Over the phone, I would have told you to go to hell."

The wind was on the rise, and the light had faded. The bright colours had dulled down, and the land had lost its early-morning glow.

"But now that you're here," said Adele, "you may as well come in."

The exterior of the house had been impressive, and the interior didn't disappoint. It reminded Thumps of some of the pictures he had seen of European cathedrals.

"We'll have coffee in the great room."

Adele led the way into a large open space with log rafters and crossbeams that towered overhead. The light came in through the windows in broad slants, but the heavy beams and posts cut it into pieces so that parts of the room were brilliant and parts were deep shadow.

"We can talk here."

The leather sofas and chairs were arranged in a U shape so that everything faced the large windows and the view west towards the Highwood and Little Belt Mountains and north to the Bears Paws.

"It's a monstrosity." Adele arranged herself on one of the sofas.

Ethan took a chair. Thumps took a corner of the second sofa, out of the sun.

"But that was Buck," said Adele. "Bigger than life. And an even bigger pain in the ass."

"But you didn't come here to talk about Buck Samuels," said Ethan.

"No," said Thumps, "I didn't."

An older woman, Mexican, if Thumps had to guess, came into the room with a tray.

"Coffee, Mr. DreadfulWater?" said Adele. "Juanita makes the cookies herself. They're quite good."

"You told my mother that you were going to look into the case." Ethan rubbed at the palm of his hand with a thumb.

"That's right."

"Because *Malice Aforethought* is paying you." There was no cruelty in Adele's voice, but neither was there any warmth.

"That is part of it."

"And the other part?"

Thumps helped himself to a cookie and a cup of coffee from the silver pot.

"I'm hoping you'd be willing to talk to me about Trudy."

"My daughter is dead."

Ethan didn't flinch. But Thumps could feel the young man's body tense.

"Technically," said Adele, "she was my stepdaughter. Do you have children, Mr. DreadfulWater?"

The sun was working its way along the southern horizon, heading west, and the shadows in the great room were on the move.

"Trudy was six when I married Buck. He needed a mother for his daughter. I needed a father for my son. It didn't quite work out as either of us had hoped."

"Dead history," said Ethan. "Nothing to be done about it."

"Can you imagine what it's like to leave a child behind?"

"You didn't leave me behind," said Ethan.

"I begged Buck to let me bring my son with me." There was no sorrow in Adele's voice, just the sharp ring of steel hitting steel. "I suppose that was the first cut."

The shifting light had crept across the floor and found his boots. Thumps tried to remember if it was werewolves or vampires who couldn't manage sunny conditions.

"After that, we just kept cutting."

Ethan shifted in the chair. "I'm sure Mr. DreadfulWater didn't come here to talk about Buck Samuels."

"Thumps," said Thumps.

"Thumps," said Ethan.

"I'm sure Mr. DreadfulWater has heard the rumours."

"Mom."

"It's all right," said Adele. "Can't control what people say. Can't change what they believe."

Thumps wanted to tell Adele that he didn't put much stock in rumours, but he knew how hollow and insincere that would sound.

"There are those who believe that I killed Buck or allowed him to die."

"How old was Trudy?"

"Twelve," said Adele. "Not even a teenager."

"How old was Ethan?"

"Eleven."

"And he came here to live with you and Trudy right after Buck died?"

Adele sat up straight and rigid. "Day after the funeral."

"It's not as bad as it sounds," said Ethan.

"I had to leave my child with my sister. He was only five," said Adele. "You think I was going to wait a second longer?"

"I hope you're not going to blame my mother," said Ethan.

"Course he is," said Adele. "Everybody else does. Poor little princess. Loses her mother and then her father. Left in the clutches of an evil stepmother and her pretender son. No wonder she fell apart."

"I wasn't here," said Thumps.

"The truth of the matter is, I was a good mother to that girl. Sure, we had our moments, but we got along. You think Buck paid any attention to his daughter? Hell, Buck was all about the business. I was the one who raised Trudy."

"And then Buck died."

"Yes," said Adele, "and then Buck died."

"And the wheels fell off."

"No," said Adele. "The wheels fell off, as you so crudely put it, when she met Tobias Rattler."

Thumps leaned back. The sunlight was streaming across his legs and threatening his thighs.

"She met him in high school," said Adele.

Ethan held up a hand. "Let me do this, Mom."

"Yes," said Adele. "My son will have a different perspective."

Ethan cleared his throat and leaned forward in the chair. "You remember high school, Mr. DreadfulWater?"

"Thumps."

Ethan smiled. "Thumps."

"Not much of it."

"But you remember the dynamics. Who was in, who was out."

"Sure."

"Tobias Rattler was a loner. Good-looking. Mysterious. Didn't have any friends to speak of. Someone passing through town on his way to somewhere else."

"Shane."

"The movie?"

"The loner."

"Exactly," said Ethan. "That was Toby. You know what they say about bad boys and good girls."

"Sure."

"Except Trudy wasn't all that good." Ethan paused and took a breath. "She had already started drinking. Maybe even drugs. We got along okay, but we didn't talk. We weren't like brother and sister."

"More like boarders in the same hotel."

"You have a way with words, Mr. DreadfulWater." Ethan made an apologetic noise. "Thumps."

"So Trudy and Rattler got together."

"Not at first," said Ethan. "I don't think they ever spoke to one another. Trudy kept to herself, and Toby was Toby."

Thumps waited.

"Second year at the homecoming game. Afterwards. Couple of guys gave Trudy a hard time. Tore her dress. Pushed her around some. Toby stepped in and stopped them."

"The hero."

"Guess so," said Ethan. "After that they started hanging out together. Toby and Trudy. T & T."

Adele's eyes flashed in the light. "You know what they call a sixteen-year-old girl who has sex?"

"Mom!"

"A slut," said Adele. "That's the word."

Ethan stayed composed. "They didn't have sex. Sure, that's what people said, but it wasn't true."

"How do you know?"

"Trudy and I didn't get along all that well, but we did talk. She confided in me."

Thumps debated his next move. "Because you're gay?"

Adele Samuels started to get off the sofa. "Perhaps it's time for you to leave, Mr. DreadfulWater."

"No, Mom." Ethan motioned for his mother to sit down. "It's

okay." Ethan smiled and turned to Thumps. "Does it show?"

"No," said Thumps. "It was a guess."

"Trudy was the only one who knew," said Ethan. "And she never told."

"But she talked to you about Rattler."

"Some," said Ethan. "If they were having sex, Trudy would have said."

Adele was hard-faced and impatient. "Why else would Rattler be with a girl like Trudy unless there was sex?"

Ethan shook his head. "Rattler wasn't with Trudy. Trudy was with him. Because he made her feel safe."

"And that was more important than sex."

"It was," said Ethan. "Trudy gave up the booze and the drugs."

"Because she was safe."

Ethan nodded. "And because she was in love with him."

Thumps thought on this for a moment. "But he wasn't in love with her?"

"Rattler wasn't gay if that's what you're asking," said Ethan.

"You'd know?"

"Trudy said Toby wasn't interested in sex."

"What about Trudy?" said Thumps. "Was she interested in sex?"

"I think that's enough, Mr. DreadfulWater," said Adele.

Ethan ignored his mother. "Anyway, Mom and Trudy had a big fight, and Trudy moved out. Got an apartment in town."

Thumps looked at Adele. "Over Rattler?"

"Yes, Mr. DreadfulWater," said Adele. "Over Mr. Rattler."

"Teenagers," said Ethan. "I'm sure you understand."

"Sure," said Thumps.

"Trudy was mad at Mom because Buck died and Mom lived."

The shifting light had found him, bright and glaring. Thumps moved across the sofa to the shadows at the far end.

"Light too bright for you, Mr. DreadfulWater?"

"Yes, ma'am," said Thumps. "It is."

"Mr. Rattler didn't like the light much either," said Adele. "Do you think that's an Indian trait?"

"Mom."

"Speak my mind," said Adele. "Always have. Not about to stop now."

"I'm told that Trudy and Tobias had a fight just before she died."

"I heard that too," said Ethan.

"Any idea why?"

"Mr. Rattler was going to leave her." Adele's voice crackled like green logs on a fire. "Off to university somewhere. Was going to dump her. Fuck the rich bitch and dump her. Is that what you wanted to know?"

"Maybe you better go," said Ethan.

Thumps stood and set his hat on his head. "Thank you for seeing me."

Ethan stepped in behind him. "I'll walk you out."

Adele stayed on the sofa. "I'm sure Mr. DreadfulWater can find his own way out. I understand that Indians are good at finding scent."

Ethan walked Thumps to the truck. "My mother has edges," he said. "For all the money, she's had a hard life." Ethan picked at the palm of his hand. "Anything else?"

"Injury?"

"This?" Ethan opened the hand and held it up. "Log house. Live in a log house and you get splinters."

Adele appeared behind them. "I said we were done."

Thumps nodded. "One last question. Why do you stay here?"

"What?"

"You said the place is a monstrosity. So why do you stay here?"

Adele turned her face to the wind. "Is that part of your investigation?"

"Probably not."

"When you get to the gates," said Adele, "make sure that they close behind you?"

"I will."

Adele stood framed against the open doorway, ready to repel friends and foes alike. "And don't come back."

THIRTY

Thumps had always imagined crimes to be rather like the puzzles you found at thrift stores, where there was no guarantee that all the pieces were still in the box. As he drove east from the Samuels estate, he wondered if Trudy and Nina Maslow were one puzzle or two. If Trudy was murdered, then the cases could be linked, but that would mean that the person or persons who killed Samuels had murdered Maslow as well. Or the cases could be separate. Trudy's death might have been suicide or an accident and had nothing to do with Maslow. But why then had the bodies of the two women wound up in the same place?

Misdirection?

Coincidence?

Edge pieces. That's all he had. Edge pieces and little else.

Thumps wasn't sure he was going to find any of the missing

pieces at Moses Blood's place, but there was every chance he'd find Moses.

The trail from the ridge to the river bottom had always been a narrow, rutted path that not even the deer or the coyotes used for fear of breaking a leg. Moses called it his "driveway," but that's because the old man had a twisted sense of humour.

However, today the dirt trail was smooth and banked. As impossible as it seemed, someone had widened and graded the track and turned it into a road, the kind of road that suggested the beginnings of executive estates and hobby farms.

Maybe this was what the billboard in Randall was advertising.

Moses's house sat on high ground banked against the Ironstone and the run of cottonwoods that followed the river. At one point, there had been about fifty trailers arranged on the flat in interesting patterns that resembled a giant maze or an enormous patchwork quilt. The trailers were long gone. The house, the chicken coop, and the barn remained.

Moses was in the yard, splitting wood. Thumps parked the car against a large cottonwood and got out.

"Should get someone to do that for you."

Moses set the maul down and wiped his face. "Cooley already put up about nine cords." Moses waved a hand at the low running wall of wood near the barn, all neatly stacked and squared off. "I figure I should have one or two more, just in case."

Next to the firewood was a pile of orange stakes with ribbons tied to one end.

"Those surveyor stakes?"

"Bunch of young boys came by and stuck them up in a nice straight line," said Moses. "Ran 'em right across the river and up onto high ground. One long line. Should have seen it. Pretty impressive sight."

"You pulled the stakes up?"

"They couldn't get their big truck down here," said Moses, "so they brought in a grader and fixed my driveway."

"Someone's not going to be happy about the stakes being gone."

"Pipeline," said Moses. "We don't need it, so I figure they don't need those stakes."

Thumps tried to keep a straight face. "And good kindling is hard to find."

Moses grinned. "Yes," he said, "good kindling is hard to find."

Thumps picked up the maul. "How about I split some wood for a while. Could use the exercise."

"Yes," Moses agreed. "Exercise is a good thing. I'll make some tea. Tea's a good thing too."

Splitting wood seemed like a good idea at the time, but it didn't take long for reality to set in. By the time Moses returned with the tea, Thumps was soaked with sweat, and his arms and shoulders ached. Somewhere in the small of his back, muscles were organizing a major protest.

"It's American ginseng," said Moses. "They grow it in Wisconsin. Supposed to give you energy for all sorts of things."

"Like chopping wood?"

"And collecting kindling." Moses set the cups on the wood plank table.

The wind was off the river. It was cutting but not that cold. Thumps buttoned his jacket up so he wouldn't get chilled. Moses closed his eyes and let the breeze flow over his face.

"You smell that?"

"The wood?"

"The snow," said Moses. "It's on its way. This week. Next at the latest. You got your car working yet?"

"Nope."

"Probably going to have to give Stas's truck back at some point."

"Probably."

"Maybe you'll be living with Claire by then," said Moses. "She has a good truck."

"Don't think that's going to happen."

"She's going to need a man around," said Moses, "even if she don't know it yet."

"Claire doesn't need a man."

"Most women don't," said Moses. "But they do it anyway."

The tea was strong and bitter. Thumps felt something that could be energy. Or it could just be his body being startled.

"Sometimes when I drink this tea," said Moses, "it helps me think."

"Maybe you can think of why someone would kill Nina Maslow."

"That's the television woman."

"It is," said Thumps.

"I fell off Belly Butte one time." Moses chuckled. "Mary Many Bears pushed me, but she had cause."

"You try to kiss her?"

Moses looked concerned. "Mary's my cousin. Why would I want to kiss my cousin?"

"What'd you do?"

"Told her she was skinny." Moses smiled. "She was skinny. But she was also quick."

Thumps tried to picture Moses going down the side of Belly Butte. "You get hurt?"

Moses shook his head. "Scraped up a bit. Tore my pants and shirt."

"It's a long ways down."

Moses finished his tea. "Come on," he said. "Throw a couple of those logs in the truck. You and me can try our hand at forensic science."

"Forensic science?"

"Just like the TV show."

THE TRAIL UP to Belly Butte had not improved. All the activity the day before had only deepened the ruts. The truck bucked its way up the hill, the front end rising and crashing down on the undercarriage, the logs rolling around in the back, banging against the sides of the bed. By the time Thumps got to the top, his fingers were welded to the steering wheel.

Moses got out of the truck first. "You might want to check the oil pan," he said. "That last hole you hit was impressive."

Thumps pried his fingers open. "So, tell me about Tobias."

Moses jammed his hands in his pockets. "Didn't catch him in time. By the time we caught up with each other, it was already too late."

"For what?"

Moses walked back to the truck and dropped the tailgate. "Most people are born into a family. Families are part of a community. You put communities together, and you got a tribe."

"Okay."

"But some people are born alone, and they grow up alone, and if you don't find them in time, alone is all they're ever going to be."

"Rattler."

"He was hitchhiking," said Moses. "Headed to Paris."

"And you took him in."

"He stayed with me a while." Moses pulled one of the logs off the truck. "And then he left. Went to that Indian university back east."

"Indian university?"

"Dark Mouth," said Moses.

"Dartmouth?"

"Grab that other log."

"Dartmouth's a private university. Expensive as hell."

Moses carried his log to the edge of the butte and set it on its end. "When Mary Many Bears pushed me, what do you think happened?"

Moses tipped the log over the edge of the butte. It slid and banged its way down the slope. A quarter of the way down, it hit a narrow ledge and became airborne, picking up speed, pitchpoling end over end, bouncing off the rocks, and crashing into the scree field at the bottom.

"Now you try it."

Thumps rolled the second log over the edge. With the same result. Slide, ledge, airborne, pitchpole, crash.

"Boy," said Moses, "not much difference."

Both logs had come to rest within feet of each other.

"That about where the Maslow woman landed?"

Thumps stepped to the edge of the butte and looked down. "More or less."

Moses nodded. "That's where we found Trudy."

"Kind of a waste of firewood."

"In experiments," said Moses, "they got control groups and subjects. Those logs are our control group."

Thumps didn't feel himself being shoved over the edge, but one moment he was standing on top of the butte, talking to

Moses, and the next minute he was sliding down the slope, grabbing at anything his hands could find, digging his feet into the side of the butte, as he slowly slid down the slope.

And then he hit the narrow ledge.

And stopped.

Moses was standing at the edge of the butte, looking down at him. "Scared the hell out of me too," Moses yelled. "Mary thought it was real funny."

"You pushed me!"

The slope wasn't as steep as it looked. At least until it reached the ledge. After that, Thumps could see that there would be no stopping. And he wasn't much the worse for wear. A couple of cuts. A tear at the elbow of his shirt.

"If you work your way to the left," shouted Moses, "you'll find hard ground."

Moses was sitting on the tailgate of the truck. "After we found Trudy," he said, "I tried it a couple of times. Just to be sure."

Thumps brushed himself off. "And you always landed on the ledge."

"'Cause I was trying to stop myself," said Moses. "Someone goes off the butte, they try to stop themselves."

"Unless they can't."

Moses nodded. "Unless they can't."

"But if you're dead weight."

Moses squeezed his lips together. "Then you're a log."

"Control group. Subject group."

"Forensic science," said Moses. "Just like *CSI: Crime Scene Investigation*."

Thumps stood at the edge of the coulee and looked down. "Too bad about the logs."

Moses stayed on the tailgate. "Yes," he said. "Going down will be pretty easy. Coming up will be harder."

Thumps winced. "You want me to get the logs?"

Moses closed his eyes as though he were thinking about a nap. "All things considered," he said, "you'll probably have to make two trips."

THIRTY-ONE

Thumps had never been pushed off a cliff before, and he wasn't sure he appreciated Moses's idea of forensic science. Not that it had been a cliff. And not that Thumps had been in any real danger. The top section of Belly Butte looked steep, but it wasn't. More a long, slow ski jump that curled up at the ledge. But after that, the plunge was quite severe, and if you didn't catch the ledge, and tumbled over, the drop was straight to the bottom.

So Thumps and the logs had been a good object lesson. Anyone pushed off the top of Belly Butte who had been alive and kicking would have been able to stop themselves. Anyone pushed off the top of Belly Butte who had been unconscious or dead would have wound up with the timber.

It wasn't really forensic science, but it was close enough, whereas carrying the logs back up the butte was pure physics.

The drive home was in complete darkness. If there was a moon, it was hidden by clouds. If there weren't any clouds, then there was no moon. And no stars for that matter. From the time he dropped Moses and the logs off and found his way back to the main road, it was dead black and the world existed only in the throw of the truck's headlights. At one point, he wondered if he had somehow taken a wrong turn, and he was relieved when he came over a rise and saw Chinook all aglow in the distance.

His house was dark. Except for the lights in the kitchen. He didn't remember turning them on that morning, but on such a black night, they were a warm welcome. Maybe he should leave them on more often.

He was almost to the porch when he saw the bag of cat food. Next to the bag was Freeway's toy. He had left both of these at the blue and white house as a token of understanding. Now here they were, thrown back in his face, dropped off like so much garbage.

Shit. Shit, shit, shit!

The first kick split the bag open. The second sent the dry food flying across the porch. If Thumps had had his service automatic, he would have emptied the entire clip into the Tipsy Twilight Owl cat toy.

He had the bag in one hand and was beating it against the newel post when the front door opened.

"Thumps?" Claire was in the doorway, wrapped in a quilt. "Are you okay?"

Thumps held up the remains of the bag, as if the ruined sack explained anything. "You've been gone."

"I have," said Claire. "But now I'm back."

Thumps set the bag down and stepped onto the porch. He could feel the kitty bits crunch under his feet. "I should get a broom."

"Good idea," said Claire. "I'll make tea."

The cat food was everywhere. Thumps swept it off the porch into the shrubs. If it was good for cats, maybe it would help the plants. He stuffed the bag and the toy into the garbage.

Claire was at the kitchen table with a teapot and two cups. "I was in Browning."

Thumps washed his hands. His fingers smelled vaguely of fish.

"You should see the fall colours around Glacier. Golds, reds, purples. The high meadows were on fire."

"Glacier's great."

Claire held the cup in front of her face. "I should have told you."

"I was worried."

"I know," said Claire. "But there were things I needed to do."

"Test results?"

"What?" Claire put the cup down. "No. I'm fine. The test results were good. Didn't I tell you?"

"Probably did," said Thumps. "And I forgot."

Claire looked around. "Where's Freeway? She's normally chewing on our ankles by now."

"She's gone."

"Oh, Thumps," said Claire. "I'm so sorry. How did she die?"

"No, she's not dead." Thumps tried to put a good face on Freeway's treason. "She's with another family."

"Another family?"

"They have kids."

Claire waited. "This is about Seattle, isn't it?"

"She was never my cat," said Thumps. "We just lived together. Sometimes."

"Sort of like us."

Thumps glanced at the clock. "You want to stay?"

"I have a room at the Tucker." Claire shifted in the chair. "I didn't want to drive home tonight."

"You could stay here."

"I could," said Claire, "but I have some things to work out."

"Okay."

"But I was hoping we could have breakfast tomorrow morning. Would that be possible?"

"Sure."

"We need to talk."

"Sure."

"Good."

Thumps took a sip of tea. His fingers still smelled of fish. "Want to give me a hint?"

"No."

"Okay."

Claire left the quilt on the chair. "Place looks good. You always did have a knack for order."

"What time?"

"What?"

"For breakfast," said Thumps. "For our talk."

Claire smiled. "Worried?"

"A little."

"Excellent," said Claire. "How about eight?"

"Will you be up by then?"

Claire went to the door and opened it. "No one likes a smart ass."

THUMPS STAYED UP late and read a Craig Johnson novel that he had read before. He liked to imagine that he was the unflappable Walt Longmire, sheriff of Absaroka County, and that Claire was his foul-mouthed deputy, Victoria Moretti. It wasn't a perfect analogy. He was not always as composed as Walt. The bag of cat food could testify to that. And Claire was hardly a bad-mannered siren with a libido the size of Canada.

Still, he liked the general idea.

It was after one before he got to bed, and then he couldn't sleep. In spite of his efforts to keep the cat off the bed, Freeway had always slept with him, and now that she was no longer here, he missed her.

He'd get over it. Maybe he'd get a pillow to put behind his legs or maybe he'd find a stuffed cat. Or one of those cuddly toy dogs for that matter. That could be the answer. A pet that didn't require any care. A pet that you could pick up whenever you felt the need and could put down when you had other things to do.

Something that would help buffer the pain and keep the world at bay.

Thumps set his alarm clock for 7:30. The Tucker for breakfast. With Claire. A talk. Thumps set the novel on the nightstand.

Where was Walt Longmire when he needed him?

Walt would know what to do.

THIRTY-TWO

Thumps was up the next morning before the alarm went off. He showered, shaved, and went on a search-and-rescue mission for the bottle of Old Spice that Claire had bought him several Christmases back.

The bottle turned up in his underwear drawer. Thumps tried to remember why he would have put it there and couldn't come up with a convincing answer. But during his search, he also found the Benchmade pocket knife he thought he had lost, a beaded belt buckle he had found at a craft store on the Blood reserve in Alberta, and $4.75 in change.

So the delay had been time well spent, and in spite of the brown residue around the little red cap, the Old Spice still smelled fine.

So Claire was back. And she wanted to talk.

Good news. Bad news.

In Thumps's experience, there were two kinds of conversations. There was the casual variety, where the topics were shallow and reasonably safe.

Weather and sports.

And then there was the serious sort, where the topics were singular and treacherous.

Commitment and feelings.

Thumps knew there were probably men who didn't mind talking about feelings. He just didn't know any.

There were two shirts in the closet that were clean and ironed. More or less. And he settled on the blue one. He hadn't worn the slacks since his last photography exhibition at Shadow Ranch, but they still fit fine. The sports coat was a remnant from his days as a cop on the Northern California coast and hadn't gotten any better with age.

Thumps wondered if the navy blue single-breasted blazer was old enough to interest Gabby Santucci. Maybe he could trade it for something more casual.

He had seen a couple of nice-looking leather bomber jackets at a store in Seattle, was tempted by one in particular, but had passed on it. Claire had been undergoing the first of the chemotherapy sessions, and buying a new jacket hadn't seemed sensitive or supportive.

So it was the green and tan windbreaker. The relaxed retro look for men who didn't own a sports jacket.

Not that Claire would care.

Thumps looked at himself in the mirror. Then again, maybe she would.

TODAY, THE QUICK CLAIM was busy. A conference in town, by the look of the name tags hanging from lanyards around the necks of the men and women in PowerPoint business attire. Maybe he should have worn the blazer after all.

"For how many?"

The woman was tall, with brown hair and thin arms that she kept cocked in front of her body. "Darlene" on the name tag. She reminded Thumps of the stick insects that bite off the heads of their mates after sex.

"I'm meeting a friend."

"Do you have a reservation?"

Thumps resisted. It was an old joke and not particularly funny. "Maybe."

"Name?"

"Probably under Merchant."

Darlene looked at her computer. "She hasn't arrived yet. Would you like to wait or do you want me to seat you?"

"Seat me," said Thumps. "Someplace quiet."

"Is this an anniversary or a celebration of some sort?"

"Probably not."

"There's a champagne breakfast for two available," said Darlene. "It comes with a red rose for the lady."

"Nothing for the guy?"

Darlene smiled. "He gets the lady."

Claire was fifteen minutes late. Thumps wanted to make an exaggerated show of looking at his watch, but he knew better.

"I know," she said. "I'm late."

"I just got here."

"Liar."

Thumps had hoped that Claire would be dressed in slacks and a blouse. Instead, she was wearing a green and white print dress with red accents and a soft yellow sweater.

"There's a champagne breakfast for two," said Thumps. "Comes with a red rose."

"You want champagne for breakfast?"

"No," said Thumps. "The woman at the front wanted to know if this was a special occasion."

Claire turned serious. "Maybe."

Okay. Now Thumps was sorry he hadn't worn the blazer.

The waiter came by with coffee and juice. "Lewis" was on his name tag.

"Hi," he said. "I'm Lewis, and I'll be looking after you this morning."

"Morning, Lewis."

"Is this a special occasion?"

Claire ordered the eggs Benedict. Thumps stuck with scrambled eggs and sausage. It wouldn't be nearly as good as breakfast at Al's, but Al's didn't have much in the way of privacy. And seeing as this was to be a serious talk, he didn't want Alvera Couteau within shouting distance of the conversation.

"Are you nervous?"

"Nope."

"You don't know what I want to talk to you about."

"Nope."

"And that doesn't worry you?"

"Nope."

"I told you that I got the test results back," said Claire. "And that they were good."

"You did."

"So that's not the reason."

"Okay."

"I wanted to talk about us."

This wasn't the first time they had had this conversation. Commitment, intimacy, moving in together. And none of these talks had ended particularly well. So far as Thumps was concerned, talking about "us" had actually hurt their relationship.

"You want to move in together?"

Claire didn't flinch. "Do you?"

Thumps wasn't sure why women liked to answer questions with questions. Maybe it was a strategy to avoid answering them.

"I asked first."

"Christ," said Claire. "Are we ten?"

Thumps put his fork down. "I'm willing to give it a try."

"What?" said Claire. "Sort of like a test drive?"

"For the both of us."

"But no commitment?"

Thumps could feel his clothes tighten around him. Having Moses push him off Belly Butte had been more fun.

"You might not like having me around all the time."

Claire sat back and wrapped her arms around herself. "How do you feel about children?"

"Children?" Thumps manufactured a smile.

"You know," said Claire, "little humans?"

"You want to have a baby?"

"Is that a problem?"

Thumps tried to hold the smile in place. "We've never talked about children."

"I had Stanley when I was young," said Claire. "Too young. I've always thought about having a couple more."

Thumps wanted to remind Claire about her health situation. But he didn't.

"But now I can't," said Claire. "I'm too old. The cancer could come back. Motherhood from scratch is too much work. Babies are twenty-four/seven."

"You'd have me."

"What part of 'too much work' didn't you understand?" Claire waited for Thumps to catch up. "But no, I don't want another baby."

Claire opened her purse and took out a small photograph. "This is Deliah Standing and her sister, Nadie."

The two girls looked to be about six and four. The sisters were sitting on a floral sofa. Deliah was holding Nadie. Neither one of them was smiling.

"Cute," said Thumps. "Nieces?"

"I'm going to buy a Subaru," said Claire. "A Forester. It's a kind of station wagon."

"Freddy Salgado said you were looking."

"I was leaning towards an Outback, but Freddy found a used Forester. Just off lease. Only twelve thousand miles."

"Supposed to be a good car in snow and ice."

"Angie Black Weasel is going to help me with the paperwork."

"For the car?"

"No," said Claire, "for Deliah and Nadie."

Thumps waited to see if Claire wanted to fill in the pieces. She didn't.

"These are foster kids?"

"Actually, they're available for adoption." Claire's eyes suddenly teared up. "Shit, it sounds like I'm picking up puppies from the pound."

"Adoption?"

"Kids need a home."

"And you plan on adopting two little girls?"

Claire nodded. Her eyes were still leaking. "Bet you're sorry you turned down the champagne breakfast and the rose."

Okay, he hadn't seen this coming.

"What do you think?"

"You have a big heart," said Thumps.

Claire carefully slipped the photograph into her purse. "What about your heart?"

"Thought you didn't want to get married."

"I don't."

"Or live together."

"Maybe you can help me change my mind."

"Raising two girls is a big responsibility."

Claire kept her voice low and even. "The father killed the mother. He'll be in jail the rest of his life. The only relative the girls have is a grandmother who's in assisted living in Great Falls."

"This is all a little sudden."

Claire waited.

"I'm not saying no."

"What are you saying?"

"Come on, Claire. That's not fair."

"No," said Claire, "it's not." She slid out of the booth with her purse. "I have to use the bathroom."

Thumps watched her walk across the restaurant. It was good to have Claire back and even better to hear that the first set of test results had been positive. On the negative side, breakfast had gone somewhat worse than he would have imagined. A little advance warning about the girls and the adoption would have been helpful, and after being held at arm's length for so long, he found Claire's sudden proposal that they might live together disconcerting.

Thumps didn't think that Claire was suggesting that she move in with him. He was pretty sure that she would want him to sell his house and move in with her. He turned the situation over in his mind, tried to figure out what he was going to say when she got back.

And came up empty.

"Mr. DreadfulWater?" Lewis was back with the coffee pot. "Ms. Merchant took care of the bill and the tip. She asked me to tell you that she had to get to the airport."

"The airport?"

"And I was to give you this." Lewis placed an envelope on the table.

"She's not coming back?"

"I don't think so," said Lewis.

Thumps opened the envelope and read the note.

"Did we leave any room for something sweet?"

"What?"

"You might want to try the pumpkin pie. It's our seasonal special."

"I'm diabetic."

Lewis nodded sympathetically. "Then pie wouldn't be a good idea."

Thumps read the note again.

"Does it come with whipped cream?"

THIRTY-THREE

By the time Thumps got to Budd's, he was in a foul mood. Breakfast with Claire had been more than a little unnerving. One minute she was a single woman not interested in a committed relationship and the next she was a mother of two looking for a partner.

Back in three days.

That's all the note had said. She hadn't even signed it. No "love, Claire" or "I'll miss you, Claire" or even a "best, Claire."

Back in three days.

The note hadn't said anything about a deadline, but it was clear that three days was the time he had in which to make a decision.

Three days.

Thumps with Claire and two small girls in her house on the reservation, or Thumps alone in an empty house in town.

Fish or cut bait.

Pearl was at her desk on the mezzanine. Calder Banks and Gloria Baker-Doyle were sitting on the sofa, going over a script.

"Hey, Thumps." Calder was off the sofa in one easy movement. "Good to have you on board."

"Brilliant," said Gloria. "Let the detecting begin."

Pearl held up a CD case. "The files you requested."

Thumps considered the case. "One disc?"

"That's right," said Pearl. She set the disc on the desk. "It's the complete file that Nina had on Samuels."

Thumps left the disc where it sat. "That wasn't our deal."

Pearl was smiling, but her eyes could have started forest fires. "What you need to understand, Mr. DreadfulWater, is that I'm responsible for this program."

"I understand that."

"And I'm the one paying you."

Thumps touched the note in his jacket pocket. Getting blindsided once in a day was enough. "Our deal was that I got everything."

"Nina was working on ideas and research for other episodes," said Pearl. "Those notes have nothing to do with the matter at hand."

"You keep the file on the Obsidian Murders," said Thumps. "That was our deal. But I get everything else."

"Not going to happen," said Pearl.

"It's your money," said Thumps.

"I'm glad we understand each other," said Pearl.

"But it's my call."

Pearl's smile slipped. "Don't be petulant."

"Fish or cut bait," said Thumps.

THUMPS CAUGHT THE sheriff in his office, playing with the old percolator.

"Are you really making fresh coffee?"

Duke had the percolator in one hand and the power cord in the other. "Something's wrong with it."

Thumps shook his head. "I've been telling you that for years."

Hockney plugged the cord into the wall and banged the side of the coffee maker. "Shit."

Thumps tried to sound sympathetic. "May have to get a new one."

"They don't make them like this anymore," said Duke.

"Praise be to heaven," said Thumps.

"You just come by to annoy me?"

"How about I take you out for coffee."

Hockney set the percolator to one side. "Which means you need my help."

"Nope," said Thumps. "All part of the DreadfulWater Howdy program. Being neighbourly and all."

"Yippee."

"I'll take you to Mirrors."

"Going to take more than a cup of coffee at some fancy café to buy my help."

"I'll throw in a muffin."

"Sold," said Duke.

MIRRORS WAS BUSIER than Thumps would have thought. But then, most of the people weren't drinking coffee. They were working on their laptops. He wondered if there was a time limit to a free work area or if you had to buy another cup of coffee every so often, like putting coins in a parking meter.

Not that anyone puts coins in a meter anymore. Everything was digitized now. The world ran on credit cards and consumer debt.

Hockney took the chair against the wall.

"In case bad guys with guns come in," said Duke, "and I have to save you."

"Did you know that this place is modelled on Café Brasilero in Montevideo?"

"Montevideo?"

"Uruguay," said Thumps. "Bottom of South America? Atlantic coast? Below Brazil. To the right of Argentina?"

"Damn it, DreadfulWater," said Duke. "You trying to piss me off?"

"Brasilero was Eduardo Galeano's favourite coffee house."

"What are you? The Google bunny?" Hockney craned his

neck at the choices on the board above the bar. "Maybe I'll get a Boozy Affogato."

"Forget it," said Thumps. "It's $8.50 and you won't like it."

"Or a Ca phe sua da."

There wasn't a reason for it, but suddenly Thumps felt exhausted. He folded his arms and put his head on the table.

"You going to sleep?"

"Just for a moment."

"That the diabetes," said Duke, "or are you just trying to play on my sympathies?"

"You don't have any sympathies."

Duke looked around the room. "Do you think they'll let us stay if we don't have a computer?"

The server arrived and departed with an order for two black coffees and one carrot muffin.

"Hear Claire is back in town," said Duke.

"She is."

"How's she doing?"

"She wants to adopt two little girls."

The sheriff chewed on the idea for a moment. "That come as a surprise?"

"Found out this morning," said Thumps. "Over breakfast."

"You got a part in any of this?"

"Maybe."

"I can't help you," said Hockney. "Macy and me never had kids."

"Don't need your help with that."

"Sure as hell need someone's help," said Duke. "I hear raising kids is like having dogs, but without the unconditional love or the cute tricks."

"I think she wants me to move in with her and the kids."

"Her place? On the reservation?"

Thumps nodded.

"She's got a nice spot," said the sheriff. "Good view of the river. Open spaces. Clean air."

"How you like the coffee?"

"Weak," said Hockney.

"The muffin?"

"Got a bunch of healthy stuff in it," said the sheriff. "Who does that to a muffin?"

The server brought the coffee pot over. "You gentlemen are drinking black coffee. Is that right?"

"It is," said Duke.

"We don't get much of that," said the young woman.

The sheriff put on his best smile. It made his face go lopsided. "Any of the staff here have kids?"

"Sure," said the woman. "Rita has three and Richard has one."

"My friend here is thinking about becoming a father."

"Congratulations," said the woman. "Bet that's exciting."

The sheriff touched the brim of his hat. "What about Rita and Richard? They find children exciting?"

The woman rolled her eyes. "Rita says she works here so she can get a break and relax."

Duke turned to Thumps. "If you lived out in the middle of nowhere, you could get a couple of dogs. They could chase the kids around and you wouldn't have to do all that much."

"You gentlemen want anything else?"

"Next time," said the sheriff, "I'll bring my laptop."

DEPUTY SHERIFF Lance Packard was waiting for them when Thumps and Duke got back to the sheriff's office.

"Mayor came by," said Lance. "Brought these."

Lance held up a bright blue T-shirt with the word "Howdy" written across the front in gold letters.

The sheriff grunted something that sounded like a truck skidding to a stop in loose gravel. "What the hell are we supposed to do with these?"

Lance held the shirt against his chest. "Supposed to give them out to citizens we see being civic."

"This ain't a state fair." Hockney settled himself behind his desk. "So what's your favour?"

"Maslow's phone records."

Duke softened his face in an effort to look stupid.

"Cell and hotel."

Duke turned to Lance. "Deputy Packard," said the sheriff, "is the Nina Maslow case an ongoing investigation?"

Lance was a little slow off the mark. And then he caught up. "Yes, sir," he said, "it is."

"And is this office in the habit of sharing information on an ongoing case with civilians?"

"No, sir," said Lance, "we're not."

Duke turned back to Thumps and spread his arms out as if the gesture was the answer.

"Cell and hotel," Thumps repeated.

"What do I get?"

"My help."

"Deputy Packard," said Duke, "have we received an official report from the coroner as to the cause of death?"

"No, sir," said Lance, "we haven't."

"So we don't know if Maslow's death was an accident or something else."

"It wasn't an accident," said Thumps. "Did the Honda have a GPS?"

"It did," said Duke.

"Then I'll need those records as well."

Hockney shook his head. "Official investigation, the results of which are to be shared only with duly appointed officers of the law."

Thumps waited for the punchline.

Duke opened his drawer and took out a folder and a badge. "I'd have to deputize you before I could give you that information."

"Come on, Duke."

"Temporary assignment." Duke held up the badge. "No benefits, but all the coffee you can drink. How does that sound?"

Thumps gestured at the old percolator. "What if it can't be fixed?"

"Suppose I'll have to shoot it," said the sheriff.

"Can I watch?"

"Figure out what happened to Maslow," said Duke, "and I'll let you do the shooting."

Thumps shoved the badge into his pocket and opened the folder. "How'd you get these so fast?"

"Friends in high places," said the sheriff.

"Lance hacked her cell?"

Packard's face turned red.

"Hacking is illegal," said Duke. "Investigating a possible murder is not."

Thumps scanned the list. "Local and international."

"It seems our Maslow got around."

"You going to make me look them up?"

"I had to look them up."

"You probably got Lance to do that."

"Same thing."

Some writer whose name Thumps couldn't remember had said that there wasn't any pleasure but meanness. Whoever it was had to have been thinking about Sheriff Duke Hockney.

"What about the GPS?"

"Got Stas working on it." Hockney stood and hitched his pants. "So what are we looking for?"

Thumps tried to picture two little girls chased by a pack of puppies across the high prairies with him in full pursuit.

"I have no idea."

"Okay," said the sheriff. "Raise your right hand."

THIRTY-FOUR

When Thumps got to the Aegean, Archie Kousoulas was standing at the register, talking with a man dressed up to look like a drugstore cowboy. Tooled boots, snap shirt, leather vest, denim jacket, and tan felt Stetson. Along with an oversized silver sheriff's badge. Thumps couldn't hear what the two were saying, but the cowboy kept tugging at the cuffs of his shirt and working his feet in the boots as though someone had dressed him when he wasn't looking.

In clothes a size too small.

The vintage suit that Archie had tried to sell Thumps was still on the rack, and while he waited for the little Greek to finish with Marshal Dillon, he slipped the coat on. It fit reasonably well. The sleeves were a bit short, but there was room to let them out. And there was a matching vest, so it was actually two outfits in one. Thumps tried to imagine an occasion where he would need a suit. Aside from breakfast with Claire, he could think of only two.

Funerals and weddings.

And he didn't go to either.

Both were depressing in their own way. With funerals it was self-evident. A dead body in a casket. A graveside ceremony under a winter sun. Ashes laid on water or thrown to the wind.

Weddings weren't much better. The whole idea of happy ever after was patently absurd. Sure, Thumps knew couples such as Duke and Macy who had stayed together, who appeared to have reached a long-term understanding. But they were the exception.

What were the figures Thumps had seen? Fifty percent? Sixty? No better than the odds you got at the tables in Atlantic City and Las Vegas.

"Let me guess." Archie appeared at his shoulder. "You didn't come here to buy the suit."

"It's a nice suit."

"Sure, it's a nice suit," said Archie. "And it looks good on you."

The cowboy was waiting by the window as though he expected a stagecoach to pull up in front of the old library.

"Customer?"

"Gofer from the mayor's office," said Archie. "She doesn't think I'm doing enough to promote her Howdy program."

"What does she want you to do?"

"Wants me to host a hoedown," said Archie. "What the hell is a hoedown?"

Now that he thought about it, Thumps wasn't sure he knew what a hoedown was either. Something to do with horses? Something to do with cattle? A dance in a barn?

"So why are you here?"

"I need to use your computer." Thumps held up the folder and the three discs. "It's police business."

"I thought you were a photographer."

"I am," said Thumps. "I'm just doing Duke a favour."

Archie grumped all the way to the office. "You know, most people have their own computers."

"I have a computer."

"Sure, but does it work?" Archie plopped himself down in front of the monitors and held out his hand.

"I can do it," said Thumps. "It's confidential material."

"You suggesting I'm not confidential?"

"You're not confidential."

"Give me the damn discs."

Thumps wanted to continue the argument, but he knew it would just delay the process. Instead, he set the discs on the desk and pulled up a chair so he could watch the screen closest to him.

Archie shuffled through the discs. "Trudy Samuels, Amelia Nash, Key West. Where do you want to start?"

"Key West."

"I remember this one." Archie squinted at the screen. "In 2007, three women were found on a luxury yacht in Conch Harbor Marina. Each of them had had the number 48169 tattooed on the back of their necks after they had been killed."

"48169?"

"It's the zip code for Hell, Michigan," said Archie. "Case was never solved."

"What about Amelia Nash?"

"You don't get out much, do you?"

"So, she was famous?"

Archie took the first disc out and put the second one in. "*Alice in Wonderland? The Lost Templar? The Red Assassin?*"

Thumps kept his eyes on the monitor.

"Hollywood star on the rise."

"But?"

"Murder-suicide," said Archie. "They were in Las Vegas for some gala benefit."

"They?"

"Nash and her boyfriend, Donny Berlin. Actor. Country and western singer."

"What happened?"

"Who knows?" said Archie. "Berlin shot Nash and then shot himself."

Thumps speed-read the story on the screen. "Why would Maslow be interested in a murder-suicide?"

"Have to ask her," said Archie. "Except you can't."

"*Malice Aforethought* only deals with unsolved cases."

Archie shrugged. "All I can tell you is that Nina Maslow was one organized woman. Look at this. Each file begins with a general summary of the case. She's got the forensics, the police reports, witness statements, news coverage, photographs. Where the hell does she get all this stuff?"

"Let's see the Samuels disc."

Archie put the last disc in. "What are we looking for?"

"No idea," said Thumps. "Are there any notes?"

"Notes?"

"Personal notes," said Thumps. "Ideas that Maslow might have had about the case. Insights? Suspicions?"

"This is a large file." Archie adjusted his glasses. "It's going to take a while to sort through all of this."

"Can you just print it off?"

"All of it?"

"All the files," said Thumps. "Samuels, Nash, and Key West."

Archie moved the mouse and worked the keys. "The Samuels file by itself is 242 pages."

Thumps nodded.

"That's half a ream of paper."

"But you can print it off, right?"

"Do you know how many trees it takes to make 242 sheets of paper?"

"Archie . . ."

"And there are two other discs." Archie sucked his face up

to one side as though he were looking for something stuck between his teeth. "If you had a computer that worked, you could read the files electronically and help save the planet."

Thumps took the printout the sheriff had given him and flattened it on the desk. "I also need you to check some phone numbers."

Archie pushed back in his chair.

"It's not as bad as it looks. A bunch of the numbers are repeats."

"Don't you have other friends with computers?"

Thumps flashed a weak smile. "No one I trust as much as you."

While the printer worked its way through the files, Archie looked up the phone numbers and lectured Thumps on the basics of responsible conservation.

"I hope you recycle paper."

"What's 34-931?" said Thumps, pointing to an entry.

"International area code for Spain." Archie marked the number with a pencil check. "Barcelona, to be specific."

"Maslow called Barcelona?"

"All to the same number," said Archie. "I hear Gaudí's Sagrada Familia is not to be missed."

"Any calls from Barcelona?"

"Nope," said Archie. "All of these are fairly old. Nothing recent."

"What about the 631 code?"

"New York," said Archie. "Recycling paper can make a big difference."

"How many calls?"

Archie tapped the pencil on the desk. "Again, the calls are all outgoing and to one number."

"Any calls to Barcelona after the ones to New York begin?"

Archie checked the printout. "What are you thinking?"

"Nothing," said Thumps. "818?"

"Los Angeles," said Archie. "So is 310."

"And 702?"

Archie worked his fingers on the keyboard. "Las Vegas."

"Okay."

"The 818 and the 310 calls go both ways," said Archie. "Probably head office? Family? Friends?"

"Probably."

"And Vegas is what? Amelia Nash?"

"Probably."

Archie stopped typing. "Could you say something besides 'probably'?"

"Probably." Thumps ran a finger down the list. "Quite a few local calls."

"Yeah," said Archie, "but only six numbers."

Thumps stretched his neck. "Can you put names to the numbers?"

"Probably," said Archie, "but all of this is going to take some time."

"So, what can I do to help?"

* * *

Even after he had walked out of the bookstore and got into the old Dodge, Thumps could still hear Archie laughing. It was bad manners at best. Sure, he didn't know that much about computers, and he could see where the little Greek might have found his offer of help amusing, but, all in all, he didn't think it had been *that* funny.

Blackfoot Autohaus was open. Stas was standing in the yard, trying to lasso a motorcycle.

"Howdy." Stas played out a loop, spun it over his head, and dropped it over the handlebars of the bike. "What do you think?"

The motorcycle was two-tone, red and white, with enormous fenders front and rear that wrapped around the wheels like helmets. On the tank was a stylized Indian head with a feathered bonnet.

"You bought a motorcycle?"

"Me? No." Stas slipped the rope off the handlebars. "Vernon Rockland. You know Rockland?"

"Sure," said Thumps. "Owns Shadow Ranch."

"Yes," said Stas. "This is him. He buys it at auction. 1947 Indian Chief Roadmaster. I am to fix it nice as new."

"It's a good-looking bike."

Stas shook his head. "Yes, beautiful piece of shit. Rockland wishes to ride it in Howdy Parade. Maybe he lives. Maybe he is dead."

Thumps wasn't sure if he had gotten the translation correct. "Dead?"

"Sure," said Stas. "Motorcycle hits car. Who is winner?"

The bike looked fine. Thumps didn't see any damage. "Rockland hit a car?"

"No," said Stas. "Not yet. First, I must to fix bike. Then maybe he hit car."

"Or he could just put it on display up at Shadow Ranch."

"Yes," said Stas. "Like Freddy Salgado and the sad story Corvette. Also piece of shit."

"The Corvette?"

"Fibreglass," said Stas. "Who makes car out of fibreglass?"

"Why is it a sad story?"

"Small boats, sure. Hot tubs, water slides, okay. Outdoor furniture and stepladders."

Thumps took a guess. "Because of . . . Elvis?"

"Elvis?" said Stas. "Rock and roll King?"

"The Corvette at Salgado's is the same model that Elvis drove in one of his movies."

"Yes," said Stas. "And now King is dead. Motorcycles. Corvettes. Piece of shit."

"Elvis wasn't killed in his corvette."

"No," said Stas. "Girl. Sad story is girl."

Sometimes it was difficult keeping up with the big Russian. "Girl?"

"Yes," said Stas. "Rich girl. Log castle. Corvette is her car."

"Trudy Samuels?"

Stas played out a length of rope. "This is why is best to buy German car."

THE GPS ON Pearl's Honda had not been a problem. Stas set his laptop on the counter.

"Honda did not come with GPS. This one is aftermarket. High end. Scary lady is good quality."

"Can we see where Maslow went?"

"Sheriff ask this question," said Stas. "Not like Russia."

"Russia?"

"In Russia, no one asks."

"And?"

"Yes, sure." Stas clicked the mouse. "Okay, here is travel information."

"How far back can we go?"

"All the way." Stas pointed at the screen. "You see? Time stamp. Each day."

"Can I have these records?"

"Sure," said Stas. "What is email?"

"I don't have email."

"You must get email," said Stas. "Everything today is email."

"Can you print off the information?"

"Ah," said Stas. "You do it old stool."

"School."

"Sure," said Stas. He clicked the mouse and the printer began wheezing. "Maybe you decide about car?"

"Do you need your truck back?"

"No," said Stas. "Not yet. Soon. Today is okay. Tomorrow maybe not okay." Stas took the pages from the printer and handed them to Thumps. "In Netherlands, many people walk, ride bicycle. Maybe you get bicycle. Maybe you wish to be Dutch."

"Maybe I should get a motorcycle."

"Lawrence of Arabia, Duane Allman, Luc Bourdon," said Stas. "All dead for motorcycles. Also Viktor Robertovich Tsoi."

"Who?"

"Russian rock musician," said Stas. "Maybe you wish to be Russian."

THIRTY-FIVE

Freddy Salgado was in the showroom, straightening a giant blue bow on a metallic red car that had been polished and buffed so that it shone in the light like a giant jelly bean. The bow could just be an advertising ploy, but Thumps guessed that the car had been sold, guessed that some lucky buyer was coming in today to see it in all its glory, to pick it up, and take it home, knowing as they drove it off the lot that the car would never be worth as much again. Or look this good.

"Hey, Mr. DreadfulWater." Freddy wiped his hands on his pants. "You just missed her."

"Claire?"

"Ms. Merchant was in yesterday. Decided on the Forester."

"Great."

"Bringing it in from Missoula. Early return on a lease.

Tungsten Metallic. Just like she wanted. And I'm giving her a good trade-in on her Ford."

"She traded in her truck?"

"I'm going to surprise her and throw in a cargo tray for the back and the rubber floor mats for the front. Help keep the snow and ice off the carpet. Those are the sorts of things that help to maintain the vehicle's value."

Thumps wandered over to the Corvette.

Freddy stayed on his hip. "Hey, you should buy the truck."

They had taken the truck to Seattle. Thumps had driven it for part of the way there and back, had driven it around the city when Claire couldn't. He had liked the bulk and the strength of the vehicle, as though it had spent its free time at a gym with free weights.

"Wouldn't that be something."

Thumps was sure that Claire had not given up the truck easily. Here was his chance to return it to her. More or less. *Hey, he could say, look what I bought.* And watch her eyes light up.

"Pickups are big sellers in this part of the world," said Freddy. "But I don't have to tell you that."

Thumps was trying to think of a way to move the conversation from the Subaru and the truck to the Corvette when a large van pulled up to the showroom doors and Calder Banks got out. Along with Gloria Baker-Doyle, two young guys, and a young woman.

"Film crew," said Freddy. "Stick around. You can pretend to

be a customer." Freddy waved a hand over the Corvette. "The reality show that's in town. *Malice* something or other. They want to film the car for one of their episodes."

Thumps watched as the young men unloaded the van. Camera, tripod, lights, reflectors. Calder had pages in one hand. Gloria was straightening his tie. The young woman was powdering Banks's nose with a puffy brush.

"Great visuals," said Freddy. "You know . . . *See the car she drove the night she died . . .* That sort of thing."

"Sure."

"Original paperwork was still in the glovebox. Bill of sale. Features sheet. Some old gas receipts." Freddy shook his head and began chuckling. "Gas was thirty-five cents a gallon back then. You believe that?" Freddy paused for a moment. "Even found an old speeding ticket in the console. I guess they don't come after you for traffic fines if you're dead."

"You get it at auction?"

"Nope," said Freddy. "Bought it off the mother. Abigail, Amelia, Adriana. Something like that."

"Adele."

"Right," said Freddy. "Adele. She called me out of the blue. Asked if I wanted to buy the car. Did you know my dad?"

"Before my time."

"Back then," said Freddy, "this place was a Chevy dealership. Dad was good friends with Buck Samuels. Sold him all his cars."

"So you bought the Corvette."

"Absolutely," said Freddy. "I'm not superstitious."

"Superstitious?"

"I mean, the last time she drove the car was the night she killed herself. There are lots of folks who would see the 'Vette as bad luck."

"But not you."

"Nope. Not me." Freddy walked around to the back of the car and opened the trunk. Inside was a large glass frame. "Had all the stuff I found in the car mounted and framed. Part of the provenance of the vehicle, part of the legend. Real important to collectors."

Freddy leaned the frame against the rear wheel. "Figured that the film crew is going to want to have this in the shot."

"Mr. DreadfulWater." Calder was through the door with his hand extended. "Good to see you again."

"Car shopping?" said Gloria.

"Mr. DreadfulWater," said Freddy, "is thinking about a pickup."

Thumps squatted down beside the frame. Whoever had mounted the items had done a terrific job. The original bill of sale was in the centre. The registration, in the name of Trudy Samuels, was in the upper right corner along with a photograph of Trudy standing in front of the car. There was a receipt for an oil change that noted the mileage and another receipt for a tune-up. The speeding ticket was mounted in the lower right-hand corner.

"They want me to stand beside the Corvette," said Calder. "But I think it would make more sense if I sat in the driver's seat. What do you think?"

"You just want to sit behind the wheel," said Gloria.

"'63 split-window 'Vette," said Calder. "Damn right I do."

"Is that what this is?" Gloria walked around the car. "Brilliant."

"That she is," said Freddy. "Not many of these babies made."

"And this is the car that Trudy Samuels drove? Yeah?"

"Got all the paperwork." Freddy picked up the frame and held it out. "This is the real McCoy."

Gloria retreated to the crew scrum and began talking to the guy who was setting up the camera. Calder opened the door of the 'Vette and slid in behind the wheel.

"They didn't make them for comfort," said Freddy.

"360 horsepower," said Calder. "327 cubic inches."

"You know your cars," said Freddy.

"I'm a European guy," said Calder. "Jaguar, Porsche, Ferrari, Maserati."

"You buy European," said Freddy. "Then you got to buy the mechanic."

Calder winked at Thumps. "What about you?" he said. "American or import?"

One of the young men hurried over. Tall and skinny in the way only young men can be tall and skinny. The muscle and bulk would come later.

"Mr. Banks," said the man. "Going to have to change jackets."

"What?"

"Oil spots, sir," said the man. "On the cuff. From the car."

Calder turned the cuff. "You can see these on camera?"

"Don't want to take a chance."

"Shit," said Calder. "Don't have another jacket."

"Do it in your shirt sleeves," said Gloria. "Yeah? Make you look like a working man."

"Maybe I should roll up the shirt. Show a little forearm?"

"Brilliant," said Gloria.

It took the film crew the better part of an hour to set up the camera and arrange the lighting. Thumps watched the whole process, intrigued by the amount of time needed to shoot a scene that probably wouldn't last a minute on screen.

Gloria touched his arm. "What do you think?" she whispered.

"Looks a little boring."

"You should be on a movie set," said Gloria. "This is exciting. Yeah."

The scene was simple. Calder would get into the car, turn back to the camera, and say his lines. And then he would do it all again. And again. And again. Each take was slightly different than the one before, but not so that anyone would notice.

Thumps stopped counting at thirteen. He had no idea how Calder could continue to say the same thing over and over again, how he was able to keep the same censorious expression on his face, the same sonorous tone to his voice, take after take.

"You knew Nina pretty well?"

"Not well," said Gloria. "Well enough, I guess."

"When she researched a case, did she share any of the information with anyone?"

"Not with me."

"Sydney Pearl?"

"Sure," said Gloria. "Sydney's the boss."

"Calder?"

Gloria put a hand over her mouth. "Maybe. Nina thought Banks was an idiot. If she had had her way, he would have never been on the show."

"So, no love lost?"

"They were both professionals," said Gloria. "Calder knew Nina didn't like him. He didn't like her. But on with the show."

"On with the show?"

"The audience liked Calder. That's the only thing that counts. Nina understood that."

"Gloria!" Calder worked his way out of the Corvette and limped over. "They've got the master. Ajay says it'll take forty-five to reset for the close-up. I want to get something to eat."

Gloria turned back to Thumps. "So have you discovered anything?"

"Yeah," said Calder. "The stuff Pearl gave you. Any clues?"

"We could help, you know."

"Right," said Calder. "That would be fun."

Archie was going to be trouble enough. He was going to

have to spend the evening listening to the little Greek complain about Thumps abusing their friendship. Maybe if there were other people in the mix, Archie would be on better behaviour. And four sets of eyes could be better than two. More importantly, Calder and Gloria knew Maslow, knew how she worked, knew how she thought.

"When are you going to be done with the filming?"

"Eight o'clock," said Gloria. "Maybe sooner."

It was a bad idea, and Thumps knew it.

"Remember the Aegean?"

"Where the party was?" said Calder.

"I'll be there."

"Brilliant," said Gloria.

Calder rubbed his thighs. "Maybe by then I'll get some of the feeling back in my legs." He put his arms over his head and stretched. "It's a classic, but there's not enough space in that thing for a shoehorn."

THIRTY-SIX

Thumps wasn't sure that Tobias Rattler was going to be happy to see him, and, all things considered, he didn't care. Rattler had lied to him. Well, the man hadn't lied exactly. He had withheld. He had omitted. And sins of omission were still sins. Of course, Thumps could only guess at the extent of Rattler's lapses and oversights, but he had several good ideas to test.

Thumps pressed the doorbell and tried to come up with a snappy way to begin the conversation that would wrong-foot Rattler, put him on the defensive, make him more amenable to the truth and full disclosure.

"Hey, Thumps." Cooley Small Elk filled the doorway once again. "You're just in time."

Thumps had expected to have a private conversation with Rattler, but as he came into the condo, he could see that that wasn't going to happen.

"Come on in," said Moses. "We've almost got it whipped."

Tobias Rattler and Moses Blood were standing at the kitchen table, working on the puzzle.

"Moses has a great eye," said Rattler. "He doesn't get fooled by the colours. He just looks for shapes."

"Found it," said Moses, and he held a piece up to the light and then set it in place. "Come on. You give it a try."

"Moses has done most of the sky," said Cooley, "but you could work on filling in the tipi."

Rattler tried matching a piece to a partially finished mountain. "I'm guessing you're not here to work on the puzzle."

"No."

"Am I going to need a lawyer?"

Thumps cocked his head. "Do you want a lawyer?"

"This about Trudy?"

"No."

"Ah," said Rattler. "Nina Maslow."

"No," said Thumps. "Dartmouth College."

"Ah, Dartmouth. I was wondering when you would get around to that." Rattler picked up a puzzle piece and tried to fit it into the pristine lake at the edge of the encampment. "Ask your question."

"Why didn't you tell me about Adele Samuels?"

"Embarrassed, I guess." Rattler left the puzzle and went to the sofa. "Dartmouth had this special admissions program for Indians."

306

"Full-ride scholarship?"

Rattler laughed. "You're kidding, right?"

"So Adele called."

"About a week or so before Trudy died. Asked if I would meet her."

"And you did?"

"Didn't see any harm." Rattler rubbed the side of his face. "I thought she might want to mend fences."

"Adele Samuels doesn't strike me as a fence mender."

"She's not." Rattler leaned forward, his elbows on his knees. "So, your question."

Thumps took a breath. "How much did Adele give you to leave Chinook?"

Rattler didn't flinch. "A lot."

"And you said yes."

"Tuition was expensive." Rattler sank back into the sofa. "It was my chance."

Thumps waited to see if Rattler was going to add anything else. "And you took it."

"Yeah, I took it." Rattler stood and stretched his back. "You have any more questions?"

"Four weeks ago," Thumps said quickly, "where were you?"

"You serious?"

"I am."

Rattler frowned. "Barcelona. Big book fair."

"And after that?"

"New York. What's this about?"

"And Las Vegas?"

"You kidding?" Rattler shook his head. "Place is a shithole. Wouldn't catch me dead in Vegas."

Cooley looked up from the table. "How about we order a couple of pizzas? We can eat and finish the puzzle in time to watch *Wilderness Gold*."

"One last question," said Thumps. "Would Adele have told Trudy?"

Rattler walked back to the puzzle. "That I took money to go away?"

Thumps waited.

"What you really mean is would Trudy have killed herself if she knew I'd betrayed her."

"Did Nina Maslow know?"

"Trudy *and* Maslow?" Rattler's smile was cold and brittle. "You really think I had something to do with Maslow's death?"

"Sheriff will be asking the same question."

"That new place near the mall makes good deep-dish pizza," said Cooley. "And they deliver."

"I didn't kill Trudy," said Rattler. "And I sure as hell didn't kill Maslow."

Moses nodded. "I'm voting for sausage and onion. Maybe pepperoni with extra cheese."

"What do you think, Thumps?" Cooley held the phone up. "You want something with pineapple?"

"Yes," said Moses. "Thumps likes that pineapple."

Rattler took his wallet out and handed Cooley a credit card. "Won't need pineapple," he said. "Mr. DreadfulWater isn't staying."

SHERIFF DUKE HOCKNEY was leaning against Stas's truck. Deputy Lance Packard was in Duke's cruiser.

"You got any doughnuts?"

Duke shook his head. "Nope."

"So this isn't a stakeout."

"Don't do stakeouts," said the sheriff. "Macy likes me home at night."

"Yet here you are."

"Still early," said Duke. "You talk to Mr. Rattler?"

"I did."

"Learn anything?"

"A little."

"Anything pertinent to Trudy Samuels or Nina Maslow?"

"Beth have a cause of death for Maslow yet?"

"She does," said the sheriff, "and seeing as you are a duly sworn-in deputy, I can share those results with you."

"Murder?"

"Lots of damage from the fall. Scrapes, bumps, cuts, abrasions."

"Falling down the side of a butte will do that."

"It surely will."

"But?"

"Maslow was killed by a blow to the head," said Duke. "Sharp, hard blow. Beth can't see how she could have sustained the injury in the fall."

"Great."

Duke pushed off the truck. "So I'm going to have to arrest Mr. Rattler on suspicion of murder."

"Don't think he did it."

"He's the only suspect I have," said the sheriff. "Maslow was out to prove that he killed Trudy Samuels. He found Maslow's body. You see where this is going?"

"Sure," said Thumps. "Your job is to arrest people."

"He in there alone?"

"Nope," said Thumps. "Moses and Cooley are with him. They're working on a puzzle."

"How many pieces?"

"No idea."

Hockney straightened his hat. "Macy loves jigsaw puzzles. The more pieces, the better. Me, I don't see the point. All those little bits of cardboard. You spend days putting the thing together and then when it's finished, you take it apart, put it back in the box, and stick it in a closet."

"The puzzle's a Bierstadt painting," said Thumps. "An Indian village with mountains in the background."

"OCP," said the sheriff. "Obsessive-compulsive puzzling."

"Don't think that's a clinical term."

"You know what a thousand-piece puzzle looks like?"

"Maybe you should wait to arrest him until we have more information."

"Mr. Rattler booked himself on a flight to Denver day after tomorrow, connection in New York City."

Thumps took a moment to digest this. "You sure?"

"I'm the sheriff," said Duke. "I'm always sure."

"You know when he made the booking?"

"This afternoon," said Duke. "It would appear Mr. Rattler is attempting to flee my jurisdiction."

"He should have told you."

"Yes, indeed," said the sheriff. "He should have done exactly that."

"You're really going to arrest him?"

"Law allows me to entertain suspicious suspects at county expense for up to seventy-two hours," said Duke. "During which time we will continue to collect evidence and interview witnesses."

"We don't have any witnesses." Thumps zipped up his jacket. "You might want to wait a bit before you raid the place."

"I'm listening."

"They just ordered pizza," said Thumps. "Seeing as it's you, they might be willing to share."

Duke put a hand on his stomach. "Hope it's not pineapple," he said. "Pineapple gives me gas."

"And I need to borrow your phone."

"You going to call Rattler and warn him that we're coming?"

"Nope," said Thumps. "Need to talk to Archie."

"Most of the time," said Duke, "you try to avoid talking to Archie."

"That's just an ugly rumour."

The sheriff slipped his phone out of its holster. "County gets unlimited minutes, but all calls should be related to business."

"You want to listen to the call?"

"Seems like a prudent idea," said Duke, "seeing as I'm sheriff and that's my phone."

Thumps took the phone and walked to the edge of the parking lot.

"Is it pepperoni?" Duke called out after him. "Everyone loves pepperoni."

THIRTY-SEVEN

It was after eight by the time Thumps pulled up in front of the Aegean. The fall skies had gone to black once again. Try as he might, Thumps couldn't find any trace of the moon or the stars. Maybe they had gotten fed up with humankind, packed their bags, and lit out for the territories.

Not a bad idea, now that he thought about it.

By now, the sheriff and Deputy Lance would have taken Rattler into custody. Or the five of them were standing around the kitchen table, eating deep dish and playing humpty dumpty with the Bierstadt landscape. Thumps was betting on pizza and the puzzle.

Sausage and onion? Pepperoni and extra cheese? Why miss a free meal?

They could always take Rattler to jail later.

Gloria Baker-Doyle and Calder Banks were in the vintage-clothing section, talking with Archie. Calder was still in his shirt sleeves, trying on a tweed jacket with elbow patches, while Gloria was working her way through a display of pill-box hats.

"DreadfulWater!" Calder waved him over. "What do you think? 1940s chic? Do I look like Bogie or what?"

"I think he looks more like Tab Hunter," said Gloria.

"And you look like Mamie Van Doren."

"Don't have the ass for that." Gloria took a dark suit off the rack and held it up to Thumps. "You could be Clark Gable."

"Or Johnny Weissmuller," said Calder.

"Tarzan," said Gloria. "Brilliant."

Archie looped a black feather boa around Gloria's shoulders. "See how much fun you can have with vintage clothing?"

Thumps checked his watch. "You finish with the filming already?"

"Professionals," said Calder. "Always faster when you work with professionals."

"I'm going to take the pillbox," said Gloria.

"And I'm going to go with the jacket." Calder ran his thumbs under the lapels. "I can write it off as a business expense."

"Office is all set up," said Archie. "Just like you asked."

"Great," said Thumps. "Hard copies of Maslow's notes? The telephone numbers?"

"Just like you asked," said Archie.

"And that fedora," said Calder. "Bogie wore one just like it in *Casablanca*."

The office had been turned into a command centre of sorts. Archie's desk had been pushed to one side, and the little Greek had set up a large library table in the middle of the room, along with a whiteboard on wheels that could be moved around.

"I only printed two copies of everything," Archie said. "I'll work off the computer, and two of you will have to share."

"I hate sharing," said Calder.

"I'll work with Mr. DreadfulWater," said Gloria. "He looks as though he plays well with others."

The top of the green metal filing cabinets had been turned into a giant party tray. Coffee. Sandwiches. Fruit. Thumps tried to remember if he had had lunch. Or dinner for that matter.

"Help yourself," said Archie. "We could be here a while."

Calder took one end of the library table. Archie took the other. Thumps and Gloria sat together in the middle.

"So," said Gloria, "where do we start?"

Archie went to the whiteboard and wrote "Trudy Samuels" on one side and "Nina Maslow" on the other.

"So," he said, "what do we know?"

"Both dead," said Calder.

"That's rather heartless," said Gloria. "Yeah?"

"But accurate," said Archie, and he wrote "dead" under each name. "And do we know how they died?"

"Nina thought that Samuels had been murdered." Calder looked at Thumps. "Any news about Nina?"

Thumps wasn't sure that this was the way to begin an investigation. It felt more like a daytime game show.

"I have it on good authority," said Archie, "that Nina Maslow was murdered."

"So she didn't fall accidentally," said Calder.

"Evidently," said Archie, warming to the task, "she died from a blow to the head."

"You're going to hit your head if you fall off a cliff," said Calder.

Archie shook his head. "If the coroner says murder, then it's murder."

"*Cui bono?*" said Gloria.

"What a bonus?" said Calder.

"It's Latin," said Gloria. "It means, who profits by Nina's death?"

"Sure," said Calder, "but what if it's not about profit. What if someone just didn't like her."

"Okay," said Archie, his marker at the ready. "Who didn't like Maslow?"

Calder and Gloria looked at each other for a moment and then Calder raised his hand.

"I didn't like her all that much." Calder smiled a quick smile. "And she didn't like me. If she had had her way, I would have been dumped long ago."

"And she and Pearl didn't always get along," said Gloria.

"That's an understatement," said Calder. "Remember the time Sydney threw that phone at Nina?"

"Stapler," said Gloria. "And she missed completely."

Thumps looked over at the table with the coffee. Now that he could see food, he was hungry. "You were at the party that night."

"I was," said Calder. "Am I a suspect?"

"What about Pearl?"

"No idea," said Calder. "Probably working. It's all she ever does."

"The problem," said Archie, "is we don't know enough yet." And he tapped the marker on each of the names. "We have two cases, and we don't know if they're connected."

"But if Samuels *was* murdered," said Gloria, "then Nina could have been killed because she discovered who did it. That would narrow down the list of suspects."

"To just one," said Calder. "Tobias Rattler."

"And if the two cases are not related," said Gloria, "then we're back to looking for someone who wanted Nina dead."

"Why?"

"The Latin thing again?" said Calder.

"Why would someone want Maslow dead?" Thumps waited for the question to settle in. "If Maslow isn't related to Samuels, why was she killed? So far as I can tell, getting along in show business isn't necessary."

"That's true enough," said Calder. "Tension helps us keep our creative edge."

"So the two cases *must* be related," said Gloria. "And we're back to Mr. Rattler."

Archie put the marker down. "How about we break for food and coffee? Then we can go over Maslow's notes and the phone records."

Thumps was out of the chair before Archie finished the sentence.

The ham and cheese on a kaiser was a bit on the dry side, so Thumps only ate two. The coffee was hot, and the grapes were hard and sweet. All in all, the sheriff and Deputy Lance had probably gotten the better end of dinner. As he ate, Thumps tried to imagine that the sandwich was a piece of deep-dish sausage and onion pizza.

With extra cheese.

"How about we work on the phone records," said Archie. "Places Maslow called in the last month. We got Barcelona, New York, Los Angeles, Las Vegas, and local."

Calder held up a hand. "I'll take L.A. and Vegas," he said. "My kind of town."

"That's Chicago," said Gloria. "Then Thumps and I will take Spain and the Big Apple."

"And I'll do local," said Archie. "Then we can all work on her notes."

Thumps had no expectations that this shotgun approach to police work was going to yield any results, but there was a comfort to the ordering and arranging of phone numbers in a column and matching them to actual locations.

"See this," said Gloria. "All the calls to Barcelona are to the same number."

"A hotel?" said Thumps.

"Probably." Gloria set her cellphone on the table. "Barcelona is about eight hours ahead of us, so if I'm wrong and it's a residence, someone is going to be pissed off."

The number in Barcelona was for the Hotel Casa Camper.

"Boutique hotel," said Gloria. "Between Las Ramblas and the MACBA. Expensive. I've seen it from the outside."

"Try the New York number," said Thumps.

The New York number was for The Carlyle. Archie had to look it up on the Internet. "Upper East Side," said Archie. "Madison and 76th. 1930 Beaux-Arts building. Some of the rooms have views of Central Park. You want to know what the rooms cost?"

"No."

"Just as well," said Archie. "You can't even afford a car."

Thumps glanced at Calder. "What about you?"

"In Vegas, we've got the Wynn," said Calder. "And WestAir."

"The Wynn is high-end," said Gloria. "And WestAir has regular flights between Vegas and L.A."

"Nothing else?"

"Just Los Angeles," said Calder. "Head office. And some of

the equipment rental houses we use. Business calls. So far as I can tell."

Thumps set the phone numbers to one side and put a hand on the printout Archie had run off. "Maslow was researching three stories."

"Samuels," said Gloria. "Key West and Amelia Nash."

"But," said Thumps, "she was only working Samuels and Nash."

"And you know this how?" said Calder.

Thumps held up the phone records. "She made calls to Barcelona, New York, Los Angeles, and Las Vegas."

"Don't forget the local calls," said Archie.

"I haven't," said Thumps. "I'm betting the calls to Barcelona and to New York were to Tobias Rattler."

"How the hell could you know that?" said Calder.

"Rattler was in both those cities," said Thumps. "It won't take much to match up the dates and the times."

"Or we could just ask Rattler," said Archie.

"Yes," said Thumps, "or that."

"Nina didn't make any calls to Key West," said Gloria. "But she did make calls to Vegas."

Archie bent over his computer and worked the keys. "Here we go. Amelia Nash. Twenty-three. Killed by her boyfriend, who then shot himself."

"Donny Berlin," said Calder. "Bad news. Drugs, booze. Man was a walking crime scene."

"You knew him?"

"Sure," said Calder. "Same business. But we weren't friends. To tell the truth, the guy scared me."

"According to this, Nash was all set to star in a new television series," said Archie. "*The Streets of San Francisco*."

Thumps turned to Calder.

"Amelia was my co-star." Calder took a deep breath. "Hell, she was the reason the series got the green light."

"You and Amelia Nash were going to do a remake of *Streets of San Francisco*?" said Gloria. "That would have been brilliant."

"I think Maslow wanted to do the Nash story just so she could rub my nose in it," said Calder. "Woman was a bit of a sadist. Doing the Nash story was her way of reminding me how close I came to prime time."

"And murder-suicide is always good television," said Gloria.

Calder made a disparaging sound. "Sure as hell beats tattooed bodies on a yacht."

"But why would Maslow do a murder-suicide?" Thumps looked at Gloria and then at Calder. "There's no case. There's nothing to solve."

"Mind of the mystery," said Gloria. "Sensational crimes are almost as good as unsolved crimes. What happened in that hotel room that fateful evening? Were drugs and alcohol involved? What drove Berlin to shoot his lover and then kill himself?"

"And Maslow had me as the narrator," said Calder. "The guy whose career was destroyed in the time it took Berlin to pull that trigger."

"Nothing like a bit of pity," said Gloria, "to tug at the old heartstrings."

"Jesus," said Archie. "Television is worse than the book business."

Calder pushed back from the table. "I have to be up early tomorrow. Big day on set. The Samuels family is coming in. Need my beauty sleep."

"Me too," said Gloria, "though I do adore all this hunting about for clues. Can we do it again?"

"Pearl expects that you'll be on set as well," said Calder. "She was quite specific about that."

"Along with Mr. Rattler," said Gloria.

"Better pay for the jacket," said Calder. "I think I'll wear it tomorrow."

Thumps stayed in the office and listened to Archie ring up the sale and close the store. He thought about reading Maslow's research, but his heart wasn't in it. And he didn't expect to find much there. Maslow was secretive. From what he knew of the woman, she wasn't going to leave important pieces of information lying around where anyone could find them. She'd keep the critical information safe in her head.

"Still hot?" Archie went to the filing cabinets and shook the Thermos.

"No."

"So what was that all about?"

"What do you mean?"

"Amateur hour," said the little Greek. "Not like you letting civilians in on a police investigation. Hell, you don't even trust me."

Thumps tried a shrug. "Extra sets of eyes help. They knew Maslow."

"Bullshit," said Archie. "You know something. There's a reason you brought them here tonight and let them see the evidence."

"Not evidence," said Thumps. "Just a bunch of phone records."

"Okay, so don't tell me."

"What did you find out about the local calls?"

"Oh, and I should share that with you?"

"Archie . . ."

Archie sighed and shook his head. "Lots of back and forth to the *Malice Aforethought* folk. Maslow and Sydney Pearl talked all the time. Calls to the Samuels place. Bunch of calls to an unlisted cellphone. Probably a burner. That could be interesting."

"Anything else?"

"She made one call to the motor vehicle office here in town."

"Motor vehicles?"

"And a couple of calls to Salgado Motors."

It took a moment for everything to fall into place. Thumps hadn't seen it. It was right there in front of him and he hadn't seen it. "Shit."

"Aha," said Archie. "You do know something."

"I need a road map."

Archie rummaged through a drawer. "What are we looking at?"

Thumps lay the map on the library table. There it was. He'd have to double-check the date and time, but he was reasonably sure he knew what had happened to Trudy Samuels. Which meant that Maslow knew. She had known all along.

Everything else had been a set-up. From the beginning.

"You always do this," said Archie. "You're not going to tell me, are you?"

"Could be wrong," said Thumps.

"This isn't a movie. You don't have to wait until the end to solve the case."

"Still a lot of pieces missing."

"Even Raymond Chandler gave his readers clues." Archie scowled. "So what's the plan?"

"Go home," said Thumps. "Crawl into bed. Sleep in until noon. Wake up to world peace."

"That's not a plan." Archie turned off the lights and left Thumps standing alone in the dark. "That's just wishful thinking."

THIRTY-EIGHT

Thumps didn't go to bed. He stayed up and read Nina Maslow's research files on Trudy Samuels and Amelia Nash. And he didn't sleep in until noon. He was at Al's early the next morning when Alvera opened the door.

"World come to an end?" Al grumped in behind the counter and fired up the grill. "Hope this isn't going to become a habit."

"What?"

"Body's entitled to a little peace and quiet to start off the day." Al turned on the coffee machine.

"You run a café." Thumps found his favourite stool. "The whole purpose of a café is to get people to come in and eat."

"Sure," said Al. "Just not first thing."

"What time do you think the sheriff gets up?"

"You want to call him?"

"Maybe."

Al started smiling as though she had just heard a funny joke. "If you're dumb enough to call Duke at this hour, I'll lend you my phone."

Thumps watched the coffee drip into the pot. So this is what Al's was like first thing in the morning. No coffee. No food.

"You solve anything yet?"

"Can I put my order in now?"

"I know what your order is," said Al. "The question is whether or not you'll get it."

"I'm diabetic. I have to eat at regular intervals."

"You really have to stick yourself with a needle after every meal?"

Thumps gestured to the pot. "Coffee's almost ready."

Al took a metal bowl from the refrigerator and dumped a pile of shredded potatoes on the grill. "I figure the blond hunk did it."

"Calder Banks?"

"Pays more attention to his looks than most women I know."

"What about Tobias Rattler?"

"Next thing," said Al, "you'll be thinking that Toby killed that Maslow woman as well."

The coffee pot wasn't that far away. If he stretched, Thumps could lean across the counter and grab it. "Could be Sydney Pearl killed Maslow," said Thumps. "Or Gloria Baker-Doyle. Sometimes it's the quiet ones who turn out to be the most dangerous."

"I'll show you dangerous," said Al, "if you touch that pot before it's done dripping."

For many years, Al had had a bell attached to the front door so that every time someone came in, the bell would ding-ding. Most times you couldn't hear the bell over the noise of the grill and the customers. But today, with the café empty, the bell sounded like an alarm.

"Morning." Sydney Pearl shut the door behind her. "I was hoping I'd find you here."

"You found him," said Al. "But he's no smarter than he was the other day."

Pearl slid onto a stool. "Is that true?"

"Mostly."

"But you've figured out a number of things, haven't you?" Pearl took a menu from the holder. "Mind if I join you for breakfast?"

"Free café," said Thumps.

"Were Nina's files of any use?"

"She had a knack for research."

"She loved it," said Pearl. "You know those puzzles that don't have a picture, where all the pieces are exactly the same size and shape, and if you put it together, you wind up with a monotone spiral?"

Thumps tried to imagine a puzzle with no reference points. Why would anyone make such a thing? Why would anyone want to put such a riddle together?

"Don't do puzzles."

"Never?" Pearl seemed surprised. "You used to be a cop. Surely crimes are a lot like puzzles."

Thumps shook his head. "With a puzzle, all the pieces are in the box. As long as you don't lose a piece, you'll be able to put it together."

"And crimes are not that orderly."

"Amelia Nash."

"Ah," said Pearl. "You read the file on Amelia."

"She was to be this season's final episode."

"She was," said Pearl.

"Okay." Al wandered down from the grill and grabbed the pot. "Iron's hot. You two want breakfast?"

"The usual," Thumps shouted back.

"Just toast and coffee for me," said Pearl.

"That ain't breakfast." Al poured two cups. "Try again."

"And one egg scrambled."

"Eat some of his potatoes," Al told Pearl. "He's diabetic and is in denial."

Pearl waited until Al had returned to the front of the café.

"Why the interest in Amelia Nash? You're supposed to be trying to find out who killed Nina."

"Why would Maslow want to do an episode on a case that had been solved? You're not solving anything. You're just going through the motions." Thumps wrapped his hands around the cup. "Like one of the old *Columbo* mysteries where you know who did it and waste an hour and a half watching the detective in the rumpled raincoat figure it out."

"Procedurals can be good television," said Pearl.

"Maybe for the middle of the season," said Thumps, "but not for the final episode. Nash is too flat. There are no surprises. Maslow was all about surprises."

Pearl poured some cream into her coffee until it was the colour of warm toast. "Do you know much about the lives of celebrities?"

"Sex, drugs, and rock and roll?"

"A lot depends on when you hit it big. If it happens when you're young, it's real easy to go off the rails."

"Amelia Nash."

"Amelia Nash," said Pearl. "She was a rocket. Talented. Beautiful. Desperately young and stupid. Donny Berlin was fifteen years older. No longer young and not so talented."

"But still stupid."

"And abusive," said Pearl. "We all tried to warn Amelia off Berlin. For all the good it did."

"He beat her?"

"Only when he was drunk or on drugs." Pearl leaned forward on her elbows. "We were in Vegas for the academy's annual benefit gala. We were celebrating. Our new series had just gotten picked up. Amelia Nash and Calder Banks. We were supposed to fly directly from Vegas to San Francisco to begin prep."

"*The Streets of San Francisco,*" said Thumps, as though he were talking to himself. "His big break."

"Not just his," said Pearl. "I was part of the production team. Maslow too. We all had a stake in the show."

"But Nash was the star."

"She was."

"Not Calder."

"Not Calder," said Pearl. "And you know what they say."

"No star," said Thumps, "no show."

"Exactly," said Pearl.

Thumps picked at a chip on the side of the coffee cup. "Maslow didn't think it was a murder-suicide."

"Nina had a sixth sense for stuff like this," said Pearl. "She was smart, curious, mysterious, secretive."

Al arrived with the food, and she had taken the liberty of moving some of Thumps's potatoes onto Pearl's plate.

"And don't be complaining," she warned. "Can't have you dying in my café."

"If I begin to feel faint," said Thumps, "I'll try to crawl out to the curb."

Al wiped her hands on her apron and walked back to the grill. "Barely enough room in the place for the paying custom-ers. Can't have a dead body taking up one of my stools."

Pearl picked at her eggs for a while. If she was going to fill in any of the blanks, she was taking her time.

"The gun Berlin used to kill Nash was a Maxim 9. Berlin had bought it at the Vegas gun show the day before."

Pearl shrugged. "Berlin was a gun nut. Offered to buy my .38 just because Tom Selleck had given it to me."

"The Maxim has a built-in suppressor. Police figure that's why no one heard the shots."

"Makes sense."

"But here's the odd part," said Thumps. "Nash was shot twice."

Pearl's expression didn't change.

"Once in the chest," said Thumps. "Once in the head."

"And that's significant?"

"Maybe," said Thumps. "Maybe not. You know what Berlin's blood alcohol level was?"

"Why don't you tell me."

"It was .30," said Thumps. "Most people pass out around .25."

"You've been very busy," said Pearl.

"Who found the bodies?"

"If you've read Nina's notes," said Pearl, "you already know the answer to that question."

Thumps nodded. "You did. At 11:10."

"And your point is?"

"The coroner set the time of death between seven and eleven."

"You know why I have that bottle on my desk?"

Thumps was tired of being polite with the woman. "Recovering alcoholic?"

"Good guess," said Pearl. "It's a prop. Like the gun. People look at the two of them together and figure they should give me a wide berth. Gives me space."

"And the Honda?"

"I'll tell you that story when I know you better." Pearl set her fork next to her plate. "But you want to know what I was doing in Nash's room."

"I do."

"I went there for a meeting," said Pearl. "Contract technicalities."

"At eleven at night?"

"Show biz," said Pearl.

"But when you got there, Berlin and Nash were already dead."

"They were."

"So who let you in?"

Pearl smiled. "That was very good, Mr. DreadfulWater. Do you know much about the lives of celebrities? Do you know what producers really do?"

"Nope."

"Celebrities are children."

"And producers are parents?"

"Simplistic," said Pearl, "but true. They're petulant, self-centred, destructive, stupid. One of my jobs is to make sure that they are where they're supposed to be and that they do what they're supposed to do."

"You had a key to Nash's room."

"Yes," said Pearl. "I had a key. And when Amelia didn't answer, I let myself in."

"Where was Maslow?"

"I had left her at the bar downstairs."

"And Calder?"

"On an early plane back to L.A."

Thumps arranged all the pieces in his head. He could see a vague pattern. Maslow would have seen it too.

"What was the meeting about?"

"All of this is quite a lot of fun," said Pearl, "but do you have any proof that Vegas was anything more than a murder-suicide?"

"No," said Thumps.

"Then there's your answer," said Pearl. "You're coming to the shoot today, aren't you? Watch *Malice Aforethought* solve the Samuels case?"

"Already know what happened to Trudy Samuels," said Thumps.

"Really."

"Maslow figured it out months ago," said Thumps. "Both of you have known all along."

"Then you can do the interview," said Pearl.

"That's not going to happen."

"Hear me out," said Pearl. "Calder's an actor. He hasn't got a cop's mind. He doesn't know what to ask or how to ask it. So, we'll block the scene and do one rehearsal with you in the lead. Calder can watch. Then when we do the actual shoot, it will be Calder on camera."

"Don't think so."

Pearl waited as though she hadn't heard the answer. "The Obsidian Murders was going to be next season's premiere episode. Now we may not have a show next year. I hate to see all that research go to waste. You understand what I'm saying?"

"You're blackmailing me."

"I told you I'd give you Nina's research." Pearl's eyes were slits. "I'll keep that promise. But I need you to do this for me."

"What if I'm wrong?"

"You don't strike me as a man who enjoys being wrong." Pearl gestured at Thumps's plate. "You going to finish those potatoes?"

"Help yourself." Thumps pushed the plate over and slid off the stool.

"What about Nina?" said Pearl. "Do you know who killed her?"

"Maybe," said Thumps.

"Ah," said Pearl. "Curious, mysterious, secretive. Just like Nina."

Thumps slipped his jacket on. "What happened to smart?"

Pearl held up a forkful of hash browns. "That," she said, "remains to be seen."

THIRTY-NINE

The lights were on at the sheriff's office. Duke Hockney was behind his desk. Tobias Rattler was sitting across from him. Both men were bent over a board.

"Checkers?"

Duke waved a hand but didn't take his eyes off the game.

"You're playing checkers?"

"Sheriff Hockney is teaching mc how to play," said Rattler.

"He's learning fast," said Duke. "Help yourself to the coffee."

Duke's old percolator was back on its table.

"You fixed it?"

"Lime deposit," said Duke. "Macy caught the problem."

"So it wasn't terminal." Thumps tried not to sound disappointed.

"Overnight in vinegar," said the sheriff, "and it's good as new."

335

Thumps wondered if the vinegar would change the taste or the texture of the sheriff's coffee. He couldn't imagine that anything could make it worse.

"Try a cup," said Duke. "It's got real bite now."

"I thought Toby was under arrest."

"He is," said the sheriff.

"I'm on temporary furlough," said Rattler. "For good behaviour."

"However," said Duke, "if he keeps beating me, I'm going to throw him back in a cell."

"It's not as difficult as chess or go," said Rattler, "but it has its moments."

Duke leaned back and yawned. "You're up early."

"You know what they say," said Thumps. "Early birds. Worms."

Duke moved one of his pieces onto the end line and turned it into a king. "You find any worms?"

"In England," said Rattler, "they call this game 'draughts.'"

Thumps looked at the board. He remembered something about men, kings, flying kings, king's row, and how men could only move forward in a particular manner, but kings could move freely around the board.

"Morgan Freeman and Tim Robbins played checkers in *The Shawshank Redemption*."

"The prison yard," said Rattler. "Right?"

"Damn it, DreadfulWater," said Duke, "you two are messing with my concentration."

"You got evidence bags?"

"I'm a police officer," said Duke. "Of course I have evidence bags."

"I need one."

"You got some evidence I should know about?" The sheriff took his finger off the piece.

"Nope."

"Then why do you need the bag?"

"It's for an experiment," said Thumps.

"Sort of like a school project?"

"Something like that."

Duke waved a hand at the filing cabinets. "Second cabinet from the left, two drawers down."

"Thanks."

"But they're old," said Hockney. "Emmitt got a whole shit-load of crime-fighting stuff on a federal grant back in the last century, and we still haven't used it all up."

"That's because you're an exceptional crime fighter."

"Oh shucks," said Duke. "Seeing as you're so sweet, you can have two."

Thumps found the bags in the third cabinet, in the bottom drawer. Brown paper stamped with the appropriate blank fill-in lines for evidence—date of collection, location of collection, type of offence, victim—and the chain of custody report—who received what from whom and when.

"These are perfect," said Thumps. "Can I have some coffee?"

Duke didn't even look up. "Help yourself. You'll be surprised by the rich bouquet."

Thumps took the evidence bag to the percolator, flattened the bag on the table, and slowly dripped coffee on it. Then he dropped the bag on the floor and stepped on it.

"What the hell!" Duke stood up. "You know how much those bags cost?"

"No idea."

"Well, they aren't free," said Duke. "You want to tell me what's going on?"

"You have any toothpicks?"

"In case you haven't noticed," said Hockney, "this is a sheriff's office, not a convenience store."

Rattler made a double jump. "Another king."

Duke looked back at Rattler and the board. "See what happens when you distract me."

"We got to watch the time," said Rattler. "Don't want to be late to the set."

Thumps blotted the bag with a paper towel. "Thought he was under arrest?"

"Not my idea," said Duke. "That producer woman said they can't do the show without him."

"Sydney Pearl."

"That's her," said Duke. "Do you know the impact national exposure can have on a local economy?"

"Nope."

"Neither did I," said Duke. "Anyway, Ms. Pearl sat down with the mayor, and the two of them had a nice chat about such matters. And then the mayor sat down with me. You get the idea?"

"Howdy," said Thumps.

"Yippee," said the sheriff.

FREDDY SALGADO WAS on the phone when Thumps got to the dealership. He waved Thumps into his office and pointed to the chair in front of the desk.

"You're kidding." Freddy tried to control the exasperation in his voice. "There are no direct flights?"

The Corvette was still in its place of honour on the showroom floor. Thumps wondered if the front seat was as tight as Calder had hinted. Maybe Freddy would let him sit in the car. Get the feel of an all-American sports car.

"Does a six-hour layover sound reasonable to you?"

The car was probably just fine if you were short and thin. But Thumps could see several problems if you happened to be tall and large. No leg room for starters. And then there was the problem of sitting with your head jammed against the roof.

Freddy was off the phone and steaming. "You ever try to fly from Great Falls to San Francisco?"

"Nope."

"Well, don't." Freddy shook his head. "First you have to fly to Seattle. But the flight from Great Falls to Sea-Tac is always late, which means you miss the noon flight to SFO and have to wait around for the evening run."

Thumps made sympathetic noises.

"Six hours," said Freddy. "Who wants to sit in an airport for six hours?"

"You could read a book."

"I could write a book," said Freddy. "And then on top of that, the evening plane from Sea-Tac to the City by the Bay will be late as well, because nowadays, all planes are late."

"Don't fly much."

"Do you know what the industry on-time average is?"

"Not good?"

"Mornings aren't so bad. After that, things start to fall apart." Freddy swung back and forth in his chair. "After five, less than 50 percent of the flights are on time. You know what would happen if I ran my business like that?"

"You'd be out of business."

"You got that right." Freddy took a deep breath and forced a smile. "So, you're back."

"I'm back."

"The pickup? Right?" Freddy tented his fingers. "Once I get it, it won't last long. Well maintained, low mileage. She's a beauty."

"So, when you fly to San Francisco," said Thumps, "do you take WestAir?"

"WestAir?" Freddy frowned. "WestAir doesn't fly this part of the country. You'd have to get to Salt Lake or Dallas to catch one of their planes."

"What if I wanted to go to Las Vegas?"

"Can't get to Vegas from here on WestAir," said Freddy. "Best bet would be to catch Delta or Alaska out of Helena."

"But not WestAir?"

"And you'll have to make at least one stop. Why do you want to go to Las Vegas?"

"I don't."

"I have to go there every year for the big auto show. Five days of hell. Deep-fried food. Grumpy people. Place is a neon armpit."

"You still have that stuff in the frame?"

"For the Corvette?" Freddy grinned. "You just want to see how much the car cost new. Am I right?"

"You got me."

Freddy opened the trunk. "Read 'em and weep," he said. "In 1963, this beauty went out the door for under five grand. Know what it's worth today?"

Thumps looked at each of the items in the frame.

"Average value today is over fifty thousand," said Freddy. "At Barrett-Jackson, this one would go for eighty, a hundred thousand easy. Hell, my first house didn't cost that much."

"How'd the shoot go?"

"For the TV show?" Freddy ran his hand along the top of

the windshield. "They had this beauty shining like a diamond. When that episode airs, my phone'll be ringing off the hook."

Thumps glanced at the clock. Just before noon. He didn't know how film crews worked, but he guessed that they wouldn't start shooting until after lunch.

"You know, when those television people first contacted me," said Freddy, "I thought it was a joke. I mean, I don't hear a thing from them for about three months, and then suddenly they're in town with their lights and cameras and it's wham, bam, thank you, ma'am."

"Think I'm going to have to pass on the truck."

"What you going to do for a ride?"

"Don't know."

"No point fixing the Volvo," said Freddy. "Good money after bad."

"Maybe I'll move to Amsterdam," said Thumps.

"Amsterdam? That the place with all the canals and the windmills?"

"Everybody rides bikes in Amsterdam," said Thumps. "Hardly any cars."

Freddy turned to the large windows that opened out onto the high plains. "This look like Amsterdam to you?"

"Can't say that it does," said Thumps.

"You got a bike?"

"Nope."

"Then," said Freddy, "I'd reconsider the pickup."

FORTY

The Samuels's living room took up much of the second floor of Budd's. The last time Thumps was here, the set had been a corpse of lumber and paint.

Now it was alive.

Lights had been hung on overhead bars, and large soft boxes lined the perimeter. A fixed camera on a dolly waited just off centre stage, while a guy in a Handycam rig prowled about, checking his shooting angles. People Thumps hadn't seen before stood in small bunches, talking to each other. A few appeared to be talking to themselves.

Chaos and order. Everywhere Thumps looked. Chaos and order.

Sydney Pearl was sitting in the eye of the storm, relaxing in an easy chair, her eyes hooded as though she were hunting rabbits.

"Mr. DreadfulWater." Pearl waved him to a seat. "So good of you to join us."

Thumps put the shopping bag next to a chair and sat down. Pearl glanced at the sack.

"We brought groceries?"

"We need to talk."

"Mrs. Samuels and her son haven't arrived yet, nor has Mr. Rattler," said Pearl. "Would you like something to drink?"

"I'm fine."

"I hope our talk isn't going to be about your not wanting to interrogate Mr. Rattler on set."

"No," said Thumps. "It's about Nina Maslow."

"Ah," said Pearl. "And you've come to the conclusion that Nina wasn't killed because of the Samuels case."

Thumps had underestimated Pearl. He'd have to remember not to do that again.

"Don't look so surprised," said Pearl. "There were only two people who knew that Nina had solved the case."

"You and Nina."

"Correct," said Pearl.

"Except there were three," said Thumps. "Nina told Rattler what she had learned."

Pearl remained silent.

"It's the only way she could have gotten him to agree to be on the show. All the rest was nonsense and smoke. Which also means that Rattler didn't have a reason to kill Maslow."

"Touché, Mr. DreadfulWater," said Pearl. "So you're not just a pretty face. So, what else do you have?"

"WestAir."

"The airline?"

"Maslow called WestAir in Las Vegas several times."

Pearl shrugged. "Nina was going to go to Vegas once we finished this shoot, to prepare for the episode on Amelia Nash."

Thumps nodded. "Except that WestAir doesn't fly to Vegas from here."

"Okay," said Pearl. "Same question. What does it mean?"

"There you are." Calder appeared in the wings of the set, looking spiffy in his new vintage jacket. "What the hell is going on?"

Pearl lowered her eyes to mouse-hunting mode. "Exactly which hell are we talking about?"

"Gloria says that you want DreadfulWater to do the interview." Calder shifted his weight from one foot to the other. "Come on, Sydney, this is my show."

"Actually," said Pearl, "it's my show, and Mr. DreadfulWater isn't going to do the on-camera interview. He's going to do the blocking and the rehearsal."

"We don't need him."

"Mr. DreadfulWater has law-enforcement experience," said Pearl, as though she were teaching a class on simple addition. "He knows how to interview suspects. He knows how to order and frame the questions. He can be your model for the actual interview."

"I don't want your job," said Thumps.

"You couldn't do my job," said Calder. "And where are my sides?"

"No sides," said Pearl. "I want real spontaneity in the scene."

"Confrontation," said Calder. "Sparks and feathers."

"Can you do that?"

At the far edge of the set, Gloria stepped into the light with Adele Samuels and Ethan Price in tow.

"We're here," she said. "Yeah?"

Pearl stood and motioned to the sofa. "Please," she said, "Mrs. Samuels, why don't you sit here. Ethan, how about you take that chair next to your mother."

Adele Samuels didn't look to be in a good mood. And her disposition didn't improve when she saw Thumps.

"Why is he here?"

"Mr. Banks will do the actual interview," said Pearl. "But I'd like Mr. DreadfulWater to stand in for the rehearsal."

"Again," said Adele, her voice sharp and brittle, "why?"

There was no rush in Pearl. She kept her voice level and calm. "Mr. Banks doesn't have the police experience that Mr. DreadfulWater has. We don't want Mr. Rattler interrogated by an actor, do we? Watching Mr. DreadfulWater at work will give Mr. Banks the methodology and the motivation that he needs to do a good job."

"It's fine, Mom," said Ethan. "Matter of fact, I think it's a good idea."

Thumps kept his mouth shut. It wasn't his show. It wasn't his life.

Adele shifted on the sofa. "And just where is Tobias Rattler?"

"Here." Sheriff Hockney plodded up the last few stairs with Rattler at his side. "Sorry we're late."

"Mr. Rattler," said Gloria. "Why don't you take the big chair. Yeah?"

"We'll put you off stage, sheriff," said Pearl. "If you don't mind."

"Nope," said Duke. "A little distance will make it easier to keep an eye on everyone."

"Maybe," said Adele, "you'll even be able to find someone to arrest."

"Yes, ma'am," said Duke, touching the brim of his hat. "It would be my pleasure."

Pearl was suddenly in action, moving about the set, talking with everyone. She spent most of the time with the two cameramen and a bearded man in his late fifties who looked as though he might be related to Ernest Borgnine. Maybe he was the director.

If reality shows had directors.

And then Pearl was back.

"How about we try a dry run," she said. "See how this might play out. Then if we need to, we can re-block and make any changes."

"What do you want us to do?" said Ethan.

"Just be yourself," said Pearl. "Answer Mr. DreadfulWater's questions. Keep it simple. I'm sure you'll be fine."

Pearl gave a signal with her hand and the set lights came on.

They were sudden and brilliant, and Thumps had to squint until he got used to the brightness.

"Do we really need this?" Adele shielded her eyes. "For a rehearsal?"

"I have to see how everything will look for the actual shoot," said Pearl. "I want to make sure we get it right."

"They're quite dazzling," said Rattler.

"My apologies," said Pearl. "All right, Mr. DreadfulWater. The set is yours."

Suddenly, what had been an abstract concept was now an unpleasant reality. How the hell had he let Pearl talk him into this?

Adele was waiting for him. "Have you ever done this before, Mr. DreadfulWater?"

"He used to be a cop," said Rattler. "Of course he's done this before."

"Yes," said Thumps, finding his voice. "I've done this before. But before we get started, I'd like to go over what we know."

"We know Mr. Rattler killed Trudy," said Adele. "Or caused her death."

Thumps could see that he wasn't going to enjoy this. He'd be more than happy to turn it over to Calder. Sooner, rather than later.

"Actually, we don't know that," said Thumps. "We know Trudy Samuels was found dead at Belly Butte. And we know the coroner found no indication of foul play."

"We do know a bit more than that," said Ethan.

"We do," said Thumps, warming to the task. "We know that Trudy was an unhappy young woman. We know that she and Tobias Rattler had formed a friendship, two loners coming together. We know that Trudy had a fight with her stepmother and that she moved from the Samuels estate to an apartment in town. We know she had a car. A 1963 Corvette split-window."

"What does the car have to do with anything?" said Adele.

"First question is for Mr. Rattler," said Thumps. "The night that Trudy died, the two of you were supposed to go to a movie."

"That's right."

"But Trudy didn't show up."

"No," said Rattler, "she didn't."

"Why not?"

"I don't know."

Thumps watched Toby's face. "That's a lie."

"Of course it's a lie," said Adele.

"You and Trudy had had a fight earlier that day, didn't you?" Rattler waited.

"But before we get to that, let's back up a bit." Thumps could feel his mouth drying out. He could use a glass of water. Or a cup of coffee. What he really wanted, now that he thought about it, was to be somewhere else. "Mrs. Samuels, why did Trudy leave home?"

"Why do teenage girls do anything?" said Adele.

"She felt trapped," said Ethan. "She and Mom didn't get along."

"Ethan . . ."

"It's not a secret, Mom," said Ethan. "Everyone knew. And we were just as happy to have her gone. She was always angry. Or she was drunk. I figured that she'd kill herself in that car of hers."

"She drove fast?" asked Thumps.

Ethan smiled. "Made the mistake of riding with her a couple of times. Didn't think I'd survive."

Thumps glanced at Pearl, then turned to Rattler. "When was Trudy supposed to meet you for the movie?"

Rattler took a moment. "It was the early show," he said. "Six-thirty, seven."

"Why didn't she come?"

"You've already asked that question," said Adele. "Christ! She didn't meet him at the movie because she was already dead. Because he had killed her."

"No," said Thumps, "Trudy Samuels wasn't dead. At 7:15 she was very much alive. And at 7:15 Mr. Rattler was waiting for her at the show. There were witnesses."

"Then he killed her after."

"Hard to imagine," said Thumps. "How'd he get out to Belly Butte? He didn't have a car. And there was no way he would have known that Trudy would go out to Belly Butte that night."

"Wait a minute," said Ethan. "You can't know that Trudy was alive at 7:15. What, you have a crystal ball or something?"

"This is how we know," said Thumps, and he reached into the shopping bag and held up a sheet of paper. "This is how Nina Maslow figured out what happened to Trudy Samuels."

"And what is that supposed to be?" said Adele.

"It's a Xerox of a ticket," said Thumps. "A speeding ticket for one Trudy Samuels, driving a 1963 Corvette, issued at 7:15 on the night she died."

"So, she got a speeding ticket." Ethan leaned forward. "Trudy collected speeding tickets the way my mother collects shoes."

"Ethan!"

"It's true," said Ethan. "It would be unusual if a week went by when she *didn't* get a ticket."

Thumps sorted through the material in the bag. "I've got a road map in here somewhere, but all of you know the geography as well as I do. Maybe even better."

"God," said Adele. "Get to the point."

"Trudy got the ticket in Randall," said Thumps. "The place is famous for its speed trap."

Ethan turned his palms up in frustration. "So?"

"When she got the ticket, she was travelling east to west. She wasn't heading to Belly Butte. Belly Butte is in the opposite direction." Thumps paused for a beat. "So, where was she going?"

Adele stiffened. "And I suppose you know."

"As a matter of fact," said Thumps, "I do."

FORTY-ONE

It was Rattler who broke the silence, his voice soft, almost apologetic. "Black Stag," he said. "She was going to Black Stag."

Adele held her ground on the sofa, still as stone.

"That's my guess," said Thumps. "Nothing much else out that direction."

"I'm afraid you're mistaken, Mr. DreadfulWater," said Ethan.

"Trudy had no reason to return," said Adele. "That question had been settled."

"She wasn't coming to stay," said Thumps. "She was coming because of the money."

"Trudy hardly needed money," said Adele. "She already had more than she deserved."

"I'm not talking about her money. I'm talking about the money you gave Mr. Rattler."

Adele turned on Rattler.

"No," said Thumps. "He didn't tell me. Maslow figured it out on her own. I was a little slower."

"I don't see how any of this is relevant," said Ethan. "So what if my mother gave Mr. Rattler a little money."

"I don't know the exact amount," said Thumps, "but it would have been mid–five figures."

"Ridiculous!"

"Not that it matters how much." Thumps kept his voice even. "What matters is . . . why?"

Adele turned away. "Surely the *why* isn't all that difficult."

"A bribe," said Thumps. "An inducement, a payoff. The means by which to get Tobias Rattler out of your stepdaughter's life."

"And you disapprove?"

"I don't care," said Thumps. "But Trudy did."

"Trudy was emotional," said Adele. "Probably disturbed if you want to know the truth. The booze, the drugs, the promiscuity. She was not a nice person."

"Did you tell her about the money?"

"Of course not." Adele's mouth snapped open and shut. "Why would I tell her?"

Thumps turned to Ethan. "Then it had to have been you."

Ethan looked at his shoes, looked poised to deny it. And then he didn't. "So what?"

"You told her?"

"Come on, Mom," said Ethan. "You know how she was. She thought she could have anything she wanted. Nice clothes, fancy apartment, a fast car. She needed to understand that she couldn't have it all."

Thumps waited for a moment. "And when you told her, she exploded."

"Oh, boy, did she ever," said Ethan. "Should have seen her. She was ready to kill someone."

Thumps nodded at Rattler. "That was what the fight was about. Earlier in the day. About your taking the money. Off to Dartmouth, jiggety-jig, while Trudy stays in Chinook."

"We were friends," said Rattler. "Good friends. She had everything she wanted right here. She wanted me to stay here."

"And here was where you were never going to stay."

"Maybe I should have." Rattler rubbed his hands together. "But I didn't."

"Remorse?" snorted Adele. "Really? Back then you were happy enough to take my money and run."

Thumps held up a hand. "So, Ethan tells Trudy what Adele has done, and Trudy finds you."

"Yeah," said Rattler. "She did."

"And you fought."

"I'd never seen her like that."

"So there was no movie," said Thumps.

"I waited for her at the theatre," said Rattler. "Hoped she would show up."

No, thought Thumps. At some point the betrayal had over-whelmed her, and she got into her car and drove to Black Stag. Along the way she got a speeding ticket. 7:15. In Randall.

"When did Trudy arrive at the estate?"

"Don't remember," said Ethan. "What does it matter?"

"Not another word, Ethan," hissed Adele. "We're done here."

"It's over, Mom," said Ethan. "Mr. DreadfulWater knows."

Thumps reached into the bag. "When the coroner examined Trudy's body, he noticed a set of fresh scratches on her right palm that didn't seem to be related to the fall. So he took a closer look." Thumps held up the evidence bag and gave it a gentle shake. "And removed these," he said, looking at Ethan. "Splinters. Just like the ones you have in your hand."

Ethan drew a deep breath. "Wood houses."

Thumps waited.

"Mom was upstairs. I was downstairs in my room, watching television. I didn't hear Trudy come in. And then the screaming started. By the time I got there, my mother was on the floor. Trudy had her hands around her throat."

"So you stopped her."

"I wasn't going to let her kill my mother."

"Ethan . . ."

"No, Mom," said Ethan. "We didn't do anything wrong. It was self-defence."

"Trudy stumbled," said Adele. "She stumbled and went over the balcony."

"Stumbled?"

"There was nothing we could do."

"You could have called an ambulance."

"She was already dead," said Adele.

"You could have called the police."

"And what," said Adele, "let them arrest Ethan? For protecting me?"

"So you took her body to Belly Butte and dumped it."

"If you want to blame someone," said Adele, "blame Mr. Rattler. He had no business with my daughter."

"Mom . . ."

Adele wavered in the television lights like a dying heroine. "Where's the sheriff?"

Duke slipped out of the shadows. "Here, ma'am."

"I certainly hope you're not stupid enough to think of arresting my son."

"I guess that depends," said Hockney. "I'm going to need him to come to the office and make an official statement."

"And if he chooses not to comply?"

"Then I'll have to arrest him on suspicion of murder."

"Ridiculous," said Adele.

"Your choice," said Duke.

"We're going home now, sheriff." Adele was already at the stairs. Ethan trailed behind. "You know where to find us."

"Yes, ma'am," Duke called after her. "I do."

It was Calder who broke the silence.

"Holy hell," he said. "Now that was something."

"Yes, it was," said Pearl.

"Shit," said Calder, "were the cameras running? Tell me we got all that on film?"

Pearl looked back at the cameraman, who held up a thumb. "Yes," she said, "we did."

Rattler leaned back in his chair. "I'm sorry about lying to you. Maslow and Pearl were both adamant that no one else could know."

"Adele Samuels had to think that Maslow was coming after you."

"Only way this could have worked," said Pearl. "You were magnificent."

"I was never the rehearsal," said Thumps.

"No," said Pearl. "You were always the main event."

"Don't much like being used."

"No. I suppose you don't." Pearl faced the sheriff. "So now what's going to happen?"

"We'll talk to the both of them," said Duke. "But I'm guessing by this time tomorrow, Adele is going to have half a dozen high-priced lawyers in harness. Doubt the DA will even try for manslaughter. Moving a dead body is the most we're going to get. Maybe interfering with a crime scene."

"So," said Pearl, "Adele Samuels and her son get away with murder?"

"You know what happened that night at Black Stag?" Hockney waited a beat. "'Cause I sure as hell don't."

"The only problem here," said Calder, "is that I wasn't in the scene."

"We'll do some cutaways," said Pearl. "Match you to the critical moments. Movie magic."

Calder slapped Thumps on the shoulder. "You got the moves. You could have been an actor."

"Let's reset," Pearl shouted to the crew. "Thirty minutes. Then we shoot with Calder."

Pearl led Thumps off to a quiet corner. "So now what?"

"You've got your episode," said Thumps.

"You know what I mean."

"When do you leave for Vegas?"

"We have more shooting to do tomorrow," said Pearl. "Then we pack it up."

"A couple of days back, Maslow called an airline. WestAir. You know why?"

"WestAir?"

"Yeah," said Thumps. "She made a twenty-minute call to an airline that does not operate in this part of the country."

"You think this is important?"

"I was hoping you might know."

Pearl worked her lips. "You seem to have a whole lot of nothing."

"Not even that," said Thumps. "But I'm guessing it has something to do with Amelia Nash."

"Because it's the only thing that makes sense?"

"Yes," said Thumps. "Because it's the only thing that makes sense."

"I expected more," said Pearl.

"Trouble is," said Thumps, "I don't see the profit in her death. She dies and the remake of *Streets of San Francisco* gets flushed. Calder loses his big break. You lose a prime-time production. The network loses money."

"So, if it's not about money . . ."

"It was about something else."

"Nina had found something," said Pearl. "This last week, when she talked about Amelia and that night in Vegas, you could hear it in her voice, see it in her eyes."

"And someone went through her room, looking for it."

Behind Pearl, the set lights came on. "I have to get back," she said. "You got any helpful ideas?"

"Shake a tree. See what falls out."

"You got any trees?"

"Maybe."

"That's what Nina liked to do," said Pearl. "Just try to make sure whatever falls out doesn't land on you."

FORTY-TWO

The sheriff and Rattler were leaning against Duke's cruiser. Thumps wasn't sure if they were waiting for him or if they were just enjoying the moment, relaxing in the low warmth of the autumn sun. If he had any sense, he would walk on by, climb into Stas's truck, and leave them to annoy each other.

"That was pretty impressive, DreadfulWater," said Duke. "Lady Macbeth meets Columbo. Almost Shakespearean."

Thumps could feel his blood sugars begin to drop. Rawat was right. Insulin was an art form. Too much, and things went south. Too little, and they went north. Neither direction was any better than the other. As appalling a thought as it was, he might have to get serious about his diet. And his eating habits.

"How about we grab a bite," said Duke. "I know just the place."

Thumps could hear little alarms go off. "Does this place happen to feature a giant squirrel?"

"Dancing squirrel," said the sheriff.

Rattler came to his rescue. "Don't know that fast food is good for diabetics."

"It's not all that fast," countered Duke. "Sometimes they let the burgers sit under heat lamps for hours. Burns away the excess fat and carbohydrates."

"You guys can go," said Thumps. "I'm heading home."

"You can't go home," said the sheriff. "We have to celebrate."

"Celebrate?"

"We solved Trudy Samuels," said Duke, "and we cleared Mr. Rattler."

"I feel like celebrating," said Rattler.

"Course we still don't know who killed Nina Maslow," said Duke. "But I think we can rule out Adele and Ethan. Neither of them knew Maslow had solved the case or that she was going to ambush them on the episode."

"If they had known," said Rattler, "they would have refused to be on the show."

"Drop me off on the way."

"That sounds like coward's talk," said Duke. "You can't go home. You haven't solved Maslow yet."

"Not my job."

"What about your deal with Pearl?" said the sheriff. "You figure out who killed Maslow, and you get all her research on that California case of yours."

"You know," said Thumps, "as an officer of the law, you could subpoena those files as part of your investigation."

Duke walked around the front of the cruiser and opened the door. "That's an interesting idea," he said, "and I'm willing to hear arguments over a burger at Skippy's."

SKIPPY'S WAS THE newest offering in the fast-food epidemic that had hit Chinook in the last decade. McDonald's, Burger King, Sonic, Taco Bell, and Wendy's had all popped up in town like pimples at a junior prom.

"You got to admit," said the sheriff, "that's one great rodent."

The entrance to Skippy's was dominated by a giant squirrel with large buck teeth and neon feet that flashed back and forth as though the animal were dancing. Thumps slid down in the back seat. Maybe no one he knew would see him.

"1950s retro," said the sheriff. "Just like the old-time drive-ins."

"Some of those drive-ins had roller-skating waitresses," said Rattler. "Did you ever see *American Graffiti?*"

Duke eased the cruiser into a parking slot, rolled down his window, and tapped his finger on a touchpad that was attached to a steel post.

"Watch this," he said.

The touchpad lit up with a menu and began playing a jingle that sounded like a dog food commercial from Thumps's childhood.

"Welcome to Skip-Skip-Skippy's," said a disembodied voice. "May I take your order?"

"Cute, huh?" said Duke. "If you order the combo, you get a Skippy's scratch card."

"Great," said Thumps.

"Chance to win a hundred dollars," said the sheriff. "So what do you guys want?"

Rattler had a Skippy's salad with ranch dressing. Duke ordered a double Acorn burger with cheese and guacamole, a basket of onion rings, and a small lemonade.

"Don't tell Macy."

Thumps read through the menu twice without finding anything that resembled food. "Is the chicken breast roasted or pan-fried?"

"Our chicken breast is broasted."

"Broasted?"

"Deep-fried under pressure," said the voice.

"I'll just have coffee."

"Would you like fries with that?"

The neon squirrel at the entrance began moving, and now Thumps could see that the red and green and yellow critter wasn't dancing at all. It was trying to run away.

"Okay," said the sheriff. "So. Maslow."

"We should look at Maslow from the perspective of a mystery writer, and work the plot backwards," said Rattler. "For example, we know that both Trudy Samuels and Nina Maslow were found dead at Belly Butte, which would suggest that the two deaths are connected."

"Except there may not be a connection," said Duke.

"And if they're not connected," said Rattler, "then whoever killed Maslow is using Trudy to throw us off their trail."

"Still doesn't tell us who killed her."

"What else was she working on?" asked Rattler.

"DreadfulWater." Duke turned around in the seat. "You waiting for a written invitation?"

"I'm waiting for my coffee."

"Nobody likes irony," said the sheriff. "You find anything in Maslow's files or phone records?"

"Odds and ends."

"Such as?"

Thumps had liked it better when Rattler and the sheriff were playing Sherlock and Watson. "Maslow was looking at three possible stories. Three women murdered and tattooed in Key West, the Amelia Nash murder-suicide in Las Vegas, and a serial killer in Northern California."

"Someone tattooed dead women?" said Rattler.

"But if you look at her phone records," said Thumps, "the

only story she was actively pursuing was Amelia Nash's murder-suicide."

"And we know this how?" said Duke.

"She made a number of calls to Vegas but none to Key West or to Northern California."

Rattler nodded. "So what do we know about this Amelia Nash?"

"Hit the pause button," interrupted the sheriff. "Here comes the food."

The smell of the hot fat filled the car. The sheriff's burger was enormous, the size of a softball. The onion rings came in a shipping container, and the small lemonade was in a quart-size cup. Thumps took a deep breath and held it. He didn't think there was any nutritional value in vapours. Still, the greasy aromas were disturbingly satisfying. No wonder Skippy was running as fast as he could. The squirrel had to burn off all the calories.

"Good value," said the sheriff, his mouth full of grilled cow. "How's your coffee?"

Thumps was thankful to be in the back seat, where he couldn't see the sheriff eat. Hearing him tear at the carcass was enough.

"You want some onion rings?"

Thumps took two. They tasted great. Warm, crisp, oily. And it only took a moment for his heart to right itself.

"Lemonade?"

Rattler leaned against the door. "So, you're thinking that Maslow discovered something about Amelia Nash and that something got her killed?"

"Let's say, for the sake of argument, that Amelia Nash wasn't a murder-suicide," said the sheriff. "Let's say that someone came into Nash's hotel room, shot her, shot her boyfriend, and made it look like love gone wrong."

"And since Maslow was killed here in Chinook," said the sheriff, "our chief suspects would, of necessity, be the folks associated with *Malice Aforethought*."

"Which doesn't make a lot of sense," said Rattler. "Why kill Maslow here? Why not wait until they got to Vegas, where there would be more suspects?"

Thumps kept his mouth shut. There was no sense getting in between Duke's burger and Rattler's salad.

"Timing," said the sheriff. "Maybe they ran out of time."

"Sure," said Rattler. "That's a good plot point. Killer doesn't want to kill Maslow here in Chinook, but something happens that forces his or her hand."

Thumps could still taste the grease from the onion rings. He ran his tongue around his mouth and found bits of crusty coating stuck to the back of his teeth.

"Sydney Pearl," said the sheriff. "Calder Banks. And Gloria Baker-Doyle. Who do you like?"

"It's *whom*," said Rattler. "And in a novel, it would be the character you least suspected."

"Gloria Baker-Doyle," said the sheriff. "She seems too sweet to kill anyone."

"Or it could be the character with the best alibi."

"Calder Banks," said Thumps. "He was on a plane to Los Angeles when Nash was killed."

"Which leaves Sydney Pearl," said Rattler. "She seems the least likely."

The sheriff picked at his teeth with a business card. "Course, *you* could have killed Maslow."

Rattler smiled. "Me?"

"Sure," said the sheriff. "Maybe Maslow's death has nothing to do with Amelia Nash. Maybe all this is really about Trudy Samuels."

"Okay," said Rattler, "I'm listening."

"Let's say that you and Trudy had a big argument."

"We did."

"And she calls you all sorts of names. Tells you that you're worthless, just another piece of reservation trash."

"You must have been there."

"Then she takes off and leaves you to smoulder."

"Smoulder?" Rattler chuckled. "That's a great word."

"Then she goes out to Black Stag and attacks Adele. Ethan pushes her down the stairs."

"Over the balcony."

"Right," said the sheriff, "over the balcony. Adele and Ethan drive her out to Belly Butte and dump the body. But Trudy

367

isn't dead. She's badly hurt, can't drive, so she calls you, and you drive out."

"She didn't have a cell," said Rattler. "And I didn't have a car."

"And rather than being grateful, Trudy starts in on you again. About leaving. About taking her stepmother's money. About betraying her."

"So I kill her?" Rattler's expression didn't change. "Because she hurt my feelings?"

"And somehow Maslow found out," said the sheriff. "So now she has two great endings for the episode. Adele and Ethan as the evil stepmother and the jealous half-brother. And you as the vengeful killer lashing out at a racist society."

"A victim of smouldering rage."

"Exactly," said Duke.

"It would have made one hell of a program," said Rattler.

"Yes, it would," said the sheriff.

"Mind you, my motive for killing Trudy seems a bit shaky. Not to mention the problem with logistics." Rattler turned around. "What do you think, Mr. DreadfulWater?"

Thumps yawned. "You didn't kill Trudy, and you didn't kill Maslow."

"Well," said the sheriff, "I'm glad we got that straightened out."

Rattler wagged a finger at Duke. "Grease."

Duke dipped his napkin in the lemonade and wiped at the grease spots on the sleeve of his jacket. "Now that's how you can tell a good burger."

More cars and trucks had arrived at the drive-in, and the place was almost full. Thumps didn't recognize anyone, but he guessed that they were people just off work, catching a quick bite, or parents with children, too tired to go home and cook. That was the lure of fast food. Price and speed. Still, Thumps couldn't imagine eating a meal that had spent most of its life at the bottom of a deep fryer.

"So, whom do you have to replace me," said Rattler, "as your number one suspect?"

The neon squirrel was in motion again, its legs swinging back and forth, its little arms pumping up and down. Somewhere beyond the run of fast-food restaurants, Thumps could hear an emergency vehicle trying to get somewhere fast.

And then there it was.

Maybe it was Skippy or maybe it was the siren in the evening light, but suddenly, he could see what he had been missing. Or at least part of it.

"They lied to me," said Thumps.

"That shouldn't be a surprise," said the sheriff. "You got to figure that Pearl knows more about Maslow's death than she's telling us."

"Not about Maslow," said Thumps.

"Who else is there?" said Rattler.

"You just figured something out," said the sheriff, "didn't you?"

"So, let's share with the rest of the children."

"Pieces," said Thumps. "Got to think about it first."

Thumps looked out the side window. A soft fog had appeared out of nowhere. On the Northern California coast, fog had been an almost daily occurrence, low clouds combining with rising warm air, especially in the morning and then again in the evening, with a burn-off in the afternoon when the sun warmed the ocean and the land. Here on the high plains, it was an advection fog, where warm, wet air flowed over cold ground and created a variation of ground fog.

There had been fog at Clam Beach the night Anna and Callie had been murdered. And for a moment, Thumps was back on the California coast.

Duke held up his sleeve. "You think Macy will notice?"

"Soda water," said Rattler. "I hear soda water will get it out."

Duke wiped his hands. "Don't think too long, Dreadful-Water," he said. "Couple more days, and those television folks are going to fly the coop."

"And I'll be back in Barcelona," said Rattler. "Did you know the actor George Sanders died in Castelldefels? It's a small beach community just outside Barcelona. He checked into a hotel and killed himself."

Thumps took the pieces apart one last time and put them back together. Samuels. Maslow. Amelia Nash. Not a perfect fit. "Okay."

Hockney turned around in his seat. He had a bit of lettuce stuck between his teeth. "Now that's what I want to hear."

"Okay?" said Rattler. "As in, 'Okay, I've solved the case'?"

Hockney started the engine. "You can tell us on the way."

"Not that much to tell," said Thumps.

Duke eased the cruiser out of the parking lot. "So," he said, "what'd you all think of Skippy's?"

"Moving target like that," said Rattler, as they passed under the dancing squirrel. "I'm surprised no one has shot the little sucker."

FORTY-THREE

The front door of Budd's was locked, and the main floor was dark. Thumps thought he could make out a hint of light on the mezzanine, but it could just as well have been spill from the street.

The lock was an old Yale, and for a moment, Thumps considered trying to pick it. He knew the general principle of deadbolts, and if he had had some of the tools he'd carried when he was a cop, he might have given it a try.

Just for old times.

But that would have required squatting down and working the picks back and forth until his back ached and his thighs burned. A better idea was to walk around to the alley to see if the back door was open.

There were two doors. A small one for employees and a large freight door through which Budd had brought in his merchandise. The small door was open. Thumps closed his eyes and waited for them to adjust. Then he stepped inside. Where he discovered that it didn't matter if his eyes were open or closed. The room he was in was dead dark. He ran a hand along the wall. Common sense told him that somewhere close to the door, there had to be a light switch.

Up and across. Down and across. Diagonals. No switch. He took two shuffling steps forward and ran into a string or a chain. With his face. He reached up and grabbed it. The light switch. The building was that old. A single light bulb hanging from the ceiling.

The room was narrow and ended in another door. Thumps swung it open and found himself on the main floor.

Mission accomplished.

He could hear voices above him.

New mission.

As he started up the stairs, Thumps considered how he would start the conversation, what he would say, how far he could run the bluff.

Sydney Pearl was sitting behind her desk, the bottle of Lagavulin 21 ready and waiting, her pearl-handled revolver snug in the shoulder holster. Calder Banks was sitting in a chair, a script in his hands.

"We're dead in the water," Calder was saying. "Vegas is dead, but I can make the Key West story work. Possible serial killer on the loose with a tattoo fetish. Lots of innuendo. Graphic visuals with crime-scene recreations. Testimony by experts. Interviews with locals."

Thumps tried to make his entrance as quiet as possible, but Pearl caught the movement as soon as he cleared the landing.

"Mr. DreadfulWater," she said. "I thought we had seen the last of you."

"Hey, Thumps," said Calder. "Help me out. Maybe you can talk some sense to Sydney."

"Mr. Banks thinks that we ought to drop the Amelia Nash story and go with Key West," said Pearl.

Thumps had decided on the direct approach to see whether he could shake Pearl just a little.

"You lied to me."

No luck. The woman sat behind her desk as still as a mountain.

"I lie all the time," she said. "You'll have to be more specific."

"The Obsidian Murders. Both you and Maslow lied to me."

"Oh," said Pearl. "That."

"Maslow didn't have a file on the case," said Thumps. "You don't have a file on the case."

"I assure you," said Pearl, "that case was going to be our premiere episode for next season."

"Sure," said Thumps. "But Maslow hadn't even started doing the research, had she? I should have seen it. No calls to Key West. No calls to Northern California. What she had was me."

"Is that the serial killings?" said Calder. "The ones with the stones?"

"Shut up, Calder," said Pearl.

"What was the idea?" said Thumps. "Pull me in on the Samuels case. We all get to be buddies, and I'd tell you everything I know about the murders?"

"You know more about that case than anyone," said Pearl. "Nina was sure you'd want to help."

"Shit."

"That's low, Sydney," said Calder. "Even for you."

Thumps held his anger in check. "And then there's Amelia Nash."

"Sure," said Calder, "but without Nina and what she knew, Nash is a dead story."

Thumps ignored Calder. "The meeting you were to have with Nash the night she was killed. What was it about?"

"I told you," said Pearl. "Contract technicalities."

"As in whether Nash could have you and Maslow removed from the production and replaced with Donny Berlin and his production company?"

Calder made a noise in his throat. "What?"

"You're guessing, Mr. DreadfulWater," said Pearl.

"Did I guess right?"

"Amelia was going to dump you guys?" said Calder.

"You're an unpleasant surprise, Mr. DreadfulWater," said Pearl. "But, yes, you are correct. Amelia wanted Berlin's pissant company to take over the show."

"And you couldn't let that happen."

"Donny had this grand idea that he had the horsepower to move into prime time, that Amelia had the juice to stamp her pretty little foot and head office would roll over on their collective backs."

"Star power."

"Sure," said Pearl, "but the head office suits aren't idiots. Donny's track record was like a demolition derby. L.A. wasn't going to let him near the production."

"And if I were to call head office?"

"Be my guest," said Pearl. "Amelia had already tried that little ploy. She had been in touch with Los Angeles the day before with her little scheme. I talked to head office that morning and called the meeting that night to set the two of them straight."

"So you didn't kill them?"

"Hey," said Calder, "that's a shitty suggestion."

Pearl's face was aglow with pleasure. She took the .38 out of the holster and set it next to the bottle. "What a lovely thought," she said. "But no, I didn't kill them. Producers don't murder the help. We just make their lives miserable."

Thumps rocked back on his heels, took his hands out of his pockets, and turned to Calder. "So I guess that leaves you."

"Me." Calder's smile was instant and brilliant.

"If Berlin and Nash were trying to dump the producers," said Thumps, "it stands to reason that they would want to dump you as well."

"Dump me?" Calder's face slowly lost colour. "That's crazy."

"Berlin wanted control of the production. That would mean the talent as well."

"Amelia wouldn't have dumped me," said Calder. "I *was* the talent. She was just a pretty face. She understood that."

Thumps turned back to Pearl. "Let's say that you're right, that Berlin and Nash were never going to get control of the production. Okay. But what were the chances that they could convince head office to replace Calder with Berlin?"

Pearl's face softened. "Better," she said. "If Amelia had pushed hard enough, she might have been able to get that."

"This is nuts!" Calder was almost shouting. "No one was going to dump me."

Thumps waited for Calder to take a breath. "I'm guessing that Berlin or Nash or both of them told you what they were planning to do, at the party."

"Very interesting," said Pearl.

"Come on, Sydney," said Calder. "You're not going to listen to this shit."

"You probably thought it was a joke at first. It would have taken a little time to sink in. And then you would have realized that she was serious and that your career was at risk."

"I was a star." Calder was out of his chair. "I was a fucking star!"

"Maybe you went to Nash's room to try to talk some sense into her. By then you would have been furious. *Streets of San Francisco* was your big chance, and they were going to take it away."

"Donny shot Amelia," said Calder. "Then he shot himself."

Thumps shook his head. "Berlin had a blood alcohol of .30. Nash was shot twice. Once in the head. Once in the heart. Precision. I doubt that Berlin was even conscious, and if he was, there was no way he could have made those shots."

"You don't know what you're talking about."

"You tried to talk to Nash, get her to change her mind, but she was drunk and mean. What did she tell you? That you couldn't cut it? That you were past your prime? That she wasn't going to do *Streets* with you?"

"I was on a plane." Calder had control of his voice now.

Thumps nodded. "The coroner set the time of death at between seven and eleven."

"My flight left at 7:15," said Calder. "And it takes twenty minutes to get to the airport from the Wynn."

"I'm sure it does," said Thumps. "But you got lucky. The flight was delayed, wasn't it? That was why Maslow made those calls to WestAir. It wasn't to check on flights; it was to check to see if your flight that night had left on time."

Calder was quick. Quicker than Thumps would have imagined. He reached across the desk and grabbed the gun before either Pearl or Thumps could move.

"Christ, Calder," said Pearl. "What are you doing?"

"Shut up, Sydney."

"You killed Donny and Amelia?"

"I didn't kill anyone," said Calder. "It was their fault. That show was mine."

"And you killed Maslow?"

Calder held the gun out, firm and steady. "She wouldn't give up. She just kept coming. You want to know something funny. She thought it was you. At first, she thought you had killed them."

Thumps could feel the fatigue return. It was late. He should check his blood sugars. "But then she figured it out."

"She found out that my flight had been delayed. She would have checked the cabs. I gave the guy a good tip to get me to the airport fast. Would he remember me? Sure, I got that kind of face. I couldn't take the chance. She should have let it go. Berlin, Nash, Maslow. They should have let it go."

Pearl leaned back in her chair and put her hands in her lap. "So now what?"

"New script," said Calder. "You killed Berlin and Nash. Maslow found out, and you killed her. Mr. DreadfulWater figured it out and came here to confront you. You shot him."

"I need a drink." Pearl reached for the Lagavulin and cracked the cap. "I've been saving this for a special occasion."

Calder pointed the gun at Thumps's chest. "I tried to stop you. We struggled, and the gun went off, killing you."

Pearl took a sip of the whisky. "God, Calder," she said, "that is the dumbest plot I've ever heard."

"It won't work," said Thumps.

"You think not?" said Calder.

"Four reasons," said Thumps. "First, no one will believe it."

"They don't have to believe it," said Calder. "It will be my word against two dead people. Nash and Berlin were trying to replace Pearl. Pearl had a key to the room. She was the one who found the bodies."

"Second," said Thumps, "your jacket."

"My jacket?"

"At the dealership," said Thumps. "The spots on your sleeve. Grease and blood look a lot alike. But when the sheriff tests the jacket, he'll find that it's splatter."

Calder shrugged. "Jackets can disappear."

"Three," said Thumps, looking at Pearl, "the pistol doesn't have real bullets."

"What?"

"I was a cop," said Thumps. "Pearl showed me the gun when we first met. The weight and balance were off."

"Bravo," said Pearl.

Calder looked at the pistol. "You're bluffing." Then he aimed the gun at Thumps and pulled the trigger.

"And four, I brought the sheriff with me." Thumps walked to the mezzanine balcony and looked over the edge. "Did you hear all that?"

"We did," shouted Duke. "Ask Mr. Banks to wait for us. We'll be right up."

"Did you find the jacket?"

"We did," said the sheriff. "And you're right. Grease and blood look a lot alike."

Calder pulled the trigger on the revolver again and again until the cylinder had made a complete circuit.

"Replica bullets." Calder was smiling again. "Fucking replica bullets."

"Real bullets are dangerous," said Pearl. "Someone could get hurt."

Calder sat down in the chair, his arms at his sides. "Well, hell," he said. "At least we got our show."

"Yes," said Pearl. "We have our show."

"So," said Calder, brightening a little, "who are you going to get to play me?"

FORTY-FOUR

Al was waiting for him when he got to the restaurant the next morning.

"I told you it was the blond hunk."

Wutty Young Beaver, Russell Plunkett, and Jimmy Monroe were in their usual places at the front, hunkered down at the counter.

"Hear you almost got killed," said Russell. "Lucky the bullets weren't real."

"Entertainment," said Wutty. "Nothing's real in entertainment."

"I said it was Mr. Fancy Face," said Al, "and I was right."

"Hear you're looking for a new ride," said Jimmy. "You interested in a low-mileage SUV?"

"You talking about your GMC?" Wutty shook his head. "You should be paying someone to take it off your hands."

"The Acadia's a classic."

"Yeah," said Russell. "Classic crap."

"Sort of like your job with the TV show?" said Jimmy.

Wutty blew on his coffee. "Bunch of lesbians."

Thumps made his way to his favourite stool and settled in. He had finally gotten a good night's sleep, but little else had changed. His car was still wrecked. His cat was still gone. Claire was still in Browning or wherever she had gone to try to find motherhood for a second time. He had helped to solve three cases, but he couldn't seem to find any pleasure in that.

Not his circus. Not his monkeys.

"Jesus," said Duke, as he slid onto the next stool. "You look like shit."

The sheriff wasn't the last person he wanted to see. And he certainly wasn't the first.

"What do you want?"

"Cranky, too," said Duke.

"Thought you were interrogating Banks."

"Hell," said Hockney. "I can't get the guy to shut up."

"So, he's told you everything."

"You were right," said Duke. "It was Berlin who told him that they were going to get him kicked off the program. Berlin wanted the part. Him and Nash. Calder went up to Nash's room to try to talk some sense into her. She was drunk and abusive. Berlin was passed out on the couch. Calder grabs Berlin's new cool toy and shoots Nash."

"Twice."

"You were right. Berlin would have been too drunk to make those shots. He probably never even woke up."

"Around seven-thirty?"

"Give or take," said Duke. "Calder panicked, grabbed a cab for the airport, hoping he could catch a flight out of Dodge before anyone found the bodies."

"And got lucky."

"Flight was delayed an hour and a half," said the sheriff. "So Calder actually caught the flight he had originally booked. Made it look as though he was in the air when Nash and Berlin were killed."

"And Maslow?"

"Like he said. Maslow was a bulldog. He followed her out to Belly Butte and killed her there. Hoped that the similarity with Trudy would keep us busy."

"So what happens now?"

"We are sending Mr. Banks back to Las Vegas."

"Vegas?" said Thumps. "He killed Maslow here."

"He did," said Duke, "but the mayor doesn't think that a high-profile murder trial will help her Howdy program."

"Calder going to fight extradition?"

"Oh my, no," said Hockney. "He doesn't want to be tried here. Too small a stage. I think he's looking forward to the climactic courtroom scene."

"You here to buy me breakfast?"

"What?" said Duke. "Because you helped break the case?"

"Three cases."

Duke shook his head. "Nope. Stopped by to pick up my badge. Your tenure as a deputy is over."

Thumps leaned back on the stool and stretched. "If you don't mind," he said, "I'd like to hold on to it for a bit."

Duke nodded. "Unfinished business?"

Al brought breakfast and the coffee pot at the same time. "On me," she said. "Seeing as how you're a hero and all."

"What about me?" said Duke.

"Howdy," said Al.

THE ROLL-UP DOORS at Blackfoot Autohaus were down and locked, but there was a light on in the office. Stas was at his desk, working his way through a stack of paper.

"Yes, please." The big Russian bolted out of his chair and threw his arms around Thumps. "You must have tea. You must interrupt before I shoot myself."

Thumps could feel the air leave his body.

"End of month," said Stas, breaking the bear hug and waving a paw at the desk. "Money comes in. Money goes out. I work on money more than I work on cars. Bills, taxes, forms for the governments, who knows how many. Little government, big government. What is 'code type 7'?"

Thumps tried to look sympathetic.

"Or 'Check box 32b' when there is no box 32b?" Stas returned to his chair and sat down with a thud. "I am mechanic. Good mechanic." He sighed. "Not *advokat*. You understand?"

"I brought your truck back."

"Yes," said Stas. "Bad news. Good news. Which is first?"

This was the moment, Thumps realized, that he had been dreading. "Bad news."

Stas poured hot water into a cup and dropped in a tea bag. "Okay. Yes. Bad news is always better first."

"The Volvo?"

Stas shook his head sadly. "You must say goodbye."

"No way to fix it?"

"Frame is bent. Drive shaft is broken. Engine block is not so good either. Car is dead."

Thumps sagged in the chair. He tried the tea. It didn't help. "The good news?"

"Ah," said Stas. "Yes. Good news. Lady is sympathetic."

"Lady?"

"Yes," said Stas. "Scary lady. One with gun? No smiling. No happy to see you. She friend?"

"Not exactly."

"Anyway, she comes here." Stas smiled. "Gives me this." Stas held up a set of keys. "Honda Element is yours."

"Mine?"

"Yes." Stas popped out of his chair. "Scary lady says to give you car. Pink slip, keys, full tank of gas. Also this."

Stas handed him a thick folder.

"She says you will want this. She says to say goodbye and good luck."

Thumps recognized Maslow's handwriting. On the label, she had written, "Obsidian Murders."

"So," said Stas. "Goodbye. Good luck."

FORTY-FIVE

Thumps stood on his porch and watched the night give way to the dawn. Nothing dramatic, a slow brightening at the edges, a brittle chill just out of reach. Winter was on the way. Snow had been predicted for the weekend. And for all of the following week.

It had been three days since Calder Banks had been arrested. Thumps had stopped by the sheriff's office.

"So he gave you a complete confession?"

"More like a script for a full-length movie," Duke had told Thumps. "Starring himself."

"Macy get the grease out of your jacket?"

"You really want to go there? Now she's talking vegetarian."

"Hear it's healthy."

"You know what tofu is made of? You ever taste quinoa?"

Claire had come home a day early. Thumps had been in the kitchen, standing in front of an open refrigerator, looking for breakfast, when the phone rang.

"I'm back," Claire had said.

"Great."

"But I'm not staying."

Thumps hadn't been able to think of what the next question should be, so he waited.

"I'm going to New Zealand."

"New Zealand?"

"With Angie."

"Black Weasel?"

"She's going to Auckland for a conference on Indigenous child care. I'm going with her."

Thumps had heard the tension in Claire's voice.

"Browning didn't go as planned. There's an aunt on the Blood reserve in Alberta who is going for custody of the girls."

"Family."

"Exactly. The aunt didn't want them at first, but now she does."

Thumps had said that he was sorry, that these situations were hard on everyone.

"No," Claire had said. "It's probably for the best. I've forgotten how to be a mother. I've forgotten just how hard it is to raise a child."

"How long?"

"New Zealand?" Claire's voice had tightened. "A month. The conference is most of a week. After that, Angie and I are going to rent a small camper and tour the South Island."

"A month."

"Angie's parents are going to look after the kids. Angie's mother is thrilled to have them. Stas and Cooley and Moses are off on their fall hunting trip, so it's a win all around."

"What about the Forester?"

"Changed my mind," Claire had said. "Freddy understood. I told him I'd put in a good word with council the next time the band looked at their lease agreements."

"So you're off."

"I'm off." There had been a long pause. Thumps had heard Claire take each breath. "You okay with that?"

"You'll have a great time in New Zealand."

"Maybe we can talk when I get back."

Thumps had slowly closed the refrigerator door. "Sounds like a plan."

"I hear you got a new car."

"Honda Element."

"I'll send you a postcard."

"Be great."

"Maybe I'll send you two."

* * *

THUMPS HAD BEEN wrong about Nina Maslow. She had researched the Obsidian Murders. The file Sydney Pearl had given him hadn't been complete, but it had been impressive. Crime-scene photos, forensics, victim information. Thumps had no idea how she had acquired the materials. Much of it had been familiar. Thumps had seen most of it before. Of more interest had been the notes Maslow had made, questions she had scribbled in the margins with arrows and circles that tried to connect disparate pieces of information into a coherent idea.

Pearl had been right. Maslow had a knack for seeing patterns and for coming at a problem from odd and unexpected angles.

He had taken Maslow's research to the Aegean.

"My computer," the little Greek had said. "Again?"

"The Obsidian Murders." Thumps had held up the file by way of explanation.

"I get it," Archie had said. "Claire's going to New Zealand, and you're at loose ends."

"Something like that."

"So what are you going to do?"

"Stay home. Wait for winter."

Archie shook his head. "It's a bad idea."

"What?"

"Going back. It's a bad idea."

Thumps had put the file on Archie's desk. "I could use your help."

Archie had picked up the file and looked at the list Thumps had paper-clipped to the front of the folder. "This is it?"

"Yes."

The little Greek had stared at him over the top of his glasses. No gesture of encouragement, no censure, just the silence of sadness. "So, when do you leave?"

"In the morning."

Archie had kept his face impassive. "It's a bad idea."

So NOW IT was morning, and Thumps stood on his porch and watched the sun break the horizon. Maybe the snow wouldn't come straight away. It might hold off for another week, maybe two. It could even turn warm one last time, a fond farewell, bon voyage, see you in the spring.

Thumps slung the messenger bag over his shoulder and picked up the suitcase. He looked up and down the street in case Freeway had had enough of small children and was looking for sanctuary.

Then he climbed into the Honda, put the promise of dawn at his back, and began the long drive to the coast.